Rope 'Em

By Delphine Dryden

Rope 'Em

Ride 'Em

Rope 'Em

A Giddyup Novel

Delphine Dryden

LYRICAL PRESS
Kensington Publishing Corp.
www.kensingtonbooks.com

LYRICAL PRESS BOOKS are published by

Kensington Publishing Corp.
119 West 40th Street
New York, NY 10018

All Kensington titles, imprints, and distributed lines are available at special quantity discounts for bulk purchases for sales promotion, premiums, fund-raising, educational, or institutional use.

Special book excerpts or customized printings can also be created to fit specific needs. For details, write or phone the office of the Kensington Sales Manager: Kensington Publishing Corp., 119 West 40th Street, New York, NY 10018. Attn. Sales Department. Phone: 1-800-221-2647.

Lyrical Press and Lyrical Press logo Reg. U.S. Pat. & TM Off.

First Electronic Edition: March 2017
eISBN-13: 978-1-60183-677-9
eISBN-10: 1-60183-677-5

First Print Edition: March 2017
ISBN-13: 978-1-60183-678-6
ISBN-10: 1-60183-678-3

Printed in the United States of America

Chapter 1

"*While you're down there, why don't you do me a favor?*"
Part of her still wanted to believe it had been a joke. A horrible joke.

Four inches of iced-over snow lined the sidewalk in downtown Providence, and a thicker, grubbier bank of the stuff marked the edges of the street where the plows had come through earlier. Victoria had grabbed her coat and bag but not her galoshes when she fled the coffee shop, and the chill had numbed her toes through her Chucks before she reached the next block. She ignored it and pulled her hood tighter against the still-falling flakes, pressing toward home as quickly as she could manage on the slippery, frozen path down the sidewalk's center.

She probably should have seen it coming. The wary, weary looks the other female barista sometimes gave her. The fact that there was only one other female employee on the roster to begin with. But Larry hadn't seemed like a creeper when he hired her. Friendly, sure, and kind of a toucher, but never overtly leering or even flirtatious. He was married, too; his wife and kids came into the shop all the time.

The job at the coffee shop had been a lifesaver for Victoria. Five weeks earlier, she'd been at a total loss for how she would make her rent another month without wiping out her savings. But a week ago she'd used her first paycheck to open a new bank account and allowed herself a moment of hope that things were turning around. True, the job only paid a few hundred a week, but it was *something*. And her landlord had been incredibly kind in letting her out of her lease early for a song—probably because the place was spotless, and he meant to jack up the price for the next tenant, but that wasn't Victoria's problem. A friend from RISD had a tiny, furnished guest room she could rent for a price she could afford on her new budget, and she was already packed and ready to move.

Baby steps toward independence, but at least she was finally learning to walk. On her own, declining all further support from the family that had never believed in her.

She had *needed* that job. But apparently it came with some requirements Larry hadn't mentioned in the interview.

"I . . . don't think that joke is really work-appropriate, Larry. Ha-ha. Anyway, my drawer is even. Yay . . ."

"Why would you think I was joking?"

Victoria kicked snow off the frozen tops of her sneakers and thought about her innocent *woot* a few seconds before it all happened, when she'd finally counted out her drawer correctly on the first try. She'd only been on the register a few weeks, and with no retail experience, it was all new to her. Figuring out the balancing procedure was a small victory. But when she'd knelt to slide the drawer into the lockbox in the office, Larry had chuckled and swiveled his chair toward her. Spread his legs. Started talking. She'd still been laughing nervously when he ran his hand down over his crotch, adjusting himself so she could see he was half-hard.

The affable smile never left his face and *that* had been creepy. *"You gotta be realistic, Vicky. You're a crappy barista, but I knew when I hired you those lips would look fantastic around my dick. And if you want to keep the job, that's exactly where you'll put 'em, Miss Woodcock. You do want to keep the job, don't you?"* He'd wrapped his other hand around her wrist, pulling her hand toward his crotch, and she'd jerked away so hard she'd almost fallen over before recovering her balance.

"Don't call me Vicky." Why that had been the first thing out of her mouth, she had no idea. Maybe because only her dad had kept calling her that after elementary school.

She stopped walking as a body-shuddering wave of nausea swamped her, a dizzy rush just like she'd felt as she wobbled to her feet in the office and edged toward the employee lockers along the wall by the door. Her fingers had been shaking so badly she'd fumbled the latch the first time, then dropped her bag as she pulled it from its hook.

"You walk out of here, you're gonna lose your chance. Don't be

stupid. We both know you need the money. How do you think Pamela made shift lead anyway?"

Swallowing the bile in her throat, she'd pulled the office door open and tried to speak. A squeak had come out, and Larry had laughed, shaking his head as she cleared her throat and started again. Loud enough so that Pamela and Andre and Jameson could all hear her. *"I do need the money. But I am not going near your dick to get it. And I quit."*

She didn't stop to watch the other employees' reactions—or those of any customers who might have overheard. Didn't care. She'd made a beeline for the door, passing Pamela, who was ripping off her own apron and shouting at Larry, "You *swore* you were leaving your wife for me, you two-timing piece of shit!"

Victoria had stumbled into the street and kept on going until the shaking and light-headedness finally overtook her halfway home.

She had twelve hundred dollars in the bank, five hundred of which she still owed her landlord for breaking the lease. She'd already sold most of her stuff that had any value—her furniture, her desktop computer, her television, most of the clothes and shoes her mother had insisted on buying her but that Victoria never wore. What she had left could fit into her car, if she abandoned her fabric samples. She had her cell phone, which she had decided to use through the end of the month, because it had been paid for before she'd realized it was on the list of expenses her parents had been covering. Ditto her car insurance. Her parents still didn't know exactly what was going on, and in the meantime, Victoria had taken the opportunity to figure out all the various ways they'd been pumping money into her life. Extrication took time. And she'd counted on her new income source to ease the way. The barista job had been the first step on her path to independence, or at least to a time at which she could reassess her priorities and figure out a new route to her eventual goal of working as a textile designer.

Her phone buzzed and she reached for it by habit, hitching up her parka and digging icy, gloveless fingers into her back jeans pocket.

Slushy snowflakes fell on the screen, obscuring her mother's picture and the green and red circles below. Reject or Accept? She'd been ignoring her mother for weeks, putting her off with vague emails and texts. But at that moment she wanted to hear her mom's voice. Even if it wasn't to tell her everything was going to be okay, because Victoria was pretty sure she was on a fast downhill slope from okay and hadn't hit bottom yet. She had to flick the snow away and tap the green button twice before putting the phone to her ear.

"Hi, Mom."

"Honey, thank God you answered. We've been so worried. What is going *on*? And don't you try to tell me it's a mix-up at the bursar's office again. Most of your first tuition payment came back to our bank this morning; they reversed the autopay. We've called them and they've shown us the accounts and it was all very clear. You *withdrew*."

It had to come out eventually. She took a deep breath, her lungs aching with the cold. "Yes."

"But Victoria, you only have one semester left. Whatever's happening, it can't be so bad that you have to drop out of college a few months before you—oh, no." Her mother gasped. "You're not pregnant, are you? Tell me you're—"

Oh, dear God. "Mom."

"I mean, Ruth Bland's daughter Jessie got through it, I know it happens, but I never thought you'd be the type to—"

"*Mom*. I am not pregnant. Okay?" A couple passing on the sidewalk glanced at her, then quickly looked away. *Jesus H. Christ.* "I am not pregnant. I am not on drugs. I haven't joined a cult. I'm *fine*." That last part was a lie, but at least the rest was true.

She hadn't been fine since Christmas vacation, and she wished for the thousandth time she'd stayed in Providence for the holiday this year instead of going home to Dallas.

The phone was silent long enough Victoria wondered if the call had dropped; then her mother finally spoke again, voice trembling. "I just want to make sure you're all right, sweetheart. I'll book the next flight I can get."

If she hadn't gone home, she'd never have been in the hallway checking the mail, never overheard her father on the phone in his study, arranging a golf date and then apparently commiserating with his good ol' boy buddy about the cost of daughters.

"*. . . might break me on the wedding itself, but my liquidity'll free up quite a bit when that girl finally lands a husband like we figured she would when we let her go all the way to Rhode Island for that damn art school. It's right next to Brown. It shouldn't be that hard to* *find a man there. Swear to God, she's a black hole where my money disappears, and I have no idea what it all goes for. Bless her heart, I don't think she knows we expected her to be banking on her looks all this time."* And then he'd made the golf date and hung up. Victoria had tiptoed up the stairs and sat on her bed in shock until dinnertime, barely able to process what she'd just heard.

The shock had lasted all the way back to Providence, when she'd found herself veering away from her first scheduled class of the new term and heading for the registrar's office instead. After withdrawing, she'd cut up the bank card for the account her parents paid into. Then she'd wandered for blocks to find a coffee shop that wasn't entirely full of students. She'd seen the "Now Hiring" sign, and an hour later she had a paying job for the first time in her life. And no plan for what happened next.

It had taken her a few weeks to figure out how little she knew about how to live self-sufficiently on her own. By that time it was too late to change her mind and reenroll for spring term, even if she'd wanted to. She hadn't, though.

"Mom." Victoria jerked her head in an effort to clear it. "You don't need to come out here. I'm really fine. Just taking time to work some things out."

"Oh, don't be ridiculous, Victoria. It's obvious something's going on and you aren't thinking straight. You need some help. I'm already making arrangements for a flight."

And that, that right there, was the problem. Always had been really. They never assumed she could think for herself. They just . . . did it for her. And she was done letting that happen. "Well, you should cancel those plans." She held up her face, letting the snow numb her cheeks and nose. First the sting, then the cold, then an illusion of heat, then nothing. "Mom, what's the weather like in Dallas right now?"

"What?"

"Is it still cold, or . . . ?" There had been a cold snap in that part of Texas over the holidays, enough to freeze the ground and make the grass ice-crunchy in the mornings for a few days.

"I can't imagine what . . . oh, it's about seventy right now. It's supposed to drop down to forty tonight and then we may get another freeze next week. I can't have the gardeners bring the plumerias out yet, but we've already started getting mosquitoes. So it's some of everything, as usual. Why do you ask?"

"No reason. Just curious." Seventy. That was a dream. Even forty sounded impossibly balmy compared to Providence in February. "I had kind of a bad day, Mom." She clenched her eyes, willing the tears not to fall. She sniffled, a useless effort, and fumbled in her coat pocket for a tissue. Her hood had slipped back a moment earlier, but the cold felt good, as if it could freeze the tears into place in their ducts.

"Sweetheart, whatever's going on, we can help you if you just tell us what it is." Her mother sounded kind, no longer irritated but merely concerned. And Victoria still couldn't bring herself to tell her mom what her dad had said. Possibly—and this was the thing that had kept her up more nights than not—because she feared her mom agreed with him. Maybe *Victoria* even agreed with him. She didn't want confirmation that his position had been valid, that she was basically a waste of space and a drain on his bank account, an incompetent who needed to be babied along until it was time to hand her into somebody else's care.

Mostly, she didn't want one more thin dime from somebody who apparently viewed her with such utter contempt. But she was starting to realize she had done a piss-poor job of making her independence happen. She'd wanted to present her family with a fait accompli, show them her self-funded, self-directed life as she explained why she didn't need them anymore. Instead, everything she'd tried to do on her own was falling apart. Because she hadn't even known how little she'd known.

Now she couldn't even tell her mom about the scene in the coffee shop without explaining about the job, and she couldn't explain about that without getting into how she'd failed so miserably at her effort to prove she didn't need anyone's help. "I have to get out of the snow. I'll text you when I get home, okay? I'm fine. Really."

"Well . . . all right. Will it be within the hour?"

"Yeah. Fifteen, twenty minutes tops." By that time she would be home, dry, and better able to think up a plausible reason her mother didn't need to come to Rhode Island. "Gotta go. Love you. Bye." She heard her mother echo the sentiments, ended the call, and stuffed the phone into her coat pocket.

At least this particular day couldn't get any worse.

A wet droplet slid down her neck from the fur on her pushed-back hood. She tugged the hood back into place, and an icy *schwip* and stinging wet trail marked the descent of a larger clump of snow straight down the back of her sweater.

No. Not snow. It was turning wetter, thicker, more painful against her face and hands: sleet.

She hitched her bag higher on her shoulder and forced herself into motion again, grimacing as she stepped out on nearly numb feet. She'd walked to work to save on gas money—what to do with the BMW, the title to which was in her dad's name, was yet another issue on her list—but now walking in the snow seemed like one more bad decision. Her friend Huey was moving to Manhattan in a month and had offered to sell her his decrepit old Honda for four hundred bucks. It ran. But she wouldn't have even that small amount of money available to buy it unless she could find another job immediately.

When she turned the corner of her block, she could spot her building through the sleet. Historic charm, featuring roomy converted "loft" studios with hardwood floors and original architectural details. Fantastic light. A mere block away from RISD and Brown. It had been the perfect home for two and a half years, but as she neared it now, all she could think of was the outrageous rent. She could probably lease a house twice the size in Dallas for half as much. Or an apartment the same size for a quarter as much. And it would be seventy degrees right now, and she wouldn't have snot freezing on her upper lip or toes that burned with cold in inadequate shoes.

Cheap. And warm. Two requirements that hadn't meant a thing before Christmas. Her needs were becoming easier to understand as they grew more difficult to meet.

She should have another paycheck coming in a week for her previous two weeks of work . . . but who knew if Larry would give it to her? And she sure as hell wasn't walking into the shop alone to ask for it. Those few hundred dollars could have kept her lights and internet on, but her standards were changing. Maybe she could do without those things for a week or two if she had to.

Cheap and warm.

Or maybe . . . maybe she'd been thinking too small. It hit her like a particularly sharp blast of sleet as she finally opened the door to her building and heaved a sigh of relief in the warm foyer. If she wasn't staying at RISD, had no job, and had gotten out of her lease, what was keeping her in Rhode Island anymore? She had friends, but she'd have left them in a few more months anyway after she graduated and got a job—presumably in New York. She wasn't seeing anyone right now—either in the vanilla dating world or in the tiny, informal local kink scene she was occasionally part of.

Dallas was warm. And cheap. And she had to get the car back to her father somehow anyway. Why not load it up and hit the road?

Her phone buzzed again as she entered her loft. Expecting her mom, she accepted without checking the screen. "Hi. I just walked in the door. Look, I really hope you didn't book a flight or something. I don't think—"

"A flight? What the fuck are you talking about?"

It was Larry. Victoria's skin crawled, and she had to resist the impulse to fling the phone away from her. "I thought you were somebody else. What do you want?"

"Are you seriously walking out without giving notice? Everybody's pissed, Pamela's walked out, too, the schedule is completely screwed, and they're—"

She hung up on him. After a moment's thought, she blocked the number.

The shuddering started again after she'd taken off her coat and wrenched the sodden Chucks off her feet. She reeled to the couch and slumped with her head between her knees, slowing her breathing until the sensation passed. She knew she ought to report the incident to somebody, but mostly she just longed for it never to have happened. To put it behind her. And she wished there were somebody around to give her a hug and tell her everything would be okay.

No, tighter than a hug. She wanted the ultimate comfort, the inexorable snugness of rope around her skin in an all-over embrace. Cradling and containing her, keeping her body secure so her mind could fly away. Providing just enough pain, now and then, to remind her she was alive. A few of her kinky friends in the Dallas scene could do that for her far better than anybody in Rhode Island had done to date. Another reason to go back.

Victoria pulled the dark red plush throw from the back of the couch and pulled it around her, wrapping it as tightly as she could. Looking around the loft, she saw a nearly barren space. A few plastic bins and boxes, plus her luggage, now contained all her worldly goods. A larger box full of fabric and other textiles sat by the door, waiting to be taken to the campus and donated. It had shocked her, in the end, how easily her life could be reduced down to these few things. In her extremity, she'd learned very quickly which things really mattered and what *need* really meant. And she hadn't needed most of what had been in the loft.

It would be a tight fit to stuff it all in the Beemer, but she could do it. Her savings should just about cover gas and lodging for the drive if she could find cheap places to stay.

She punched out a quick text to her mother, stressing that she shouldn't book a flight because Victoria planned to come home in a few days and they could talk then. Her mom's first response was a terse, *"So relieved!"* and Victoria quickly forestalled any further discussion by replying that she was about to take a nap but would be in touch again later to let the family know when she'd be *"getting in."* If her mother assumed that meant a plane flight instead of driving halfway across the country within the next few days, so be it.

Within minutes she was deep into plotting her route on her laptop, while a mix of swing and big band played in the background. But the stress of the last hour, and the physical toll of the eight hours of work preceding it, started to weigh in. Her eyes grew heavier and she jerked her head up a few times while doggedly chasing down motel rates in the various towns along I-81 and I-40.

When her playlist reached Ella Fitzgerald singing Cole Porter, she gave it up and put the laptop down on the couch beside her, tugging the blanket even more tightly around herself. Still not enough, but it would have to do. She let her eyes close and softly sang along with Ella—to the rope she wished were binding her, or to whomever might do the binding, "You Do Something To Me."

Chapter 2

It was just about everything Ethan Hill loved best in the world, all in one place. The view over the main grounds of Hilltop Ranch. The feel of a well-balanced tool in his hand. The smell of freshly sawn cedar and an underlying whiff—when the fall breeze was just right—of horse.

When the breeze wasn't right, he caught an underlying whiff of himself, which was less pleasant but still somehow right. He'd earned that sweat, and the project he was working on was worth every drop. Not to mention the blood and, yes, even a few tears that had gone into the process of building his very own tiny house from the ground up.

Or at least from the trailer base up.

His older brother, Logan, thought he was nuts. "So lemme get this straight: You're gonna build a two-hundred-square—"

"Two-twenty," Ethan had corrected him.

"Two-hundred-*twenty*-square-foot RV—"

"Tiny house."

Logan shot him a look. "On a trailer bed. And live in it. In the middle of Tornado Alley."

Ethan had shrugged. "Technically, we're way south of Tornado Alley, and also if we get a warning I can come down to the main house. Or find the nearest safe structure if I'm out on the road. Which is part of the point."

He'd wanted a tiny house ever since he'd first read about them nearly a decade earlier as an undergraduate. The idea had taken root. Ironic that he'd thought of it like that, given that part of the structure's allure was its mobility. Don't like the view? Hitch up the trailer to the truck and find a change of scenery.

"Besides," he'd pointed out to a still-skeptical Logan, "if I work out the kinks building one for myself, we could do a whole *village* of them as an alternative to building more cabins. It's getting to be a *thing*. It'll be cheaper than site-built, we won't have to worry about septic, and it'll make Hilltop a destination for a broader client base. Not just dude ranch guests but people who want to try out tiny houses. Or ecotourists. The fact that there aren't any oil rigs in sight adds value."

"Hipsters."

"Paying customers." Ever the little brother, he hadn't been able to resist a dig. "Hey, I remember a certain Houston-based engineer who spent a whole year talking about his Chemex and making everybody taste test the difference between coffee beans grown in one field and coffee beans grown in a field two miles away, so I don't think you have any stones to throw at hipsters, bro."

"Hey, I appreciate simple, functional, elegant engineering, and full-sun coffee is a scourge on biodiversity . . . okay, fine, point taken."

In the end, Ethan had found a plot of level, mostly treeless ground about a hundred yards up and around the hill from the old barn, parked his trailer base there, and started building. He was part owner of the ranch anyway, and he had as much right as Logan or their cousin Chet to do whatever he liked on the land. Today that involved finally installing the first section of reclaimed cedar planks he'd salvaged to use as part of his siding.

Soon, he'd have the exterior completed. Which meant it was almost time to have a talk he'd been putting off with the partners at the vet practice. Let them know they needed to start looking for a new associate. He hoped to stay on as relief staff until the spot was filled and be first on the list any time they needed a locum. But he couldn't keep up his current heavy schedule of ping-ponging between the practice and Hilltop. Close as Bolero was to San Antonio, it was still too far to be a workable commute.

They knew it was coming—he'd never planned to buy in, that was understood from the start—although they probably didn't anticipate his leaving quite so soon. Or under these circumstances. Ethan had always expected to take over the local practice from old Doc Taylor in Bolero one day; everyone knew that. What he hadn't expected was that his investment in his grandparents' old guest ranch would turn first into a time-consuming hobby, then pretty much a second career.

Pity was, he couldn't exactly explain to the folks at the practice how a rinky-dink dude ranch and a sideline selling hand-dyed rope halters could provide him a living wage, much less one that would compete with his salary as an associate vet for one of the most highly regarded large animal practices in the state. So when he told them he was leaving to focus on the ranch—as he really ought to, sooner rather than later—they would probably think he was nuts.

Except that one weekend out of every month, Hilltop hosted a private event, by invitation only, with heavy security. And those weekends—the now infamous Giddyup events—put the rest of the month's earnings to shame. Just as Ethan's biggest return on time and materials didn't lie in selling handmade tack but in peddling batch-dyed handmade bondage rope.

A kink mecca. That's what Hilltop had grown into as Giddyup had become more widely known. They had guests from all over now, and Robert had put a special world map in the office; you could scrape a gray film off any state or country, kind of like a scratch-off lottery ticket. They'd started scratching off all their visitors' points of origins and been amazed at how much of the map was exposed.

Giddyup was the funding secret behind Hilltop Ranch's success. It was amazing how neatly the operations overlapped, and how much equipment could serve dual purposes. Leather care was leather care, whether you were maintaining a saddle or making your submissive or slave polish your boots . . . or condition your whips. The soft, pliable hemp rope Ethan preferred for bondage was nothing like the stiff cord of a lariat, but either way he had the skills to do a great class in knot tying for the guest ranch visitors. The kids loved it, and the local scoutmaster had even asked him to do a demonstration for some of the kids working on a badge.

Human ponies didn't have to make do with pretend barns or paddocks at Giddyup; they could have the real thing. And the amusing stocks the tourists liked to stage pictures in usually had a waiting list ten deep on Giddyup weekends. Getting the opportunity to put your sub in genuine stocks and whip them in public, outdoors, for a crowd of enthusiastic onlookers? Priceless.

He might not make as much money on Giddyup and rope sales as being a vet, but at Hilltop he didn't have to pay rent. Or shell out gas money to drive back and forth to San Antonio all the time. The salary cut seemed worth it.

Ethan still planned to take over for Doc Taylor of course. Someday. He'd always planned to, *someday*. For now, though . . . He hefted the hammer, shifting his grip around the handle and frowning at the sensation of an incipient blister on his palm. As part of this rare full weekend off, he was doing a rope-making demonstration for the ranch guests the next day. It was time to either get some heavier gloves or lay off the construction, or he'd be miserable working with the jute yarn he planned to use for the demo.

But it was okay. He had time. Finally, he had time.

He exhaled slowly, scanning the horizon again, smiling at the perfection of it. The *rightness*. This house. This place. This work. The people here. The possibility of taking his rope to kink conventions across Texas, even across the country, and spreading the news about Giddyup as he sold his wares. Leaving the practice would give him time for all that.

Ethan descended the ladder, put his hammer carefully back into his toolbox, stripped off his work gloves, and picked up his cell phone to make that call.

Doing any kind of rope demo for the pure-vanilla Hilltop Guest Ranch clientele was always an exercise in cognitive dissonance for Ethan. Sunday morning, as he kept an eye on the volunteer turning the crank and carefully walked the wooden traveler back from the hooked jack to keep an even tension on the twisting jute strands, he was thinking of his recent attempt to dye a hemp rope multiple shades of red. He thought a gradation from scarlet to a deep merlot or even black cherry would look fantastic against bare skin and make the knotwork really stand out. But he was having trouble getting the shades to come out the way he wanted. When he'd hung the length of rope to dry the night before, following the latest stage of dyeing, he could see already that the colors were muddy instead of blending from one to the next smoothly, as he'd hoped. None of which should be on his mind while he was monitoring how that nice Mrs. Fedelman was doing with the pacing on the crank.

"Okay." He brought the traveler to a halt and quickly whipped the end of the slender new rope with a piece of string from his pocket, securing the twists before taking off the slack. It was about twelve feet long according to the gauge he'd set along the path. "We have a rope. Gather 'round if you like, see how it feels."

He fielded a few more questions, laughed at a few jokes from the small crowd, and quietly pondered how he would get the red dye stain off the jeans he'd been wearing the night before. Maybe those would just become the dyeing jeans. But how to get that color fade right . . . ?

He turned the group's attention to his horse, Sackett, who'd been dozing next to the fence a few yards from the ropewalk.

"So, once you've made your rope, what can you do with it?" *So many, many things.* "Sackett here is wearing one great example, and this is certainly a way lots of cowboys used handmade rope back in the day. Sackett can't wear a bit, and usually I ride him with either a flat halter or a hackamore. But today he has on a simple rope halter, handmade by me." He patted the buckskin's beautifully arched neck, then scratched his fingers into the horse's somewhat fuzzy, lingering winter coat before moving his hand up to the undyed hemp around Sackett's long head. "He's a good horse and I've worked with him a lot, so you'll see this halter is very simple. But if Sackett here were an ornery type, and I were an old-time cowboy, I might have added knots in sensitive areas to get more control over the horse. Mostly on the nose and along the jawline." He slipped his hand under the rope over Sackett's cheek, touching the jaw beneath, and suddenly got a face full of curious equine nose for his trouble. He held up an open palm, letting Sackett explore with his sensitive lips: no treats at the moment.

"Wouldn't that hurt?" asked one of the guests.

"It would and does, especially if you don't have a light hand on the reins. It's not something I'd advocate as a training method. Fear and pain don't help you build a relationship with animals. They aren't good ways to communicate long term." They weren't his jams anyway, for the most part; he liked *control*, and healthy respect built on trust. With horses, with kink partners. "It can also injure the horse. But there was no SPCA back then. And if your job, maybe your life, depended on getting control over a horse fast, moving it where you needed it to go, this was a way to accomplish that. Some people still use basically this same rope halter, which is one continuous piece, but there are adaptations."

Resisting the string of warnings he wanted to give—he already knew most of this crowd didn't have horses, and he could talk to the ones who did later on—he pulled a heavier, flat-woven green halter off the nearest fence post. He traded it out for the bare-bones model on Sackett as he explained the differences and the greater safety of the more involved version. Then he said he would be happy to take commissions for similar halters if any of the guests were interested.

"Handmade by me in any color you like." He added with a grin, "Any *solid* color, at least."

Ethan's usual Monday involved a staff meeting, then a lot of paperwork unless he was in the field—which, in his line of work, often meant a literal field.

He'd expected things to feel different that week, after he'd dropped his bombshell about leaving the practice. To his vague disappointment, everybody took the news in stride. Nobody even seemed surprised or put out. It was just another item on the agenda.

"Way to make me feel needed, y'all," he'd finally let out, when the whole practice seemed ready to move on to the pressing issue of who would be vetting the latest round of new calves at the Schultz farm.

The office manager shot him a quelling look over her reading glasses. "Ethan. Don't be petulant."

Malik Winston, the managing partner of the practice, chuckled. "So glad I got you that word-a-day calendar, Beverly. That was a good investment."

One of the other associate vets, Angelo Torres, made a kissy face at Ethan. "You know we love you, man. But exactly no one here is shocked by this. Old Doc Taylor's what, five hundred and three, now? He's been talking about retiring for at least ten years."

"Longer," Dr. Winston corrected him.

"Okay," Angelo went on, "so you didn't want to buy in here because you were always planning to take over for him, right? Since you were in kindergarten or something, and he cured your pony."

"Third grade," Ethan grumbled, "and it was one of my grandparents' mares. He hasn't retired yet, mind you." They'd all made the assumption that he had an understanding with Taylor and was leaving to start working at his practice; Ethan hadn't corrected them because it would be true eventually, right?

Dr. Winston leaned over the conference table, shaking his head. "Yeah, I'll believe it when I see it with Taylor. He'll be out doing jobs until he keels over. But hey, congratulations on the move, and

I'm glad to hear the ranch is doing so well. Sorry if we all seemed underwhelmed. You'll definitely be missed."

"Thanks." Ethan felt like a complete asshole. "Sorry, I didn't mean to derail things."

"You've derailed the spring schedule more than the meeting, but we'll figure things out. Uh, in fact, Bev, after we finish the meeting, let's you and me look at the calendar and try to carve out some time for interviews. Okay, so where were we . . . calving time at Schultz's?"

Ethan spent the rest of the morning on state vaccine reporting forms, one of his least favorite parts of the job. He couldn't lose himself in that, the way he could when he worked with animals. He had to take frequent breaks, move around, remind himself how important the information was. Hard-learned study skills that continued to come in handy.

He had sent his resignation email after the staff meeting: two weeks' notice, but he was flexible about the end date if they had trouble with scheduling. Apparently they didn't. By late that afternoon, when he came back in from a follow-up visit to a horse with a snakebit nose, he saw Dr. Winston and Dr. Abelard, the other partner, leaning over Bev's shoulder as she studied her computer monitor.

Dr. Abelard was pointing to the screen. "And if she can make it by then, she can also help with the yearling stuff at Lockwood's. She's got a great bedside manner. Maybe she can actually get along with Rusty."

Bev nudged the vet's finger aside gently. "Trudy, I love you, but if you touch my screen one more time . . ."

"Sorry. Hey, Ethan! We think we found your replacement!"

Trudy Abelard was beaming, and Ethan pasted on a smile he didn't feel in return. "That's awesome. Who?"

"It's amazing. I was editing the job posting to get it ready when my niece pinged me out of the blue. You know Marguerite, the one who was up in Oklahoma? She'd mostly been doing relief jobs up there. Her husband just got transferred back to San Antonio, and she was asking me to keep an ear to the ground for any associate spots because now that they're moving back, they plan to stay. They're in town right now, house-hunting. Can you believe the timing?"

"Wow." That timing was pretty astonishing. "That's like . . . fate."

Fuck. No take backsies now, even if he'd wanted that. Not if they were bringing in a relative. Trudy's protégée no less. She'd been so proud when her favorite niece decided to follow in her footsteps; now she was beaming at the prospect of bringing Marguerite into the practice.

They focused on the schedule again, chattering brightly, hardly noticing when Ethan waved and headed into the back office area to write up his notes on the horse.

It was as if they'd already started to work around him. He was as good as gone. And free to pursue his kinky entrepreneurial dreams.

Chapter 3

Victoria was surprised by how easy it turned out to be to completely uproot her life. She'd thought herself so settled in Providence. But after the month she'd already spent purging the excess from her studio—selling off what she could, in the end giving away things to avoid having to move or store them—she had little trouble fitting the stuff that remained in the trunk and backseat of her car. She'd allotted an hour for loading up and last-minute emergencies; she wound up leaving Providence thirty minutes ahead of schedule.

At five-thirty on a Sunday morning, there wasn't much traffic. She made it out of the city, down through Cranston and Warwick, her car a deep blue shadow in the pre-dawn chill. When she spotted a Starbucks sign near Mystic, she exited and made a loop to find it. She knew it was an expense she could ill afford, but something about it fed her soul. One last fling to wash down the nutty granola bar she'd been saving for breakfast. One last middle finger at Larry, too, who had always bitched about his primary competition, even as he refused to add wi-fi or any food options beyond the barest minimum of morning pastries.

When she finally got back on the I-95 and had a chance to take a sip, she realized with a start that she could have made a better latte herself. Maybe not such a crappy barista after all, even if she had still been kind of a slow one.

The early start got her through New London and a few more towns before the traffic started piling up. New York and a hefty chunk of New Jersey were one long nightmare, and by the time she hit the farm country again she was beginning to wonder if she'd ever make it off the East Coast. But by midday, when she stopped somewhere in Pennsylvania to stretch her legs and buy some chips, she took one deep breath of the air outside the car and knew she was in a different climate. The crisp wind bore a distinctly new flavor, pine and spruce and woodsmoke and frost that had never mixed with sea air.

She didn't have time to stop and sightsee. It wasn't even particularly scenic—just a gas station across the street from a few houses that had seen better days, and wintry-bare trees all around with evergreens peeking through. Snow patched the ground, thin and grimy, more of it gray or sand-colored near the parking lot than white. Through the trees, she could see some better-preserved stretches. When she walked closer to the edge of the lot to get a better look, she spotted a set of marks crossing the surface of one low drift: perfect bird tracks, so clear she could practically envision the thing hopping along. A cardinal maybe. Or something less vivid, but she liked to think it was a cardinal, dangerously cheerful against the white background.

Cardinals were small. How did they get away with being bright red anyway? A question for the internet to answer later, if she remembered to ask. It felt good to notice things again; since Christmas she'd been so wound up over leaving school, working, selling things off, trying to make ends meet, that she'd had no time to do so much as sketch, much less anything truly creative. With the moment-to-moment tension gone, her artistic mind was awakening again. This drive, crazy though it might be, was a short vacation from the harsh realities of her new life as an actual adult.

It felt like vacation now because she wasn't used to it, but it had been her way of life up until five weeks ago. One long vacation from reality. No wonder she'd done well at design; she'd never been distracted by having to deal with the entire bottom half of Maslow's hierarchy. Sure, she'd worked for her grades, and even if she sometimes doubted her talent—what artist didn't?—she had plenty of objective affirmation that she was good at her chosen field. But in a way, her dad wasn't wrong. She had been taking without thinking. Stuff had been handed to her. *Opportunity* had been handed to her. She'd known that before, but she'd always thought of the *big* opportunities as the important factor: the chance to get a great private education with tutors whenever she needed them, the chance to attend the best design school. Getting to stay in a family friend's Manhattan loft while she'd done two of her summer internships, instead of in a tiny, shabby apartment shared with five other people. Accepting last summer's Paris internship with Balenciaga without a thought for the expense. She'd flown first class and she'd appreciated that. But it hadn't occurred to her that the distinction wasn't between flying first class and coach. It wasn't even between flying first class or not flying at all. It was between never having to worry about anything and having to worry about *everything* because you weren't sure you would have the money to eat that day if you paid the electric bill. Which expense was more important? Which could be put off another day or week? And how could you get the money to cover at least one expense, to take one massive, pressing concern off the endless list for a short time?

She'd thought *hardship* meant not getting to do things in style, or sometimes not getting to do the things you preferred. So naïve. Hardship meant your choices were between bad and worse, if you were lucky enough to get those choices at all.

Now she was driving straight back to her parents, after barely over a month of trying to make it on her own. Sure, she'd told herself it was about returning the car and living on the cheap in Dallas, but . . . what about once she got there? For twenty-two years they'd kept her in a bubble and she hadn't even realized it. She wasn't sure *they* had realized it. They weren't awful people; they meant well and only wanted to protect her. If she went back home and they offered her an easy way out—as they almost certainly would—did she have the strength to refuse?

A pickup truck drove into the station, its tires scraping the salt-and-sand-strewn asphalt as it turned. The harsh sound broke the reverent winter stillness, and with a sigh and a final stretch, Victoria returned to her car. She scrolled through her playlists, finally settling on a mix of show tunes, and then pulled back out onto the road, pointed toward the narrowest overlapping segments of Maryland and West Virginia.

At a certain point it all started to look uniformly Appalachian. Ridge-and-valley country, the part that looked like ripples on a relief map. In real life it was mile upon mile of nearly straight road edged by endless ranks of winter-bare trees, only the evergreens hinting at the colors the landscape might provide in another month or two. The land looked completely fed up with the whole stark winter beauty deal. At least the good weather had been holding since she'd left

Rhode Island; the sky was a flat, pale gray-blue, as bland and drained as if it, too, was sick and tired of winter.

Grungy little towns loomed up, unmemorable and quickly passed by. When she hit Lexington, Virginia, it was near sunset, and she scanned the chain motels along the highway. They looked clean, well-lit. From her admittedly brief research, she knew most of them were within her tiny budget.

She had never stayed in a motel before. She started to pull into the one she'd picked, heard her mother's gasp of horror, and drove right past, hating herself.

People do this all the time. This is what people do. And her only other affordable option was to sleep in the car: not a risk she was willing to take.

She swung into a drive-through burger place and defiantly ordered off the value menu. A burger, some fries, a weirdly large soda.

With dinner cooling, she was motivated to act quickly. She circled back to the motel, parked, and practically jogged to the reception desk inside. Paid cash up-front for the room, then found it and quickly unloaded all her things from the backseat.

Not quickly enough. Her burger was already stone cold by the time she'd dragged the last suitcase inside, double-checked that the car was locked, and then closed and bolted the door to her room.

She munched on a clammy French fry as she sized up the place. It looked clean enough, although it was a bit musty; the bathroom smelled of disinfectant, but there was nothing obviously gross happening there.

The bed checked out as reasonably comfortable; when she flopped onto it faceup, spread-eagled, it didn't poke or sink in or squeak. She lay there for a moment, then giggled and moved her arms and legs, tracing an angel shape on the orange-and-brown bedspread. Rolling over to examine the shaved-chenille fabric, she decided the design wasn't too bad: a pattern of overlapping rings that neither drew nor deflected the eye in any dramatic way.

"Way to turn orange into a neutral."

Or the way to camouflage something . . . Her mother's fears rose up as if they were her own, and she practically flung herself off the bed with a curse, then reapproached it with her heart in her throat. She flipped up one corner of the coverlet by the foot, mumbled *please, please, please* a few times, then plucked the sheets back from the mattress.

No brown or red flecks. Even in the crevices between the piping and the fabric, or tucked under the pillow top, when she finally steeled herself to start exploring further. The rest of the corners, the sheets and blankets, and the nooks and crannies around the headboard checked out, too. As did the two chairs and the curtains. No telltale spots, no tiny beasties fleeing from the glare of her cell phone flashlight.

The burger was a semicongealed lump, but it was calories she'd paid for, so she ate it anyway, slumping in one of her bedbug-free chairs with her feet propped up on the equally vermin-free bed.

Something had gone her way for the first time in a while. Sure, her standards had sunk pretty low if the highlights of her day were *saw some cool bird tracks in the snow; didn't encounter bedbugs.* But she would take what she could get.

Halfway through her meal, she paused long enough to pull up a video on her laptop—*She's a Good Skate, Charlie Brown*, one of her favorite comfort watches, especially the part where Snoopy turned out to be a whiz with fabric and design. She needed a moment to chill out before the task ahead.

By afternoon the day after tomorrow, she'd be in Dallas. She'd already chickened out on calling her mother with a specific arrival time, instead texting her the vaguest details she thought she could get away with and saying she didn't need a ride from the airport. But at some point on the drive, she'd realized she wasn't ready to go home at all. It was childish and cowardly and probably meant she had a rotten character. But she didn't think she had the strength to go running home with her tail between her legs after massively fucking up her brief and ridiculously ill-considered bid for independence.

Her parents would probably take her right back to a string of psychiatrists and psychologists, just like they'd done when she was a little kid struggling in school. Struggling compared to her older sister, Alexandra, at least, who had apparently come out of the womb reading and writing legal briefs and doing trigonometry in her head.

The experts had all insisted there was nothing wrong with Victoria; she just wasn't performing like her older sister because she was a different child with different strengths. She excelled in art, in visual-spatial tasks, and some verbal skills, but not in pencil-paper work and standardized tests . . . which meant she was hard to quantify. Her parents had taken all that to mean she would never be able to achieve much academically. They'd sent her, along with a huge chunk of money, to the best school they could find . . . a girls-only boarding school. In small classes, with intensive tutoring, her grades naturally improved. As far as Victoria could tell, her parents never credited her hard work or considered that their assessment of her ability had been wrong; they'd praised the school and made a lot of jokes about how funding that additional computer lab had been worth every penny.

Soon her biggest problem was homesickness. Her parents lined up extra sessions with the school psychologist, who counseled her to make friends and find a "family" at the school. Eventually she had, in a way. Mostly she'd given up feeling like her parents would ever validate her the way they did Alexandra, but she didn't really resent it. Those were the breaks, and at boarding school her teachers loved and nurtured her passion for the arts as they would any form of gift-edness.

Victoria's parents loved her very much. She knew that. But she was a lateish afterthought of a child who hadn't been the perfect follow-up they'd expected, and they didn't like it when they felt they were having to *deal* with her. They didn't like a lot of cause for concern. Or a lot of questions. They liked things that went smoothly, according to the manual, and required only routine maintenance for optimal functioning. The newest model of any electronic device. A fresh-off-the-lot BMW. A child who either blew the roof off all standardized testing and went on to clerk for Supreme Court justices before vaulting into one of the youngest junior partnerships in the history of law firms . . . or perhaps a daughter who might have been an unobjectionable English or business major and had the equivalent success in sororities, then the Junior League, after finding a husband who was the male equivalent of Alexandra.

Those weren't things Victoria had ever said aloud to her parents. Mostly because after a few years away at boarding school—they'd put her in the residential program for "socialization", even though they lived not five miles away from the school—she'd learned not to talk to them about anything that mattered to her. It never went well. They were nice people who loved her, but they didn't get her and she didn't get them. She didn't particularly crave their approval anymore . . . but she didn't want them to hate her.

Unfair, ungrateful, ungracious, immature . . . Victoria was probably all of those things for wanting to throw away the advantages her parents had given her, but she couldn't handle hearing the words from them yet. Not after the events of the last few days. She didn't want to hear them say—or at least imply, yet again—that she was *their problem.* She didn't want to be *anybody's* problem. She didn't even need to be anybody's solution. She just wanted to be herself, and have that be enough.

However . . . practically speaking, she did need to stay somewhere for at least a few nights until she found a job and some sort of cheap living situation. Once she had her feet under her, she would be in a better position to talk to her parents. It would be nice to have an intermediary, someone to smooth the way with them in the meantime, reassuring them that she was safe and they didn't need to worry. And only one person could fill that role.

Victoria and her sister Alexandra had never been particularly close. Too many years separated them, and they were so different in almost every way. But since Victoria had moved to Rhode Island they'd started to email and text each other more frequently about other things. Less like a much-older sibling with a pesky teenage sister and more like peers. Almost like friends.

Victoria paused the video and dragged her cell phone toward her; it slid easily over the Formica table that hugged the corner of the motel room. She would miss the phone horribly when she had to give it up; it had been a lifesaver this past week, and she wasn't sure how she would function without GPS and the internet always at her fingertips. People did, though. So she would learn to.

It dawned on her that some of the self-proclaimed Luddites at RISD who eschewed smartphones and carried around only the barest-boned, dumb models probably weren't being hipsters at all, as she'd always assumed; they were doing it to save money. She'd had this realization about so many things the past month that the sensation had grown familiar, but it never got any less horrifying when she looked back and considered how insensitive she'd probably been in her blind privilege; sometimes she felt the entire world was one big conspiracy about thrift that she hadn't been aware of for twenty-two years. Now her eyes were opening slowly, and the light was painful on her previously shaded retinas.

She took up the phone and navigated to her contacts, taking the long way around to get to the information she needed. It really wasn't a time for email or texting, but she hated phone calls, and this one wouldn't be easy. But it would be easier than showing up on her parents' doorstep in two days.

Finally, she steeled herself and made the call. As it rang, she pulled her legs up into the chair and hugged her knees, constricting herself as much as possible.

"Hello? Vic?" Alexandra sounded busy and distracted. She always did, though.

"Hey, Alex. How's it going?"

A heavy sigh overloaded the phone for a second, then a muffled thump and curse. "Gimme a second." More thumping, then the distinct sound of a door closing. "Okay. What the fuck is going on, Victoria? And make it quick. I have to get back to a meeting."

Shit. "I'm sorry. I can call you tomorrow. I—"

"Are you pregnant?"

"What? No. Why is that the first thing people keep—?"

"Mom's convinced you're knocked up and suffering from temporary pregnancy insanity. I told her that wasn't a thing, but she didn't seem receptive."

"I am neither pregnant nor insane."

"Then why are you on this weird-ass road trip? She's hiding something, I can tell."

Victoria's stomach clenched. "R-road trip? How . . . how do you . . . what makes you think that?"

Another sigh. "Oh, baby girl. For fuck's sake. You're carrying an iPhone on a plan in Daddy's name. You're driving a BMW he owns. Do you really think he doesn't know where you are at every minute of every day? Oh, and Mom's alternate theory is drugs. I think she's been binge-watching *Intervention*."

"No, not drugs." Victoria's face was numb, her lips icy and tingling. God, she'd been so stupid. No, ignorant. Layers and layers of ignorance, and just when she thought she was getting to the core, she looked around and saw she had barely dented the surface of the . . . life onion, or whatever people meant when they talked about layers all the time. "Hey, what's that thing where you're so stupid you don't even know how stupid you are? It has a name . . . something hyphenated?"

"Oh my God, your jackrabbit brain. *Creatives*. Are you talking about the Dunning-Kruger effect?"

"Yes!"

"You don't have that. That's people without skills thinking they *do* have skills. You have some skills, but you have . . . unconscious incompetence or something. I don't know, I'm not a psychologist. Vic, what is Mom hiding and why are you calling me at . . . God, I can't believe these people are *still* in my conference room. I was going to say *at work*, but probably you thought I would be at home by now, like a normal person."

Victoria rubbed her lips, fleetingly wondering when she'd last washed her face or put on lip gloss. Her skin felt dry, her lips chapped. "I called to ask if I can stay at your place for a few days once I get to town the day after tomorrow. Only until I find a job and have a chance to talk to some friends, see if somebody'll let me couch surf for a bit. Oh, and if you and Paul still have the truck, could I . . . borrow it or rent it or something for a little while?"

A voice called in the background of Alexandra's phone, no more distinct than the *Peanuts* grown-up voice. *Wah-wah-wah-wah-waaaah.*

Alexandra answered the voice. "Rashid, just tell everybody to take a ten, okay? We'll reconvene at eight-thirty. Vic? I'm skipping the part where you're apparently coming back to Dallas and living like a drifter. Tell me *now* whatever it is that our parents haven't been telling me. Because I have had a *very* long day and I don't have time for this. If I can help you I will, but I need you to cut to the chase."

Victoria didn't blame her. Nobody ever had time for it. She swallowed, took a deep breath, then spilled. "I overheard Daddy calling me the black hole where his money goes and saying I was too dumb to realize I was supposed to be trolling the Brown campus for a husband. So I cut up my bank card and withdrew from school. I've been working as a barista to cover expenses and I thought I had it all under control, but a few days ago my boss told me I had to blow him to keep the job, so I quit. Then I realized I'd already talked the landlord into letting me out of the lease. And Providence is tiny and expensive and really, really cold. And Dallas is big and cheap and warm, and I know people there with pool houses and garage apartments I could maybe stay in. Plus, I need to give the car back to Daddy anyway. So I just . . . hit the road."

"Jesus. Okay. Okay, so . . . okay. God. Are you all right? Physically, from the thing with your boss?"

"Yeah. He didn't really touch me. I mean, he tried to put my hand on his dick. Mostly he was just an asshole."

"No. That isn't *just* being an asshole. That is sexual assault. Did you report it to anybody?"

"No," Victoria admitted. "Well, except kind of the other employees, as I was leaving. Including his girlfriend, apparently. Who I think will probably tell his wife."

"*Ooh.* All right. We probably have some time . . . I'll research the laws and statutes for Rhode Island. You should *definitely* get some therapy about that or a support group or something. Meanwhile . . . ugh, I can't even get to the main thing. There are so many layers of men being dicks in this situation."

"I *know*," Victoria commiserated. "We both knew Daddy could be . . . well, kind of a sexist frat bro, let's face it."

Alexandra snort-laughed. "Jeez, Vic. Okay. Fair enough. He's a *type*, for sure. He's ethical at least, I'll give him that one."

"For sure. But it did catch me off guard to be . . . okay, I wasn't surprised to hear him being a misogynist, I just never expected to hear it aimed at *me*. It threw me." She ran her fingers through her hair and realized that was overdue for a wash, too. "I acted hastily and in anger, and it was probably stupid."

"No probably about it. It was absolutely stupid. You had one semester left and all your bills were being paid. Do you have any idea how fucking lucky you were to have that?"

"I'm starting to. I think I have a way to go yet."

"I . . ." Alexandra paused, and Victoria could hear tapping. Fingers on a keyboard, absurdly fast. "Of course you can come to my place. I'm going to look into some things. I have to go, though. What time will you get here, do you think?"

Victoria smirked. "Couldn't you just ask Daddy?"

"Touché. Are you going to call them? They're really worried."

"I texted Mom. I can't . . . do more than that right now. I just can't. And I should be there sometime between lunch and dinner. It depends when I leave that morning. I'm hoping to make Memphis by tomorrow night, so I'll be heading out from there."

"Okay, kiddo. Paul should be at the house, so he'll make sure you have something to eat and set you up in the guest room. He may be out picking up the kids, but he's usually back home with them by four."

Paul, Alexandra's husband, was a political blogger who worked from home.

"I'll time my arrival accordingly." Victoria revived her laptop screen, traced her finger over the trackpad, then pulled up *She's a Good Skate, Charlie Brown* again, hitting pause before it could restart. "And thank you so much."

"Okay. I have to go, I have several testy Norwegians and Brits in my conference room. Not to mention the locals."

"What you get for picking oil and gas law. See you day after tomorrow, Alex."

"It chose me. But I think that may work out in your favor, with what I have in mind. G'night, Vic."

She hung up before explaining her last, cryptic remark.

Victoria put her phone facedown on the table, sliding it behind the laptop so she wouldn't see it if it lit up again. She had run out of mental energy to even wonder what Alex was talking about. She rattled the ice in the bottom of her ridiculously large Value soda, dug for the last few bits of French fry, and hit Play.

Victoria had grand plans to fuel her entire drive's caffeine requirement the next day with one small Styrofoam cup of free coffee from the motel room coffeemaker; that didn't even get her out of Lexington. She found the closest open drive-through, bought a big cup of the cheap stuff, and loaded it with all the sugar and cream the guy at the window would give her. Cost-effective and filling. Forty-five minutes later, at the inevitable rest stop, she got to appreciate the sunrise from a nearby scenic overlook.

It was a long haul to Memphis, and in some ways the reverse of the previous day's drive. Mile upon mile of thinly populated Appalachian wrinkles, finally giving way to relatively flatter land with a lot more concrete and cars.

That night, unable to face another "value" meal, she pulled into a grocery store before settling on a motel. The past month had taught her the beauty of the clearance aisle, and after she'd grabbed some peanut butter, crackers, and a box of store-brand granola cereal, she spotted the best find of all: a rack of cheap, oversized insulated mugs, half off their original low price. Three bucks. If she'd gotten one before leaving Providence, it would've already paid for itself.

She snagged one that read *"Memphis, Home of the Blues."* Would it leak? Probably.

But she only had one important question for the motel clerk when she walked up to the desk. "Is there complimentary coffee and a coffeemaker in every room?"

There was indeed. Victoria had to stifle the urge to fist-pump as she paid for the night.

This time she checked for bedbugs *before* bringing her stuff in. She counted it another small victory, or at least the absence of a failure, which seemed to be her new standard.

Chapter 4

Victoria was worn out from her road trip by the time she finally hit Dallas. If she'd been a bit more alert when Alexandra got home from work, she might have asked her sister about the plan she'd fleetingly mentioned on the phone. As it was, exhausted and emotionally bruised, Victoria spent most of their evening unloading about her past month or so, especially about the incident with Larry. Then she fell asleep on the couch in midsentence and didn't budge until the smell of coffee woke her the next morning.

Fortunately, Alexandra had been able to shift some meetings and get the day free. The Beemer made amazing time between Dallas and the little town of Bolero, where Alex swore Victoria would be able to chill, regroup, and figure things out in her own time. In a quiet, bucolic setting where the guys looked like cowboys and probably wouldn't act like douche canoes.

Victoria was experiencing some déjà vu on the half-day drive across central Texas. The landscape was different, but the navigation was the same: pick a road—in this case, I-35—and stay on it until your eyes were about to cross from boredom. At least she had company this time. "But aren't *most* cowboys a little bit . . . I mean, it's not like I haven't known plenty. They're great on old-school chivalry, but it's not the group I'd associate with deep respect for women in the modern, feminist fashion, you know?"

"They aren't *real* cowboys. Have you been listening at all?"

"Honestly, not until about eight? Before that you're lucky I kept the car in the lane and stayed more or less awake."

"God. Why didn't you just ask me to drive?"

"Too sleepy to think of it." She slid to one side of a semi, racing up the left lane to get ahead of it, then eased back into the right lane, appreciating the responsiveness of the steering. She would miss the car's handling, the smell of the leather seats, the ergonomics. But Alex had implied there would be vehicles she could borrow at—what was it called? Hilltop? "Fine. Tell me again where we're going and why I can't just stay at your place?"

"Will you listen this time?"

"I'll give it my best shot."

Alex sighed—her hard-put-upon sigh. She sounded a lot like her six-year-old daughter, Piper. "It's a guest ranch. Like a dude ranch. But they've only started up again the past year or so, and there are cabins that aren't ready for hotel guests yet, aren't up to code or standards or whatever. I don't know. Mindy said they had a place you could stay as long as you liked, to figure things out. Um, except for one weekend a month, when there's a big private event at the ranch or something. But apparently you can house-sit at her place in town on those weekends. 'Town' being Bolero."

"Mindy's the friend who's also an oil and gas lawyer, right? Or . . . wait, no, not a lawyer."

"She was a landman."

"She? Was a . . . huh?"

"A landman. It's just what the job is called, Vic. It's an oil-and-gas thing, okay?" Alex slurped at her tea ungracefully; their mother would have tsked in disapproval. "So that's how I knew her. But she went up to Hilltop for a weekend and it turned out she'd gone to school with the owner—who *isn't* a cowboy or a rancher, he's a former petroleum engineer, so basically a nerd in redneck clothing. They fell in love, she quit a job she hated, moved to his ranch, happily ever after. Now she helps him run the place. There's horseback riding, nature hikes, even camping. We've come up a few times with Piper. She loves the place."

"Do you and Paul camp?"

"Oh fuck no. Are you insane? We get one of the fancy cabins."

Victoria glanced at a road sign, then at the gas gauge. They had over a quarter tank, so they should be fine as long as Alex remembered to fill up before starting back to Dallas from wherever in the boonies this town turned out to be.

When Victoria had started to unload her car the night before,

Alex had stopped her. "*Don't bother. We'd just be packing it into another car, then unpacking it when we get there. I'll drive the Beemer back to the city and get it to Daddy, don't worry.*"

Alex's plan, as far as Victoria could make out, was for Victoria to hang out at this Hilltop Ranch place, chill for a while, figure out her next steps, possibly get some therapy. And it would be far enough away from Dallas that their parents wouldn't be in her face the whole time, asking questions. Or, more to the point, Victoria suspected, wouldn't be at Alex's place all the time pestering both of them. But that was fine. Victoria didn't mind some distance. If she had to venture into San Antonio to find a job, she'd need a vehicle, but Alex had made it sound like that wouldn't be a problem.

"Okay. It does sound like a great place to get my head together. But what about when I come back to Dallas?"

Alexandra sipped her tea, then made a production of consulting the GPS on her phone. As if they weren't on the same road they'd been on for the past four hours and wouldn't be on it for quite a bit longer before they had to do anything resembling navigation. "I think," she said at last, "you should focus on yourself. Don't worry about a deadline for getting back. Take your time to work things out and get your finances in order. Or . . . whatever."

That would have sounded supportive and reasonable if she hadn't taken so long to say it; as it was, Victoria's neck prickled with unease. "Okay."

"See the signs for Loop 1604? We'll be taking that exit, so head's up."

"Oh." Sooner than she'd expected, somehow. "We aren't even to San Antonio yet."

"We swing north of town. Hopefully avoiding some traffic, but we'll see. Google Maps says it's green, but one wreck and that's shot to shit."

"Thanks again for setting all this up." Victoria was still stunned with relief at having a little time to figure out what to do next without being practically in her parents' backyard.

"Don't thank me yet." Alexandra swirled the remainder of her tea in the cup lid, then swigged it back and reached for a tissue from the box on the floor to swipe it dry before replacing it on the vacuum flask.

That prickle up the spine again. "And . . . why not?"

"Oh, you know. Just . . . rustic accommodations. Scorpions, probably. Definitely some massive spiders."

"Ah. Great. Well, beggars can't be choosers, I guess."

"That's true. Literally." Shifting in her seat to face Victoria, Alex sighed and gave her an earnest look. "And you should remember that once we get there, okay?"

What the actual fuck? Exactly how big were those spiders? But . . . Alex had gone out of her way to arrange this, had even taken the day to make the drive with her little sister. "I'll remember."

"Good." Alex turned front again and pointed at a road sign on the next overpass, tapping the roof as they swept under it. "That's 1604. Get over to the far-right lane."

Victoria changed lanes, scanning the stores on the feeder road as she glanced behind her to check the blind spot. "Hey, look, a Spec's. Can we stop?" Not that she had any extra money to spend on liquor, but she had a sneaking suspicion that at some point in the next few hours she might be in the mood for a shot of something mind-numbing.

Alexandra treated it as the rhetorical question it probably should have been. Victoria kept driving, wishing she knew what awaited her at her destination.

Ethan had only planned to stay at Hilltop long enough to exercise Sackett, let his dog Roxie have a good run, then head back to work. He was on call, technically, but Trudy had Marguerite handy to assist if anything came up. The practice's prospective new addition had shown up bright and early that morning and seemed to be making herself right at home.

Turning Sackett back toward the barn after a quick loop around the hilltop trail, Ethan decided on a brief detour. He angled the horse in the direction of his tiny house build site and dismounted near what would soon be the front deck. A fine old pecan tree was perfectly positioned to shade the area when the summer days were hottest; now, in February, there was still a bit of a glare in the afternoons. But he could already feel the potential. He couldn't wait to have the deck complete, to sit outside his own front door of an evening and watch the sun go down.

He slid off Sackett and let the reins down, ground tying the horse, then circled the house and satisfied himself everything was secure. The coppery roof and new solar panel frames reflected the sunlight, as did the white moisture wrap around the sections of the exterior that hadn't been sided yet. He hadn't made as much progress lately as he'd hoped; now, maybe he'd have more time to work on it. It might even be done before the hot weather really kicked in.

Leaning against the side of the house, he indulged in a deep sniff of the old cedar he'd already placed along one wall. The smell was strongest along the new cuts, but even the weathered sections were faintly aromatic, and it was a *good* smell. Wholesome, authentic. Like something homey and built to last. He reached out and rubbed his hands along the rough surface, knowing the smell would linger on his skin. Even half-completed, the house was starting to feel like *his place*. Everything felt like it was clicking into alignment, the whole universe going Ethan's way.

Roxie, sniffing around the trailer's base, suddenly lifted her head and pricked her ears, her compact black-and-white form going instantly into alert mode. A few seconds later, Ethan heard what seemed to have set her off: raised voices carried on the fitful breeze. Licking his forefinger and raising it, he tested the wind's direction before it could die down again. The yelling had come from the main house, apparently. Good to know his secluded hilltop grove channeled sound from that area. He might have to move to another spot if he wanted peace and quiet.

Over by the pecan tree, Sackett seemed interested in the noise too; his big ears strained in the same direction as Roxie's. Fitful gusts of breeze carried a few clear words to Ethan and his animal companions. Enough words to suggest that something unpleasant was going down at the main house.

"*Mumble UNBELIEVAgarble garble garble NOT YOUR DECISION garble mumble TELL YOU TO FUCK OFF IF I mumble garble . . . DAMMIT!*"

Ethan winced. "Yikes." It hadn't sounded like Mindy, but the wind could play tricks. He hoped his brother wasn't at the receiving end of . . . whatever that was.

Glancing around at the view, the house frame, the siding planks still waiting to be placed, he gave himself a moment to fix the scene in his mind. It had been, for a few moments at least, near perfection. His animals nearby, the smell of cedar and pine and hard work in his nostrils, a reminder of his physical accomplishment and that he could soon leave his town house behind for good. He hated to step out of that magic bubble of unexpected, simple enjoyment. But the babble of raised voices wafted toward him again and he sighed in resignation.

He whistled sharply, grabbing both animals' attention. Roxie shook herself out and pranced toward the trailhead, circling in readiness as Ethan gathered Sackett's reins, then swung into the saddle.

"Maybe we'll get to ride in and save the day."

Sackett snorted, and Ethan chuckled at the perfect timing. Then he urged the sturdy buckskin into motion down the trail that led toward the horse barn and the main house.

The worst part was, Victoria knew Alexandra was right. This *was* a golden opportunity. She *should* be grateful she had a place to go and people willing to take her in and give her work. She *had* acted foolishly and put herself in this position, more or less. She was, in fact, behaving exactly like the spoiled little princess everybody thought she was. Yelling, cursing on a stranger's lawn, being not only unkind but ungracious. Inexcusable.

But *dammit*.

"Dammit!" She stomped a foot in her frustration, wincing as her toe came down on a rock. Out of spite—and because she was wearing cowboy boots anyway, so what the hell—she kicked the rock. It skittered only a few feet. Wholly unsatisfying.

"Are you finished?" Alexandra waited, eyebrows raised, arms folded over her chest. Not *really* looped together, but in that fancy way where the top hand rested lightly in the opposite elbow crook, fingers fanned to better display her manicure. She looked 100 percent unruffled, but also 100 percent done with the situation.

Victoria wished she had another rock to kick. "Yes, I'm finished." She crossed her arms, folding them carefully in conscious imitation of her older sister. Time for some damage control. "I apologize for my outburst. I just wasn't expecting to be offered up for manual labor to strangers for an indefinite period. A little warning would have been nice." Like at any point during the five hours they'd spent in the car that morning.

"Sure would've."

Ha-ha. "Fair enough."

"Look. You showed up on my doorstep and I found you, pretty much overnight, a place to live. Three squares a day. A job, provided you can make yourself useful." Alexandra sounded like she doubted it but was being too polite to say so. "All without having to ask Daddy for a bailout. And the weather's even nicer here than in Dallas most of the year. I realize it's not the vacation you probably hoped for, but it's not like I'm forcing you into indentured servitude here. I was only trying to help. You're free to walk away anytime you like."

Walk away. Literally, because Alex would be driving back up to Dallas in Victoria's former car once they'd hauled her stuff out of it.

A bailout . . . God, it was so tempting. Even now, Victoria could probably go back to RISD if she wanted to. She'd lost the semester, and because of the way the capstone courses were scheduled, that would probably set her back a full year on graduation, but she might be able to fill the time with additional interning, extra classes, *something*. It was ridiculous to get so close to graduation, then throw away the whole thing in a fit of pique; she knew that intellectually . . . even if her parents might scoff at the term *intellectual* as applied to her.

Then she pictured going to her father and confronting him with what she'd heard. Enduring his critique, his dismissal, his condescension. Or, maybe even worse, his excuses or rationalizations. She couldn't make herself do it.

Hilltop was way more beautiful than Alex had given it credit for, and Logan Hill and his girlfriend Mindy seemed genuinely nice. They had been more than willing, at a day's notice, to let a friend's wayward little sister stay on the ranch indefinitely as long as she helped out around the place. They were being incredibly generous, and she was being a huge asshole to have responded to Mindy and Alexandra's initial discussion of Victoria's job description—"*as we discussed on the phone yesterday*"—with a tight smile, a tug on her sister's arm, and a curt, "*Alexandra, can we speak outside for a moment?*"

She'd just been so startled to hear Alex calmly outlining *her* plan and discussing it all with these two strangers as if Victoria didn't even have a say. Agreeing, on Victoria's behalf, that she would be more than capable of mucking out stables, doing laundry, serving food.

Those were all things she was willing to do to earn her keep . . . but *she* wanted to make that decision herself. Not have it listed to her as if she were a child being handed a chore chart. And especially not have it sprung on her this way—like a kid lured into Mom's car with a promise of ice cream only to be taken to the dentist. Or to the new boarding school.

To their credit, neither Logan nor Mindy had batted an eye when Victoria had first walked in and they'd all recognized each other from a kink club in Dallas. The introductions had been perfectly polite, as though Wildcat and Ariel had never seen Velvet wound from head to toe in rope and spinning, inverted, from a suspension scaffold while a top carefully caned her ass once on each rotation. And as if she'd never seen Wildcat flogging Ariel into a deliriously joyful orgasm. The unexpected secret acquaintance was a curiosity, though; it didn't factor in to the bigger issue of Alexandra trying to make decisions for Victoria. Even if it had helped to ramp up Victoria's anxiety about the whole situation to the point of her storming out for a perhaps not entirely deserved rant at her sister.

"Look." Alexandra's fingers tightened around her own upper arm to the point where her knuckles whitened. She was apparently trying to keep her cool. "You can't get something for nothing, Victoria."

"I didn't *ask*—"

"You're going to have to earn your keep here. That was the choice you made."

As if she hadn't already realized that months ago. "If you had just told me what the deal was, I would have—"

"Would have what?" Alex shifted her hands to her hips. "Refused to get in the car with me? Tried to couch surf somewhere and get another minimum-wage job at a . . . what was it, a *coffee shop*?" She might as well have been saying *cesspit* or *bordello*. Disgust tightened her lips, marring the plastic-perfect lines of her face. "You can't live like that."

Frustration rose in Victoria's gullet like bile, hot and thick and bitter. "I would have known in advance and not been surprised. That was all I was going to say. I could have made an informed decision. Instead, you assumed you knew best, just like everybody else does, and you tried to do everything *for* me. When I asked you for help, I wasn't asking you to take over and arrange my life. I didn't ask you to find me a job, or even a permanent living arrangement; I just asked if I could use your guest room for a few days." She exhaled, closing her eyes, trying to release some of the sick tension in her gut. "I appreciate the help. I really do. I'm sorry I was startled and angry, and I'm sorry I told you to fuck off. But I am *just so tired* of people assuming they know what I need better than I do. Assuming that I'm incapable of deciding for myself instead of giving me tools to make good decisions."

"I . . ." Alexandra bit her lip, then shrugged. "Okay, fair. I guess I was doing that. I should have let you know everything Mindy and I talked about before we came here. But you have to admit, you've made some deeply questionable choices recently."

Victoria wasn't sure that was true. She thought she'd made some hasty decisions that came from the right place and had unforeseen consequences. But how was she supposed to learn about consequences if she never got the chance? Her bills had always been paid and she'd never had to worry about a thing, but that meant she hadn't known how many things there were to worry about out in the real world. She hadn't merely had a safety net all her life; she'd practically been enveloped in Bubble Wrap and stored in a vault.

Some time she would have to ask Alexandra how she'd borne it long enough to get through law school. Whether she'd had to fight to learn this stuff, too, or whether their parents had simply assumed she'd be able to handle it because she never had any of the early school struggles Victoria had. But right now, Victoria had some ground to make up with her potential employer. Because angry though she might be with Alex, it really was too good an opportunity to pass up. Especially if her new employers could help introduce her to the local kink scene. "We should get back inside."

Alexandra looked about as thrilled at the prospect as Victoria felt. "I really hope you take the job. But I'll try to let you do the talking this time."

"Thanks, Sis." Victoria gazed up the steps to the farmhouse, unsure whether she was heading to her destiny or her doom. "I appreciate it."

Chapter 5

The yard in front of the house was empty when Ethan pulled Sackett to a halt and slid off. As he looped the reins around the hitching post, he scanned the clearing from the horse barn to the trailhead. Nobody was out there, and not a creature stirred in the dusty afternoon light except his brother's dappled gray, Charley, who was dozing at the rail.

"Huh."

With Roxie at his heels, he took the porch steps two at a time and opened the front door right on time to see his brother, Logan, lean out of the office down the hall and say the words nobody wants to hear when they've come to investigate a ruckus.

"Ethan! Just the person I was looking for."

Ethan caught the screen door before it could swing shut and started to back up, but he was too late to escape and he knew it. Roxie, puzzled by the sudden direction change, circled at his feet and nearly tripped him on her way back out the door.

"Ah, shit. Sorry, Rox."

Logan grinned—bared his teeth really. "Roxie! Bring 'em on."

Ethan groaned as his dog shifted position behind him, claws ticking on the wooden porch. She closed on his ankles, bumping one boot with her snout. Not quite a nip but close. *Damn Border collies.*

The last of his everything's-coming-up-Ethan high fizzled out. Sighing, he gave in and walked inside toward the office, following Logan. "What?"

"C'mon in here, bubba. I'm glad you happened by. Got some folks I want you to meet."

Logan's voice had gone extra-Texan, which usually signaled he was either angry or up to no good. Given the earlier shouting, Ethan feared it was some combination of the two, so he approached the office with considerable trepidation and stopped in the doorway.

Mindy waved at him, smiling way too broadly, just as Logan had. She nodded toward the couch, where Ethan recognized a comely brunette friend of Mindy's who'd visited the ranch a few times with her family. He couldn't recall her name—Adrian, Athena, Alexa?

"You remember Alexandra?" Mindy chirped at him.

He nodded and tipped his hat. "Nice to see you again." The last time he'd seen her, she'd been in jeans and boots, with a plaid shirt tied at her waist. Now she was wearing a buttoned-up blue Oxford, dark slacks, dusty flats, and looked out of place on the ranch.

Mindy moved on with the introductions. "This is her sister, Victoria Woodcock. Victoria, this is Ethan Hill, Logan's brother. Our vet, and also our semiresident rope-making expert."

The woman sitting next to Alexandra leaned forward, waving one hand with a casual "Hey," and Ethan finally saw her face.

She was the most beautiful woman in the world.

Okay. He wasn't quite sure what to do with that. He took off his hat and held it in his hands, nodding at the woman, blinking a few times to make sure she wasn't an illusion. Nope. She was really there and she really looked like that.

Logan was saying something, but Ethan couldn't focus on the words. He tried to break down exactly what it was about the woman that struck him as perfect. Her hair wasn't quite blond or brown but some in-between color with sunnier streaks in it. Dark gray eyes; it looked like maybe she'd been crying recently. Symmetrical features. Her cheeks were flushed, but he couldn't tell if it was from too much emotion or too much sun. No one element stood out. So what was it?

She was looking at him like she was uncomfortable, and he realized he was openmouthed, staring, about the same time Logan cleared his throat loudly.

"Sorry, what? I've, uh . . . I'm kinda worn out. Probably should've taken a lunch break." True, though unrelated to the staring thing.

"I *said*," Logan repeated, with a look that made it clear he suspected where Ethan's mind had been, "since you're going to have a bit more spare time on your hands, you get to be in charge of helping Victoria here learn the ropes . . . uh, so to speak. Help us figure out where her skills can best be used to help out around the place. She'll be shadowing you when you're here. Obviously, when you're at work, she can hang with Diego or Lamar. Maybe Robert. Victoria, do you cook any?"

"Well, I—" she started.

Alexandra broke in, snorting. "Are you serious?"

Victoria cleared her throat and shot her sister a glare that could strip paint from the side of a barn. *"Alex."*

"Sorry. Sorry. Go ahead." Alexandra sighed and fidgeted, sliding her hands under her thighs.

Victoria continued. "I've never cooked for large groups, or a restaurant or anything, but I cook for myself. And I bake a lot."

"You do?" Alexandra seemed genuinely surprised.

"Yes, I do."

"Okay, then." Logan clapped his hands, clearly satisfied with her answer. "So you can spend some time with Robert, too. Maybe you'll end up being the new part-time pastry chef or something. Excellent."

Mindy groaned and put a hand on one hip, pinching her waistline. "Just what we needed. More delicious food."

Logan grinned and slapped her on the butt, sharp enough for the sound to ring in the small room. Mindy chuckled. Alexandra put a hand to her mouth, her eyebrows lifting halfway to her forehead.

Ethan looked at Victoria, curious to see her reaction, but she was staring down at her clasped hands, playing with one of the half dozen or so silver rings adorning her fingers. Each ring was different, and she wore some of them at the middle knuckle. Weird. Her jeans had fashionable rips in them, which he'd always thought was the dumbest thing imaginable. And her boots looked sort of like cowboy boots, but they stopped at the ankle and had *zippers*. Useless. So . . . despite her looks, she was probably *not* part of the universe's recent decision to favor him, since it was pretty clear the last place she belonged was a ranch.

He had a house to build, rope to make, *plans*. He hadn't made a drastic career decision so he could become his brother's flunky; he had to get out of this. "I'm only here to exercise Sackett today. I was about to head back to the practice. Uh, and is she—sorry, was it Virginia . . . ?"

"Victoria," she replied softly, not looking up.

She sounded sad. *Fuck.* He wanted to cheer her up, even with her stupid jeans and the boots made for city girls. *Retreat, retreat.* "Victoria. Sorry. Are you . . ." How did one ask that? Especially with her sister standing there? *How kinky are you anyway*? Because if the answer was not at all, she was in for a shock the following Friday. He turned back to Logan. "Is she going to be here on *all* the guest weekends?"

"Yes," Logan said briskly. "I think we can find some things for her to do at the private functions."

Victoria propped her elbows on her knees, her chin on her hands, and shot him a quick smile that didn't reach her eyes.

"Great." Ethan rubbed the brim of his hat, needlessly reshaping the dip in the front. So the world's most beautiful woman was also kinky. That didn't give him any ideas at all. Nope. None. *Jesus, please let her be a bottom. Please please please . . .* "Good to have that cleared up. Anyway, I've really got to get my horse put up."

"No problem." Logan responded too quickly and easily for Ethan to trust him. His smile was pure evil. "Victoria needs to see the barn anyway. You can give her the grand tour. Then, on your way back here, you can point out cabin fourteen."

"I—"

"And you were planning to be here tomorrow to work on your trailer, right?"

"Tiny house," Ethan corrected automatically. "Right." He was going to set up camp there, actually, now that the exterior was all but finished and he'd started on the interior. A sleeping bag and a few weeks of roughing it appealed more than the idea of yet another night at the main house or a bleary midnight drive back to his place in the city.

"You're building a tiny house?" For the first time Victoria's eyes shone with interest. A hint of a real smile touched her lips, and fuck if it wasn't like a sunbeam lighting up her face. "I'm fascinated with them. I'm a little claustrophobic, but it's still such a great concept. And some of them seem so open."

I am so fucking fucked. "Yeah."

"The idea of voluntary simplification really appeals to me." Victoria leaned forward, ignoring her sister's disbelieving snort. "I mean, my supplies and work always take up space—I can't really help that—but in terms of personal goods. *Things.* People get so invested in quantity or novelty instead of meaning, you know?"

He nodded, thinking immediately of his apartment back in San

Antonio and all the junk he still needed to make decisions about. Extreme downsizing came with a lot of challenges, and getting rid of crap was one of the worst for him. "Exactly, and there's the whole deal where you think it's 'perfectly good.' This is a perfectly good hammer, and someday one of my other hammers will probably break, so why get rid of it even though I have three of 'em?"

"Yes! It's hardest with practical objects because we know they're intrinsically useful."

Alexandra cocked her head. "What are you two even talking about?"

Victoria blinked at her sister, her lovely face going blank. No expression beyond a faint, fake smile. The light died in her eyes as she said, "Minimalism."

She's about to get shot down hard, and it isn't the first time.

"Sweetie." Alexandra shook her head. "I don't think you know ... well, minimalism can mean different things to different people, I guess." She squeezed her sister's arm gently, kindly, ending with a fond pat.

Victoria's expression never changed. She didn't even look angry or sad or ready to argue. As far as Ethan could see, she'd simply tuned out. There was a light in the window, but nobody was home.

"So I guess I can show you the main house first," he found himself saying. "Introduce you to Robert if he's around. Then the barns. You can check out the horses. Then the cabins." Jesus. What was he getting himself in to?

Logan clapped his hands once. "Okay, we have a plan. Victoria, welcome aboard. And enjoy your tour."

The clap startled Victoria from her zone-out and she blinked at Logan, trying to shift her mind off hammer weights and textile colors and everything she knew about tiny houses. He mentioned something about a tour—apparently, the interesting, horsey-smelling tiny-house guy was going to show her around the place.

"Thanks," she said to Logan, knowing it was probably a few beats too late and sounded odd. "I really appreciate your giving me a chance."

"We're glad to have the help." His smile was warm and genuine, as was Mindy's. They seemed like truly nice, happy people, and for one distinctly catty moment Victoria wondered how the hell Alexandra had managed to score such great friends.

She was being so unfair. Alex was right to be pissy about the situation and had gone way above and beyond to help. What Victoria needed to do was find a way to repay her kindness, instead of indulging in childish, bitchy pouting because her big sister didn't understand her. Why should she understand? How much of her own tween and teen years had been spent waiting for attention while her parents dealt with Victoria's issues? And by the time Victoria was in high school and had more or less sorted things out, Alexandra was practicing law and married and rarely saw her sister except at major holidays.

So Alexandra might know a thing or two about Victoria, but she still didn't *know* her. The fact that Victoria had chosen an art school instead of a "real" college only cemented her reputation as a flake in the family's collective mind, never mind RISD's sterling reputation. To the rest of the Woodcocks, it was only a lesser school conveniently situated next to an Ivy, where she was supposed to have been finding a man.

It was what it was, though, and she couldn't change it by wishing. She forced her attention into the present moment and smiled at the tiny-house cowboy. He looked like somebody's stereotype of a guy from Texas: Wranglers with dirt ground into the hems, boots too dusty to determine the original color, a sweat-stained hatband, a sunburnished neck, and forearms that no doubt gave way to pasty white just past the collar and rolled-up sleeves of his plaid shirt. She would be surprised, when he turned around, if he *didn't* have a ring worn into one back pocket from carrying a tin of dip. Not quite as tall or fair-haired as his brother, and his features weren't as classically even. He looked less like a movie star cowboy and more like one of the folks a production team hired locally to play extras. Decent-looking enough to score a line or two, maybe. Too fidgety and quirky to pull the big box-office numbers.

"Ethan, right?" She smiled at him, trying to convey generic, brisk friendliness. "I guess I'm all yours."

He opened his mouth, then snapped it shut, pressing his lips together and scowling before he finally spoke. "All right. S'go." He put his hat back on his head a bit too firmly, then adjusted it as he pretended to tip it at the assembled group. "Y'all."

He backed out of the doorway, then nodded for her to follow before disappearing down the hall. With a hasty smile and wave to the other three, she rushed to catch up.

What have I gotten myself in to?

She swung around the doorway in the direction Ethan had turned and saw him standing at the end of the hallway. In the room behind him she could spot a counter, a tiled floor. The kitchen maybe? That wouldn't be the worst thing in the world. The kitchen—she could smell it as she got closer, a history of garlic and onions and things fried in heavy oils—looked spotless and professional as far as she could see.

The dog at Ethan's feet wasn't a kitchen staple, though. Black and white Border collie, tail tucked but wagging and ears pricked, looking way more optimistic about Victoria than her owner currently did.

Forget the dude. Victoria dropped into a crouch and held out a hand, palm up, clucking softly. "What's her name?"

"Roxie." Ethan sounded reluctant to give up the information. Or maybe he was just chronically taciturn.

"Roxie," she called softly. "Hey, pretty girl."

The dog wagged her tail harder and came forward, claws clicking on the dark, patinated hardwood. She sniffed Victoria's fingers, then sat abruptly in front of her.

"Um." Ethan pulled his hat off again, scratching his fingers through his hair. It was longer than she'd realized, and more of a light golden brown than it had appeared in the dimmer light of the office. "Sitting dogs get petted."

Brilliant. "Good girl, Roxie! What a good girl." She started behind the ears, giving the dog a thorough scritching on both sides before moving down to the shoulders and finally the spine. Roxie's fur was sleek and thick. By the time Victoria was through giving her way too much attention, a halo of loosened undercoat surrounded her, clearly visible on the polished hardwood floor.

When Victoria stopped, the dog thumped her tail hard and nudged Victoria's hand, trying to angle her nose under Victoria's palm.

Ethan was apparently over it. "Roxie. That'll do."

The dog turned to him and then came to his gestured command, a hand signal so quick and subtle it might easily have been missed if Victoria hadn't known what it was. Ethan's demeanor didn't holler *dominant* the way Logan's did, but he definitely gave off a subtle toppy vibe, and the dog seemed to respond to it as instinctively as Victoria did.

She also couldn't help but be impressed, even sheerly from a pet management standpoint. She'd tried to train her mother's spoiled-rotten Pekingese, Noodles, but the silly dog had never even managed to sit without being told out loud several times and offered treats.

"This here's the kitchen." Ethan gestured behind him, then backed off a step so she had room to enter. When she passed him, the smells of horse and wood resin—pine, cedar?—momentarily overpowered the garlic and oil. But once inside the room, she forgot the man smells and focused on the culinary possibilities. Long stainless counters, professional cooktop, huge refrigerator, and a giant butcher-block island running down the middle of the room. One section of the counter was set lower than the rest for ease of kneading and rolling. Plenty of free space to set up cultures for sourdough or even vegan cheese.

"It's perfect." She smiled at him, trying to get a read on his sudden change in manner. One minute he'd been eagerly discussing downsizing, the next he'd been frowning when she made friends with his dog. Was he always so mercurial or had she done something to piss him off? She seemed to be doing a lot of that lately.

Ethan shrugged and glanced around the kitchen, as if seeing it for the first time. "It gets the job done. Robert seems to like it okay. He doesn't seem to be here, though, so—"

"Yes I am," trilled a voice from another doorway across the room.

Victoria heard what sounded like a clothes dryer door slamming; then the familiar rhythmic thrum of the appliance started up. A second later, a slim, dark-haired young man swished into the kitchen from what she assumed was the laundry room. He wore distressed jeans so tight they had to be endangering his circulation, leopard-print high tops, and a ringer T-shirt with a bright splash of rainbow watercolor under curly script that read *Gayus ex Machina*.

"Hey, li'l jefe." The new arrival fingertip waved at Ethan, but his eyes were trained on Victoria with keen interest. Ethan seemed poised to respond, but the Gayus ex Machina kept talking. "And who have we here? Honey, you have Roxie hair all over that nice cardi. Do you want a lint roller?"

"Robert, she doesn't need a lint roller."

Victoria pursed her lips and looked at Ethan, then back at Robert. Tempted though she was to ask for the lint roller just to be contrary, she resisted and forced a smile instead. "Hi. I'm Victoria Woodcock. I guess I'm going to be working here for a little while."

Robert nodded, his face solemn except for the sparkle in his eyes. "Is that your real last name?"

"Yes." And she had heard every joke about it at least three times.

"I like it. But then I would . . . co—"

Ethan cleared his throat noisily. "*Robert*. Victoria says she's good at baking. After dinner maybe she can help you with cleanup and the two of y'all can make some plans about that."

"Lord yes. Is there enough in the budget for a baker, though?"

"She'll be doing different things. Filling in around the place, figuring out what she's good at. I'm giving her the grand tour right now."

"All righty. Well, I assume there's a story here." Robert winked at Victoria. "But you can tell me later while we're up to our elbows in dishwater. Welcome to Hilltop, Miss Victoria."

"Thank you." She didn't have to fake her smile this time; Robert's was infectious. "I'm glad to be here." Strangely, as she said it, she realized it was true. Everything was new and different and overwhelming, but this seemed like such a good, solid, wholesome place. The kind of place people might come to learn something about themselves.

Maybe she'd spent too long perusing the guest ranch's promotional literature while Alexandra had been catching up with Mindy earlier, before shuffling Victoria into manual labor. The brochures were full of glossy photos of happy guests on horseback, close-ups of local wildflowers, impossibly beautiful sunsets over the hills. Not to mention phrases like "rugged, authentic settings," and "steeped in local tradition." She wondered if they had brochures for the *other* events, too, the ones that apparently occurred during "private" weekends. Given Logan and Mindy's predilections, and the way Ethan had asked about it, she was 99 percent sure that meant kink. Maybe she'd find out the following weekend. Those brochure pictures would look a lot less like motivational posters, that was for sure.

Robert crossed to the big commercial refrigerator and yanked the door open, pulling out a tray with what looked like enchiladas on it. "Where're you taking her next, li'l jefe?"

Ethan growled. "Would you stop?"

"What? You said I couldn't call you 'baby boss' anymore. Diego suggested an alternative for me."

Victoria tried to stifle her giggle but didn't quite succeed. Ethan shifted his frown her way for a moment, then shook his head. "Is everybody still out on the trail?"

"As far as I know." Robert gestured toward Ethan's belt as he walked to the oven and flicked it on. "Where's your radio?"

"I'm not really here today. Okay, Victoria, we can hit the horse barn next, I guess. But Lamar's up on the high trail with the guests— uh, did you see the whiteboards by the desk in the study, with the magnets that have names on them?" At Victoria's nod, Ethan continued. "One is the employees and where they're assigned throughout the day. The other is the guests: where and when they're staying, any extras they've paid for, any special needs. The calendar next to that shows when we're dark—nobody staying—and when we have folks booked. So we have four guests left right now from the weekend group. They'll leave Monday morning. There's a midweek package deal and there'll be about twelve people here for that, Tuesday through Thursday. Then a large group arrives Friday and stays through Sunday, if I remember right. You'll hit the office here each Tuesday morning for a staff meeting and to get your work assignments."

He went on for a bit, talking faster all the time, and she lost track of the details. After a few minutes of nodding as if she understood and would retain everything he was saying—and wishing like hell she'd brought something to take notes on—Robert threw her a sympathetic glance, then tilted his head and batted his eyelashes at Ethan.

"Ethan? Would you mind terribly? I need to focus on finishing the mole poblano next, and I concentrate better in silence."

"Oh, sure. Sorry. Okay, we can head out this way." Ethan led the way to the back door, which stood propped open. A screen door kept the bugs and critters out while letting the cool air in; though it was only February, Central Texas was currently enjoying daytime temperatures in the seventies. Victoria wore a long, loose-woven cardigan of her own design and making, but she hardly needed it. After Rhode Island, the seventies felt like summer. It would have been even more delightful if she hadn't known all too well that actual summer in this part of Texas would be about thirty degrees hotter.

"This is the back door," Ethan explained as he closed the screen behind them and jumped down the three stairs of the stoop. "The laundry room"—he pointed back toward the kitchen in the direction Robert had first appeared from—"is also the mud room, and the door into that is the *back-back* door. You'll get used to it. Come in that way if you need to take your boots off. I'll show you when we head in this direction again after the barn."

"Okay. Will I need to take my boots off then? Will they get that dirty in the barn?"

He quirked his mouth and bit his lip, casting his gaze down at her ankle boots, then back up to meet her eyes. His whole face changed, humor transforming it from mildly attractive to dangerously appealing in an instant. Lord help the person who tried to resist if this guy ever made puppy dog eyes.

Then he shrugged, shaking his head as if there were nothing he could do to help her. "You're probably gonna want some more serious boots."

Chapter 6

The horse barn—the name seemed to suggest there were other barns—was located perpendicular to the main house, across a wide-open area that started as a gravel trail through lawn and opened into an expanse of typical, dusty, barnyard dirt. To one side of the barn Victoria spotted two corrals, one large, one small; a brown-and-white horse stood in the small one, head down, reaching through the fence rails to feed on the surprisingly lush growth of native grasses beyond.

In a month or so the place would probably be alive with wild-flowers. Beyond the wide-open yard, the hill country spread out in shades of green and brown under an impossibly large, clear-blue sky. White powder-puff clouds floated nearly overhead; on the horizon, a darker area hinted at storms traveling closer or departing.

Ethan gestured around them with his free hand as they walked, pointing things out; with the other he led his horse by a reined halter that looked like hand-dyed, handmade rope. Nice stuff. She wondered where he'd gotten it.

Ethan gestured toward the small corral as they walked past it into the stable yard. "So . . . that paint over there is Diego's horse, Spock. His first name isn't really Spock."

Victoria chuckled. "He'd tell us the first name, but we couldn't pronounce it?"

Ethan did a double take at her, clearly astonished at her *Star Trek* acumen, then turned resolutely forward. "Original series fan?"

She shrugged, then squinted to let her eyes adjust to the gloom when they entered the barn. "*Next Gen* is my favorite, but I have an appreciation for origin stories. Oh, wow. That smell brings back some memories."

Sweet, oaty, only faintly tainted with the less-pleasant smells of poop and sweaty horse. She'd been steeling herself against a negative reaction; instead she kind of hoped they stayed in the barn a good long while.

Ethan looked amused; the puckish, half-boyish, half-wicked smile ghosted across his lips again, and Victoria had to look away quickly when her heart started pounding faster. Not a helpful response to have to her new boss's brother.

He led Sackett into one of the first few stalls, taking off the halter thing and then the saddle, which he plopped on top of the stall divider as if it weighed nothing. Then he moved around the stall, settling the horse, passing a brush over his coat. Victoria glanced down the corridor that split the long barn. It was clean, tidy, and airy, with a dozen or so stalls on either side, then another open double door at the far end.

Ethan finally emerged from Sackett's stall and closed it behind him, saddle over one arm. "Be right back. Hang tight." He disappeared into another stall—or room, she supposed, as it looked closed in—then came back out with empty arms and returned to the main door, nodding for her to come over.

Next to the door, bolted to the wall, was a big plastic bin. Ethan lifted the lid and scooped out a handful of grains, passing them to her. They were faintly sticky and obviously one source of the sweet smell. Curious noses were already peeking over nearby stall dividers; the horses seemed to know the sound of the bin opening quite well.

Ethan took a handful of the grain mixture for himself as well. "If you remember the smell, I take it you've spent at least a little time around horses?"

"I took riding lessons for a few years when I was pretty young." She sniffed the handful of stuff more closely, trying to parse out the smells. Molasses maybe? Oats, corn, some sort of pellets. "Then I went to . . . well, a different school, and had to stop."

"Do you remember how to feed them?"

"Uh." A vague memory brushed her mind: soft, fuzzy lips against her palm. "Hold your hand flat? And don't ever walk behind them."

"Words to live by. Can't always avoid it in some lines of work, mind you." He winked at her, then strode toward the nearest stall, making a ticking noise with his tongue. The dark bay—yes, bay, she remembered that one. Dark brown body, black mane and tail—stretched its head toward him, clearly anticipating nice things.

Ethan obliged, putting out one hand with a clump of the sweet, grainy stuff on his palm and letting the horse take it. He kept the rest of the goodies in his other hand, well behind his back, as he patted the horse.

After a few seconds Victoria felt obliged to say something to fill the silence. "He's beautiful."

"She."

Of course. "Sorry."

Ethan shrugged, then wiped his palm on his jeans. "The horse doesn't care. She is beautiful, though. This is Poppy, Mindy's horse. Well . . . my mom's, I guess, technically. But now she's pretty much Mindy's. You already saw Logan's guy, Charley, parked next to my ride back at the house."

"Oh."

"It's cool, there won't be a quiz or anything. You want to give her some of that sweet feed you got there? We use different feed for actual nutrition, by the way. This is only for treats if we don't have any fresh stuff handy. Usually no more than a handful a day. Go ahead, she's waiting."

"Sure." The horse was bigger than she remembered horses being, but if she was going to be working here, it was probably something she needed to get comfortable with. She transferred a small amount of the oat stuff into one palm, then held it out flat toward the horse, flexing her fingers back hard. Poppy took the offering with a damp flutter of lips, then snorted gently on her wrist. Emboldened, Victoria stepped closer and stroked the horse's sleek, dark cheek as she'd seen Ethan done. The horse didn't seem charmed, instead leaning past her and almost nudging her off-balance.

"Whoa, there." A hand grabbed Victoria's other wrist, pulling, and she yanked away as hard as she could, stumbling back a few steps and clamping her free hand over her mouth too late to stop a short shriek from breaking the stillness of the barn. The horse threw her ears back, grunting her surprise as she jerked her head away from the stall door.

Roxie, who'd been napping by a bench a few stalls down, leaped to her feet, instantly alert.

Ethan held up both hands, feed dropping from one of his hands to the floor. "Hey. Hey, sorry. Sorry. She was reaching for your other hand. For the feed? I was worried she was gonna nip you, she does that. Sorry."

"You—" Victoria couldn't squeeze words out of her throat. Her heart was pounding too fast. Her stomach lurched, just the way it had when she'd walked home from the coffee shop. She forced herself to exhale, willing her shoulders down and away from her ears. "Use your words next time."

"Yeah, I will. I'm so sorry." He was still holding up his hands, as if she were robbing him at gunpoint. She mirrored him, hands up, palms out, in a back-off gesture. She'd dropped her oats, too, and they lay in a broken crumble next to his.

He hadn't done anything wrong. He'd been trying to keep her from getting bitten. It was okay. She could breathe. "You can . . . you can stand down. It's cool."

"What? Oh, right. Um. Let me just . . . so this doesn't draw rats or bugs. Lamar'll get ticked if he sees a bunch of . . ." Ethan crouched and swept all the dropped feed into one hand, then deposited it in a trash can near the big door, rubbing his hands against his thighs to clean them as he returned to her. "So . . . are you okay?"

"Yeah." She said it quickly, then gave herself a few seconds to consider whether she'd meant it. "Generally, yes. I've had a really bad week, though. Month. Month and a half. The last week was the worst. My boss, uh . . . ex-boss . . . asked . . . me to . . ." Saying it to Alexandra hadn't been this tough.

Ethan shoved his hands as deep into his front pockets as they would go and rocked back and forth, up to his toes, then back onto his heels. "If you don't want to tell me, you don't have to. If it helps, though, shoot."

The scene was still sharp in her mind, so she told him exactly what she saw. "I was down on my knees, putting my cash tray away in the lockbox thing. He was in his desk chair, right"—she gestured with her hand, marking a point a few feet away—"about there. Turned around and said I should blow him if I wanted to keep the job. He grabbed himself and kind of . . . stroked. Then he pulled my hand, like he was gonna put it . . . there. I had to walk around him and the desk to get out of the office. It was . . ." She closed her eyes, which didn't help, so she opened them again to see Ethan looking aghast. "It was a bad day."

"That *fucker*. What a—pardon my language. What a . . . I can't . . . aarrghh, I shouldn't say any of the words that are coming to mind, but trust me, they're awful. Oh my God."

"I've probably thought all of those words since it happened."

"I mean, I'm so sorry that happened to you. There's just no . . . nothing I could possibly say or do would make it any better, but I . . . wait." He had an idea; she could practically see the lightbulb go on over his head and his body jolted with sudden eager energy. "I know what might help. A little, at least. Follow me, and you have to be real quiet, okay?"

"Okay." She had no idea what to expect, but she followed him past several more horses in stalls, down to the opposite end of the barn, and out the other set of large doors to a paved courtyard of sorts, with some other, smaller buildings around it. He was almost bouncing as he walked.

"Guest horse tack room, feed storage." Ethan pointed to each door in passing. "That over there's for washing, obviously." The hose and poles with eye hooks for attaching horse-holding things were a fairly dead giveaway. "And over here . . . shh . . . is the hay barn."

The building across the courtyard was a miniature version of the horse barn, and only the top half of one side of the double door was open. Ethan unlatched and opened the bottom half as quietly as possible, silently signaled Roxie into a down stay in the shade beside the building, and then gestured for Victoria to follow him into the gloomy space.

He murmured as she caught up to him. "When we catch 'em in time, I move 'em to a nice, clean box in one of the empty stalls so they'll be safer and we can keep an eye on things at first. But li'l Mabel is wily. She always finds a way to do it somewhere on her own."

"Do what?"

"Shh." Ethan paused by a stack of hay bales higher than his head, then peered around the corner they formed. "Hey, Mabel. Pretty kitty. Yeah, you know I won't hurt you." He moved forward slowly, talking in a low, even tone as he went. "Brought a friend, but she won't hurt you either. Preeeeettttty kitty. Hey, kittykittykitty."

"*Mbbbraow*?"

Victoria looked around the corner. In the near darkness past

Ethan, who was dropping slowly into a crouch, she could make out a nook between stacks of hay, and a small tabby-and-white cat walking toward Ethan. The cat paused to arch her back and stretch before deigning to let Ethan pet her; then she forgot to be aloof and started purring and rubbing herself against his knee.

Soft mewling started up. The kittens, probably, missing their mother's warmth and milk.

"She's cool today," Ethan said. "C'mon over; take a look. No touching yet."

Victoria tried to move as slowly as he had, finally crouching next to him. Mabel hunched and started back toward her litter when Victoria approached but seemed to relax again once the strange new human was parked next to the familiar one she liked. The little cat stalked back for more attention from Ethan, who spoke softly to Victoria as he petted Mabel.

"When my brother and cousin and I bought this place, it was pretty overrun with cats. Our grandparents hadn't been keeping up with it. We started catching and fixing 'em as we could, but we'll always need a few around to help with the rats, so we're letting a few breed. Just trying to be selective. Sadly, we do also lose some to coyotes, hawks, stray dogs, accidents. But we're aiming for a stable population, and we'll be cross-breeding with some neighbors' animals, too. This'll be Mabel's last litter, and I've already retired Spike, the daddy."

Eyes adjusting, Victoria could make out four kittens nestled in the hay. Two were Mabel's colors, another pure tabby with no white, and the fourth was calico.

The loudest mewled—one of the Mabel clones—then lifted a wobbly head and cracked its tiny eyes open. It started to commando crawl in its mother's direction, then managed to stand up for about a second before thumping back to the ground.

Seeming to sense her short break from motherhood was up, Mabel slunk back to the kittens, ending up on her side somewhere between the adventurous one and the other three. She groomed her front paws, apparently utterly uninterested in the four tiny creatures that squirmed their way to her belly to nurse. Then she accosted one of the kittens after it latched on, bathing its body roughly; it kept nursing, apparently resigned to its mother's ministrations.

Ethan stood as slowly as he'd bent down and backed carefully away from the scene with Victoria in his wake. He waited until they were both out of Mabel's sight before whispering, "Pretty cool, huh?"

She realized she'd just followed this strange man into an unknown, dark area with no idea what he had in mind—trusted him without a second thought, even after the earlier scare. And it was good to know she could feel that way about anyone right now. Probably not the outcome he'd intended, but it was almost better than the kittens. "Yeah, pretty damn cool. Thank you."

The kittens had also been insanely cute. Teensy baby animals with their eyes barely open? Please.

It was as if he could read her mind. "Kittens make everything better. In real life, as on the internet." Ethan led her back into the light, then pointed to the gap between the washing station and the barn. "That way next. On with the tour."

Chapter 7

It had been such a promising start, Ethan thought sadly. Even with her weird boots and funky rings and inexplicable preference of *TNG* over *DS9*, Victoria had seemed amazing when he first met her. But after a week of trying to work her into the routine at Hilltop, what he mostly felt when he observed her stunning appearance was bafflement about how any grown person with most of a college education could be so very, very uneducated about some of the most basic things. Not because she was willfully ignorant or unintelligent but because a lot of things had apparently been so far removed from her existence that she hadn't even known they needed doing. Much less how to do them.

Like scrubbing the toilets.

"You want me to ... what?"

He'd rolled his eyes. "Can't start getting squeamish on me now, Vic. It's just part of the job. C'mon, you just do it and get it done. It won't kill you."

"What? No, I don't mind cleaning it, I mean ... I ...." She looked at the cleaning cart, scanning the various bottles and equipment with a furrowed brow. "I hadn't closed yet at the shop. I've never had to do it, so I don't ... I don't know how. What things do I use?"

He'd blinked, trying to process what she'd just said. "You don't ... even know what a toilet brush looks like?"

"Oh, okay, so a brush? Oh, wait, it's this thing, right?" She gripped the handle of the toilet scrubber, clearly pleased with herself for getting it right. "And you use that squirty bottle of cleaner that bends at the top, to get under the rim part. I mean, I *have* seen commercials obviously. Okay. I got this." Her cheerful expression fell when she looked at him, and he realized he must've been making a sour face.

He tried to look reassuring instead. "Yeah, that's what you use. Okay, so, if I can ask just one background question? You lived in an apartment for two years, right? So . . . who cleaned your bathroom?"

She shrugged, as if the answer should be obvious. "The maid service."

"The maid service." Of course. Because that was a thing every college student had. In their "loft." Which Ethan had quickly figured out was Victoria's word for fancy-ass hipster apartment that probably cost twice as much to rent as his place in San Antonio.

"They came weekly. I went a few weeks without in February, after I realized it was on the list of expenses my parents were still covering and put a stop to it. But I was pretty tired from working and packing, and I'd sold most of my stuff anyway, so there wasn't much cleaning to do by that point."

And there was the twist, the weird contradiction that kept him bouncing between finding her insufferable and finding her admirable. She'd done a dumb thing, to be sure, but she had acted on principle and stuck to her guns. Done what she had to, to see it through. Gotten a job. Sold most of her stuff to keep up with her bills. Hadn't asked friends for money or handouts. She hadn't even asked her sister to line up the gig at Hilltop; Alexandra had done that without asking, but Victoria had seen it was a good arrangement and gone along with it. So Ethan couldn't scoff too much. At twenty-two, he'd never have had the balls to make the kind of leap Victoria had. Hell, he didn't know if he'd be that brave now. Especially given her complete lack of the necessary skill set for survival as a minimum-wage earner.

His reluctant admiration had lasted until it came time for her to use a vacuum cleaner; then the cycle had started anew. He still couldn't believe he was the only one Logan could find to show her all this stuff, except . . . everybody else already *had* their assigned work. Ethan was suddenly around all the time. So he supposed it made a certain amount of sense. And it wouldn't last forever obviously; he'd help train her, then he'd get back to the important business of making rope and figuring out how long he could get away with not taking over Doc's practice.

Strangely, Victoria *had* known how to muck out a stall. She'd had to do that when she'd taken riding lessons as a little girl—because of course—although she quickly learned that mucking out one stall for one pony twice a week was poor training for helping to clean an entire horse barn daily.

She could drive a stick shift. But she'd never changed a tire. And when Ethan had mentioned she might need to add oil occasionally to the beat-up truck she'd be borrowing for trips to town, she'd gone as wide-eyed and stuck as a deer in headlights. So he'd shown her how to pop the hood, how the dipstick worked, how to add more oil without getting it all over the engine. And she had seemed to take it all in, but God help the woman if she got a flat out on the road. Thank God she'd decided she had to keep some kind of cell phone; even on an outdated model with a pay-as-you-go plan, at least she could call for help if she got stranded between the ranch and town.

She didn't know how to check the other fluids either. Or how to get new car insurance once she was no longer on her parents' policy—which she'd cursed about when she realized and added to the list she was making of stuff people had to pay for on their own. For somebody who wanted to go it alone, she was woefully uneducated on how to actually accomplish that. She kept finding ways her parents were apparently still sneaking help to her by simply paying for things until she discovered them.

But dammit, her determination was commendable. Because as soon as she found out, instead of whining about it, she would sit down with her horribly lean budget plan and figure out when and how to cut off that line of support, even if she couldn't replace it right away.

"Plucky as fuck," Logan described her when they met to try to work out the following week's schedule.

Mindy cleared her throat. "Plucky? Really?"

Ethan raised his hand, waving it to get Mindy's attention. "I didn't use the word *plucky*. Just want that on the record." He was lying on the couch in the office, boots propped against one arm of the couch, head on the other, one hand pressed to his forehead melodramatically.

"Noted."

"Wait," Logan said. "So we can't say *plucky* anymore?"

Mindy opened her mouth as if she were about to explain it, then sighed instead. "No. Sorry, hon. Another heroine stereotype bites the dust. You can also strike *spunky* and *feisty* off the list."

"It's almost like you women are people or something."

"Crazy, isn't it?" She turned back to the scheduling board.

Logan leaned back in the leather desk chair, swiveling it from side to side. "You're still my manic pixie dream girl, though, right?"

"I was *never* your manic pixie dream girl."

Logan swung to face Ethan, pointing with his thumb over his shoulder and nodding, mouthing *manic pixie dream girl.*

Ethan shook his head. "Dude, no. Okay, so we can't have her on cleaning duty because she takes *forever*, and I'm seriously worried she's gonna accidentally mix chlorine and ammonia or something and kill us all. Or some guests. Or herself. She's fine with laundry, though. Robert adores her, but there's only so much room in the kitchen or the budget for baking supplies, so that's definitely a small time commitment per week." After Mindy moved some magnets around on the board, he continued. "Weirdly, of all the stuff she's done, I'd say helping out in the barn has gone the best. But Lamar and Diego already have most of that covered. They love her too, by the way. The animals love her. Everybody loves her. She's like a frickin' Disney Princess." Why that made his headache worse he didn't know.

He covered his eyes, pressing the lids as if he could squeeze the tension out. His phone was in his back pocket, uncomfortably digging into his butt, as though reminding him he still needed to listen to the voice mail Doc Taylor had left him earlier. And tomorrow he needed to finish cleaning his stuff out of his old office so Marguerite would have more room for her things. He wasn't sure whether to take the stuff to his apartment in San Antonio or store it here at the ranch or . . . All he really wanted to do was spend some time alone, working with some rope and the new batch of dyes he'd ordered. He might even start tonight.

Logan's chair squeaked and Ethan could feel his big brother's eyes on him, but he refused to look.

"So, Ethan." It was Logan's wheedling voice. "You know . . . the guests love her, too. Mindy and I had a thought about that."

"Oh?" What fresh hell was this?

"Official demonstration helper and living history liaison. Apparently she's also got some experi—"

"Nope."

"You didn't let me finish."

"You want her to help with the rope demo. Nope. She'll lose a hand or something."

Mindy made a disgusted noise. "Ethan. Stop being such a drama queen. It's not that hard. She'll be helping Lamar and Logan, too. And it may help you sell some halters. Suck it up."

Tuesday, Wednesday, Thursday . . . then Friday was the start of a Giddyup weekend. For four days he could suck it up. But then it would be time to blow off some serious steam.

Of course it always depended who showed up to the event. Trekking out to Bolero took more planning than a trip to the local club in San Antonio or Dallas; they got some completely new faces each Giddyup but also a lot of dedicated regulars, and none of those familiar visitors offered quite what he was in the mood for at the moment. He'd be doing a suspension demo early Friday evening with the wife of one of the regulars, but after that he wanted to *play*.

Preferably with some nice red-gradient rope. Yeah, he could definitely start on that tonight.

Victoria could tell Ethan was tiring of the "caught red-handed" joke.

His own fault for neglecting to glove up while conducting his latest dye experiment. All it took was one time; she'd been there. Sometimes it was just too much trouble to find the gloves, or just too tempting to get your hands on the material. Whatever he'd been using—different reddish hues of fiber-reactive dye, apparently, but she wasn't sure what brand or quality—seemed to have particularly miraculous skin-staining properties. His cuticles, in particular, were a lovely deep wine shade. His fingernails, however, looked like something from a horror movie: such a bright red he looked almost like his nails had been peeled off. The rest of his hands were pink, either from the lingering dye or from his various efforts to remove it.

She'd seen him trying regular soap, pumice hand cleaner, and saddle soap at the ranch on Tuesday. After he'd come back from his clinic Tuesday evening, she'd smelled a sharp whiff of something like nail polish remover—she didn't know why a vet clinic would have acetone, but he seemed to have tried it at some point. And heaven only knew what else.

If he'd used a specialized dye remover right away—in the past she'd used one called ReDuRan, but there were others out there— he'd probably have been able to get most of the stuff off. As it was, anything he did now would probably only set the dye further or damage his skin. Too bad he hadn't asked the one person on the ranch who knew.

When Victoria showed up at the ropewalk Wednesday afternoon to go over her role in Thursday's rope-making demo, she hadn't seen Ethan immediately. But she'd noticed that the drying rack—a long line of fence posts behind the rope walk area, with pegs and hooks for hanging the rope—sported some pretty unfortunate experiments. The lighter ends of some of the ropes were a lovely, rich, true red. But all the darker ends were muddy, brownish-purple messes, and it was clear Ethan had no idea how to blend from one color to the next. He'd blown quite a bit of hemp on the experiment, and she wondered if it was the first such disaster or only the latest in a series.

She examined one of the shorter lengths, testing for wetness with a fingertip before picking it up. When she unraveled the dark end slightly, she could spot the deep red core. He'd tried to go over the true red with the wine color and lost the best of both shades. If he was going for a smooth blend from one shade to the other, that sort of dip-dying would never work with the colors he seemed to have in mind. He needed to learn some color theory. And learn that gravity and varying dye viscosity could be his best friends.

Still, she admired some of his other finished work. Solids, a few two-toned jobs, a couple of color-blending experiments that had gone better than the reds. Now that she'd connected Hilltop's upcoming private event with the fabulous Giddyup kink fests she'd seen people talking about on Kinkbook, she couldn't wait to see what Ethan could do with all that pretty rope.

A crunch on the gravel behind her signaled that someone had joined her.

"Um. Hi. That's not part of the demo," Ethan said. "That was a personal project."

"I can see that." She carefully draped the rope back over its pegs and turned, unable to resist glancing at his hands. Yep, still pink and red. "It's been hard to miss."

"Please don't say it." He closed his eyes, looking weary. His eyelashes were insanely long. The tips were lighter than the rest, like the hairs on an expensive paintbrush. "Don't say the red-handed thing."

"I wasn't," she reassured him. "I was going to say that it's clear you love dyeing rope. And you ought to know by now the rule is 'no glove, no love.'"

He frowned down at his hands, lifting them and examining the backs, then the palms. Then he pointed to one of his cuticles. "See that shade?" When Victoria nodded, he continued. "Marguerite liked it so much she ordered a custom-dyed halter for her palomino. Who arrived at Bewliss's yesterday, apparently."

"That's the stable in town, right?"

"Right."

"Well, at least you have the halter-making excuse built right in. Most bondage rope makers probably have to come up with elaborate explanations for why they're always walking around . . . blue-handed or whatever the case may be."

"That was close. I don't know if I should let that one slide."

She nearly broke, then, and told him the whole process he needed to use—and why she knew all that. Part of studying textile design was studying the history of textiles, and she'd loved that part of her education so much that one of the few pieces of equipment she'd kept other than a sewing machine was her portable spinning wheel. But watching him try to work it all out reminded her of her own current struggles. And he seemed to enjoy having a project to focus on.

"How about you set up some twine on these hooks and show me how to slide this traveler down the walk instead?" *Oops.* She might have given too much away there.

Ethan looked startled, then pleased. "You've been studying up."

That was certainly true. "I have."

"That's great! I usually get some volunteers to help crank, then work the traveler myself, but I guess you could do that part. Let's give it a whirl."

Together, they set up the components and managed to produce a decently uniform ten feet of six-millimeter jute rope. Once Ethan had knotted the ends, he turned to Victoria with a challenging eyebrow raise, holding her gaze as he found the rope's center by feel and then pointed to her with the bight.

She shrugged and offered her hands, wrists pressed together. "I thought we were doing a demo for the vanilla guests."

He chuckled and slipped the rope quickly around her wrists, wrapping them together. "We could role-play an outlaw kidnapping the rancher's daughter. That'd get their attention. Or a rancher's daughter apprehending the outlaw, I guess, if that's more your thing. My preference is for the other direction."

The rough jute scratched her skin, making her catch her breath. It had been far too long. "I'd be the one getting tied up, but I'm really not in to role-play. You should grab their attention with bright colors instead. Off, please." He hadn't knotted the wrap into place; when he let go, she was able to slip the rope free herself. "We could even show the dying process. I could help with that. Get it set up in the background while you're working on the ropewalk. We could have samples at different stages in the process. Then maybe you could sell some in bundles, as souvenirs. Not everybody wants a rope halter, but I'll bet some of the folks would buy a length in their favorite color for craft projects."

He was already shaking his head. "Not a chance. I know you have health insurance, but I don't think Logan wants the paperwork involved in having an employee covered in scalding dye. Or inhaling a bunch of soda ash, which is a chemical that goes in at a certain part of the dying process. It's not part of your job description." He moved, perhaps unconsciously, to stand between her and the area where he'd set up the electric burners and big pots he used for his dye projects—as if she couldn't simply walk around him in either direction to get there.

He wasn't exactly mansplaining her own field to her, not knowingly; he had no idea that she'd been hand-dying things for years, so it didn't really count. But the very fact that he assumed she couldn't do it suddenly made her determined to show him her expertise.

"I still don't have a job description. And I could show you what—"

"Nope. I'm sorry, Vic, but the answer is no. This isn't like dyeing Easter eggs or something. You have to know what you're doing. And I don't know it well enough to feel comfortable teaching you."

The last bit made her feel almost bad for hiding her knowledge from him. Almost. Except that he'd been insulting with the Easter egg comment, and with assuming that she didn't know how to do this; she'd *always* been upfront with him about her areas of ignorance. She wasn't a general incompetent and she resented being treated like one. Plus, he'd interrupted her, which she hated. And he looked so somber she almost laughed in response; she had to put up a hand to cover her mouth for a second. The man took his dyeing *very seriously.* She briefly wondered if he was as diligent about the bondage part, then stuffed the notion firmly back down.

"Okay, then," she relented, smiling in the sweet, bland way that had seen her through so many family dinners. "How's that ombre project of yours coming along, by the way?"

"Hombre?"

"Ombre. The color gradation. You know, the rope that's supposed to go from the shade of your fingernails to the shade of your cuticles?"

He uncrossed his arms from his chest and stuffed his pink-and-red hands into his back pockets. "Just fine, thanks."

"Glad to hear it. By the way, could I have some spare lengths of rope? To experiment with? Don't worry, I won't blow anything up. Just practice cat's-paws and whatnot. I have my own safety shears and everything."

He blinked, and then his gaze flicked up and down her body and he shifted his weight as if his pants had suddenly started to chafe him. "Um. You could buy some off me."

Victoria frowned. "You know I don't have any money to spare. Come on. You *make* the stuff. Give me some rejects." She wanted to accomplish his ombre project for him. It was a show-off move, but dammit, she needed a little validation right then.

"It's not safe to practice alone. You can play with rope all you want this weekend at Giddyup."

Oh, she planned to.

Victoria's back pocket vibrated and she reached for her phone automatically, flicking her gaze away from Ethan to check the name. The new, cheap phone felt odd in her hand, but it seemed to get the job done okay.

"I should take this." She took a few steps away and accepted Alexandra's call, wishing she had texted instead. "Hello."

"Hey! How's it going?"

Alex's voice sounded too bright and hard, as if she was forcing a smile. Something about it put Victoria on alert. "Great! I think I fit in here better than you ever thought I would." She ignored Ethan's snort and the swish of a rope near her leg.

"Awesome! So, listen, Mom and Dad have been calling me a lot, and the thing is, they know you're safe and that you'll be in touch, but they really want to check on you for themselves. Uh . . . so there's a chance they might be visiting you."

Oh fuck no. All the no. No no no no. "Noooooo."

"Yeeeeaaah. They were talking about driving up this weekend—"

"Nope."

"Vic. They just want to make sure you're okay."

"No, it isn't that kind of nope." It was *also* that kind of nope. She didn't feel ready to face her parents yet. But mostly, this weekend was out of the question for reasons that had nothing to do with her own preferences. "It's a nope because it can't happen this weekend. It's a private function for a . . . club. The whole place will be completely closed off to nonmembers and ranch staff from Friday morning through Sunday night. And I won't have any free time to talk to them anyway. I'll be working." Or flying, if she got lucky. Either way, no free time.

Ethan walked into her field of view, his brow furrowed. He looked from the phone to her and mouthed something she couldn't make out. She shrugged and waved him off, mouthing back *It's fine.* She hoped that wasn't a lie.

Alexandra gave a groan of frustration. "I told them it was a bad idea. Look, can't you get a lunch break or something to spend with them? If you'd just *talk* to them, they wouldn't be so worried, and Mom would stop asking me about you. Couldn't I at least give them your new number?"

"They'd stopped calling on the old one, but apparently felt fine tracking my location across country on it, then calling *you* to discuss me behind my back. So, no, I'd rather you didn't. I'd rather you let me decide when to do that. Okay?" Petty? Yes, probably. But at the moment, Victoria was mainly concerned with keeping her parents away from Giddyup weekend at all costs.

"You're entitled to work breaks, you know. Is there an employee handbook? Do Logan and Mindy—"

"*Alex.* I will get breaks. No employment laws are being broken. But I'm not using any of those breaks to drive into Bolero to talk to Mom and Dad about stuff that I'm not ready to discuss yet." Victoria was still figuring out how she felt about the whole thing—her parents' choices and attitudes, her own choices and attitudes, how those all fed into and fed from one another. "Especially not on a . . . private weekend."

Alex paused, and Victoria could almost visualize her sister's expression as the lawyer brain engaged. "What kind of event is this weekend thing anyway?"

Fuuuuuck fuck fuck fuck fuck. "I'm really not sure. It's some private club. They organize their own events, this is just the venue." Partial truths were always better than outright lies. "I gather Mindy knew some of them in Dallas. Maybe the context was work? I have no idea. I've been too busy shoveling horse shit and washing sheets and making rope to worry about what the private clients are planning to get up to."

"Hmm. If it's work-related, maybe I should look into it for myself."

Shit. The last thing she needed was a suspicious Alex looking into what sort of events might be held at Hilltop that weekend.

Maybe sensing her distress, Ethan covered his mouth to make his voice sound more muted and distant and called out, "Hey, Victoria, can you give me a hand with this?"

She sent a grateful smile his way. "I'll be right there! Alex, I have to go. If you want me to, I can find out what the thing is this weekend and email you about it or something."

"No, that's ... it's fine."

"But Mom and Dad *really* can't come up here during the event. Or you."

"Yeah, I got it. I'll tell them. What about the next weekend?"

"I'll email you. Really gotta go. Sorry!"

"Okay. 'Bye."

"'Bye."

Victoria ended the call, then closed her eyes and exhaled slowly. When she opened them, Ethan was raising his eyebrows at her, a sublimely amused expression on his face.

"Family trouble?"

God, he's cute.

Shh, ignore that.

"Nah." She pocketed the phone and forced her lips into a smile. "Everything's under control."

Chapter 8

This, at least, she knew.

By the time the sun was close to the horizon and the main yard had started to fill with kinksters, Victoria felt more at home than she had since arriving at Hilltop Ranch. Since midafternoon, when a crew of rough-looking but extremely congenial bikers had ridden up to manage security for Giddyup, the ranch had taken on a whole new feel, and it was like sinking into a warm bath.

Instead of horses in the big corral, there were three pony players cavorting around. Another one stood in one of the temporary stalls she'd helped Ethan, Diego, and a few early-arriving volunteers set up; his handler was carefully applying sunscreen to his many exposed parts, while he stomped and occasionally sent a playful nicker toward his potential friends in the corral.

Subs in big, functional-looking locking collars strode around, chatting and greeting friends; no street collars necessary, no need for hiding or discretion. From her vantage point on the porch, Victoria could see two of them trying out the stocks, giggling, then joking with a leather-vested dom type who stopped in passing.

Victoria rubbed her hands against her bare thighs; she still recalled the Rhode Island snow and sleet well enough to marvel in bliss at the warm weather. It was cooler than it had been recently—the forecast said highs in the low seventies and lows in the low fifties for the weekend—but it felt like summer to her, and in her experience people wore less, rather than more, at kink events. She'd had to dig deep into her off-season clothing box to find the denim shorts. She wore those and a Hilltop Ranch T-shirt over a plain black sports bra and yoga shorts; comfortable as the increasingly kinky surroundings might be, she still didn't plan to get naked, even though Logan had told her to take the night off and enjoy herself.

Not everyone had the same reservations about nudity. As the sun started to melt into a blazing puddle over the hills, and Diego fired up the four big outdoor heaters around the wide space between the main house and the horse barn, more and more skin was bared in the gathering crowd.

"Quite a sight, isn't it?"

She startled at Lamar's voice, then smiled as the old horse whisperer sat down beside her and stretched out his legs.

"I'm more used to this than the ranch stuff, to be honest," she admitted. "It's pretty cool to see such a big outdoor event, though. That's new to me." It occurred to her, finally, that she ought to be surprised Lamar was there on a Giddyup weekend, calmly surveying the scene, chuckling at a guy in head-to-toe gloss red latex stopping to complain to his partner about all the dust and pieces of "hay or straw or . . . ugh, *nature*" that clung stubbornly to his outfit.

"Welp." Lamar pulled a toothpick from his shirt pocket and stuck it in his mouth; it bobbed up and down as he kept speaking. "Nice thing about gettin' old. Nothin's that surprising anymore. Seen it all before. It comes and goes in cycles."

Victoria assumed he meant metaphorically. "I have a hard time picturing bondage nights at the ranch back in the fifties or sixties or whenever." How old was Lamar anyway? He was one of those sun-cured guys who looked ancient but had probably looked exactly like that since about age forty. Timeless.

He turned his head, looked at her for a second, adjusted his hat, and then turned front again. "Nothin' new under the sun, Miss Victoria. So, you gonna take me up on those riding lessons soon? It's like riding a bicycle; it'll come back to you. You get good enough and you could be leading trail rides instead of scrubbing toilets and doing laundry. Don't stop makin' the kolaches, though, please. Robert never did have the best hand at pastry."

"I don't know if I'll be here that long." She had sent résumés everywhere she could think of. Not just Dallas but New York, Paris, Milan. Anywhere she had the remotest hope that somebody remembered her from one of her internships or from an alumni event or from a contest or award or *something*. "But I'll keep making the ko-laches as long as I stay."

"Fair enough. You think you could maybe do some o' them . . . croissant? Plain, not that fancy chocolate business."

He said *croissant* perfectly, with a better French accent than Vic-toria's. Hidden depths, Lamar had. Victoria nodded. "Yes, I can. It's been a while. Give me a few practice batches before you judge me."

Lamar smiled, toothpick wiggling. "Can't wait." He slapped his palms on his jeans, then pushed up and away from the porch and tipped his hat. "Bonfire lighting's in about ten minutes. That's when the party really gets started. You enjoy the evening."

"Thanks! You too."

She didn't know, and wasn't sure she wanted to know, how much Lamar participated in Giddyup. But she didn't have long to think about it. Ethan ambled over to the porch from the direction of the old barn, hands in his back pockets, irked expression on his face.

He nodded his head at her, eyes flicking to her bare legs and her impractically short boots for a fraction of a second before he caught himself and made eye contact. "Hey."

"Hey yourself. Something wrong?"

"Eh." He glanced toward the trailhead leading to the parking lot, as if he was looking for somebody. Clearly he wasn't finding who-ever it was. "Did anyone give you a rundown of how this goes? Like a schedule? What's Logan got you doing, concessions or water bottle patrol or . . . ?"

"For tonight, I've been instructed to enjoy myself." She stretched her arms over her head, enjoying the popping along her spine, won-dering if it would be worth it to go for a warm-up walk and do some stretching before it got any cooler. Just in case she got a chance to play. "Tough job, I know."

"So you're off tonight? Hmm . . ." His expressive face was ridicu-lously easy to read sometimes; now, he looked like a cartoon villain plotting something. Not in a Skeletor way. More of a Doofenshmirtz vibe.

She shouldn't find that endearing. He could be kind of a tool sometimes. He still didn't think she knew much about anything—al-though he had been downright complimentary of her after their rope-walk demonstration. When his attitude changed it showed up on his face instantly, every time.

Victoria found that transparency refreshing. After years of spending all her time around designers and artists, she was used to artifice—to people who wore the image they wanted to project like costumes, with every move and garment and expression cultivated to fit a particular aesthetic. She had thought her own aesthetic was voluntary simplicity, paring things down to their essentials, form following function, organic flow. But every day of the past few months had shown her a new way in which she had failed at that. There had been nothing organic about her life, her choices, her opportunities; she'd been a hothouse flower, sustained through a complex artificial system. Now she was going through a hardening-off process. It was nice to spend time with someone who knew how the real world worked . . . how to do practical things. Someone genuine. And funny and patient and mostly *nice*.

Even if the person in question was, currently, being a bit of a Doofenshmirtz.

"I'm off." She side-eyed him. "Why?"

He was getting the eager, full-body tension she'd noticed on other occasions, when he got happy or excited about something. Ready to pounce. "You still want some rope for . . . whatever?" He waggled his eyebrows, putting a world of lascivious meaning into that *whatever*.

She'd mostly wanted the rope to play with dyes, but she shrugged. "I guess so, sure."

"My stunt bunny had to bail on me." He took his hands out of his pockets, obviously forgetting about their lurid coloration in his need to gesture. "She couldn't get a babysitter last minute or whatever. And I'm supposed to do a thing after the firelighting and the mingle. Suspension demo of a rig I'm supposed to teach a workshop on tomorrow." He traced invisible ropes with his hands, sketching the rig in the air. "Wouldn't even need much flexibility, no predicament stuff, easy peasy. I was looking around for a volunteer. The main pose is just—" He approached her, hands up, palms facing her. "May I touch your arms?"

"Certainly." *That's all you wanna touch, cowboy?* Now where had that thought come from? She needed to stop kidding herself; she knew *exactly* where that thought had come from, and it was nowhere helpful.

Gently, Ethan pulled her hands from her knees, where they'd been resting, down her calves, coaxing her hands to curve around her ankles. Then he pushed her elbows closer together as he explained the tie. "Your legs would be bound together at the knees and ankles. Suspension is from a chest harness and a loop around the hips, but you're bent this way and bound elbow to knee, wrist to ankle. Your hair is bound to the central point too, but there isn't too much weight on that; it just keeps your head positioned with the chin up. And then . . . uh, you're hanging with your back almost parallel to the floor, facing down. For, you know . . ." He pulled his hat off and ruffled his hair, a move of his she'd come to associate with embarrassment.

"For, you know, spit roasting?" It was the first thing that sprang to mind, and her mind wasn't the only thing that reacted to the imagery.

"Or whatever."

Victoria nodded, pulling her own hat off—she'd purchased one at the local general store, a cheap straw tourist number that really did help keep the sun off—and ruffling her hair in imitation of Ethan. She resisted the urge to fan herself with the hat or squirm against the unforgiving wood of the porch step. Instead, she curled her toes hard inside her boots until the tingling thrill behind her breasts and between her legs subsided enough for her to think again.

Ethan looked hopeful. In about one second he would hit puppy dog eyes, and she wasn't ready to learn whether that would be as devastating as she suspected.

"What would be in it for me? You said something about rope?"

"Yes!" He fist pumped.

"I haven't agreed yet."

"Oh. Okay, so, I was going to use some of the dyed rope we've been selling here. As part of the demo, you know, kind of free advertising. But I could just use only a length or so of that, and then for the rest use some undyed stuff if you prefer. And whatever I tie you up with, you would get to keep."

An offer she couldn't refuse.

After the traditional lighting ceremony at the fire pit, Ethan gestured Victoria away from the crowd and made for the old barn—now, inevitably, dubbed the Bondage Barn—to get set up. They had to talk about limits, but fortunately they wouldn't really be doing that much. He only hoped she was more experienced with suspension than with most of the stuff he'd tried to show her around the ranch the past few weeks.

"Okay, what are you gonna wear?"

She pulled her Hilltop shirt off without breaking her stride. "This sports bra. Yoga shorts. Which I have on under these."

"Yoga shorts?"

"They're like . . . trunks? Like boxer briefs."

"That one I know."

Victoria laughed, a pleasant lightness over the growing cacophony of the crowd behind them at the fire. "Now I don't have to ask you if it's boxers or briefs."

He blamed the outdoor heater they walked past just then for the flush of heat on his cheeks. Had she been *planning* to ask him that? He'd kind of worried she was getting fed up with him, fed up with Hilltop maybe. But she came back each morning for more, and he didn't get the sense it was masochism or submissive eagerness to please that motivated her. She wanted to learn the nitty-gritty. Part of him had to respect that, even as he winced at the sheer amount of nitty-gritty she didn't know.

Back in undergrad, his crowd had a set of descriptors—borrowed, if he recalled correctly, from another friend at Cal Poly San Luis Obispo. It had started out gendered, but the girls had appropriated it almost immediately. Some people were *chromy*, like a shiny new king cab truck with expensive trim that looked like a beast but had a uselessly small engine under the hood. The California version of all hat and no cattle, basically. And other people were *doers*, like a horse that'll go and go without complaint until it drops. He'd been in a lot of conversations that went something like, *How'd it go last night with Jessica? Aw, just okay. She's chromy, but she's not a doer.* Or, sometimes, *Why'd you break up with Jason? He thinks he's a doer and he's not. And he isn't even that chromy.*

He'd estimated Victoria as chromy from the first moment he'd seen her—she was, after all, the most beautiful woman in the world—and shortly after determined that she wasn't much of a doer. But over the past week and a half or so, he'd realized that wasn't quite true. She *wanted* to be a doer, and she was getting there. Hair shoved up in a knot, borrowed galoshes on, sweat staining her back and armpits, shoveling horse apples out of a stall and never saying a word even though it was obvious she was hurting from several hours of doing the same thing the previous day. Somehow, she was still chromy as fuck. *As fuck.* But she didn't give a shit about the chrome at that moment.

Or possibly ever. That was her dilemma now, he suspected. She had thought of herself as a doer before this. And when she'd realized she wasn't, she'd set about remedying it and was working her hardest at that. Sure, she wasn't always effective. But she was genuinely trying and she learned fast, and he really hadn't given her enough credit.

Tonight, after spending hours doing God only knew what to help set up for the weekend, she'd still managed to do something to her hair and face to make her look . . . fresh and pretty and sexy and *damn*. She was really good at the chromy thing when she wanted to be. *And* a doer. A chromy doer was . . . the gold standard. The dream, the myth.

And maybe she wanted to know what kind of underwear he wore? Thank fuck she wasn't planning to do this demo naked, because he was way too old to be sporting a crush boner in front of a crowd of happy perverts. Plus . . . she was only twenty-two. With her life kind of in the toilet.

"All right." *Back on track, get back on track, Ethan.* Without pausing his progress toward the barn, he hopped a few times, rolling his shoulders and shaking out his hands. They were tingling, partly sore from all the cleaning efforts and partly anticipating the rope. "All right, all right, all right. Any parts of your body I can't touch during the scene?" As she continued toward the barn, he jogged ahead a pace or two, then turned, walking backward, gesturing with his hands as if suggesting various areas that might be off-limits.

"Uh, nope. Well . . . no sexual touching. I mean, touch whatever you need to for the demo. But once I'm tied up, please don't jack me off in front of the crowd or tweak my nipples or anything."

Oh, God, he would have more than a crush boner happening soon if that kind of talk continued. "Right. I wasn't planning to." He turned around, facing the barn again so he wouldn't have to deal with visual stimulation and putting on his most clinical vet demeanor. "In order to do the chest harness, I'll probably be touching your breasts quite a lot. Obviously your upper thighs, knees, pretty much your whole legs. And your buttocks, to do the hip part of the support."

"My buttocks?" She snorted. "Hot."

"Fine. I'm gonna have my hands all over your ass and tits, in front of God and everybody. You got a problem with that, missy?" Everybody had a default setting, and Ethan's was being a straight-up smart-ass.

"I am actively looking forward to it, Mr. Convenient Rope Top." She turned her head to shoot him a look, like *whatcha gonna say to that, bud?* Then she stumbled over a pile of horse crap, nearly fell, and recovered only after a few running steps and jerking herself upright like a marionette. Knocked the shit off one boot toe and kept on walking. "I meant to do that."

He refused to find it adorable. *Refused.* "Safeword. The house words are red, yellow, green. Yellow me if you need to slow down or talk about anything or have any questions. Or have any circulation issues whatsoever. Uh, you don't have any physical problems I need to know about, right? Or allergies?"

"The safewords are fine with me, and nope. Healthy as a horse. A healthy horse."

"Well, feel free to let me know if something's too much or you want information. I'll have some background music, so the audience won't necessarily hear if we're talking quietly."

"What, like some ambient stuff? Or the traditional Japanese thing or . . ."

"You've probably never heard of it." Aaand now he sounded like a hipster douche.

She paused at the edge of the square, packed-earth area in front of the horse barn, turning to the left, where a trail of solar lights was starting to show up in the gloaming. "That way, right? And why don't you try me, cowboy?"

"Oh . . . you say that right before I'm about to have you tied up at my mercy?"

"You've promised not to do any sexual touching. My breasts, buttocks, and presumably my vulva and anus are safe from anything other than what is necessary for the suspension."

"Be still my heart. Clinical language does me in." Because really. Clinical language did, in fact, turn him on a bit. Actually, it seemed that just about anything Victoria said turned him on a bit when they weren't talking about how to get hair out of drains or shovel horse shit. When they were just two people strolling through the cool night air, planning some friendly bondage.

He hadn't been drinking. It wasn't a moonlit night. He didn't have a single rope on this woman yet. But he realized if he'd met her at a club or a kink convention or in just about any other setting, he'd already be in big trouble. Because he just . . . had never felt this way about anybody before. The knowledge hit like a ton of proverbial bricks. It wasn't even the boner. It was the intrigue. The delight. The unexpected continual rightness of her.

He wasn't dumb enough to think that *she's different from other girls* was a thing. He liked women in general, always had. He didn't think he'd only fall for somebody who was *different*. But *he* felt different with her. It was weird.

"Are you going to tell me about the music or not?" Victoria forged ahead of him on the path, looking down to mind where she stepped. "These lights need to be brighter. Isn't there, um . . . What is it, low wattage or low voltage? Might be better than solar? Less green, I guess. Oh . . . you could do solar-powered low voltage. Right? Because you have solar up at your place you're building, so I know you'd be able to wire that and figure out the . . . meter, or the controller box thing, converter, whatever it's called. And there are plenty of places around here to put the panels where the guests wouldn't see them. Then you'd have brighter lighting and no problem with it going out after a few hours."

"Oh. *Oh.*"

"What?"

"Hang on . . ." He stopped right there, pulled his phone from his pocket, and texted Logan. Because they'd been talking about the light situation and they'd known the cheap solar stake lights weren't enough for the long haul, but they hadn't really gotten creative with thinking about alternatives. "I think you . . ." He looked up at her, startled, then schooled his features because he knew his being startled that she'd thought of it was kind of offensive. "I think you may have just solved a problem we've been talking about for a while. About the path lighting. So . . . thank you."

"You're welcome. Are you gonna tell me the music, though?"

He sent the text and then continued up the path. "Uh . . . it's this big band song. It's called 'Sing, Sing, Sing,' but it's all instrumental."

Victoria looped her thumbs in her belt loops and nodded. "Mm-hmm. Gene Krupa's cover or GTFO."

He almost stopped in his tracks. "No, the Benny Goodman live Carnegie Hall version. It's twelve minutes long. Then I go to some Cole Porter to finish up. The demo is about fifteen minutes."

She shot him some fairly significant side-eye. "Cole Porter, huh? Are we talking Frank here? Or are we talking Ella? You will be judged by how you answer this question. Because you've already disappointed me with your 'Sing, Sing, Sing' choice. And let's not even get started on *DS9* again."

Sweet holy fuck. Marry me. "Um. Ella?" *Please let that be the right answer.*

"Good job. You pass. I mean, Frank has his moments, too. Don't get me wrong. But . . . *Ella.* You know?"

They were nearly to the top of the rough road that led up from the new barn to the old one, which had been farther from the main house. But Ethan had to know one thing before he tied Victoria up. He stopped, putting one hand near her shoulder and then letting it rest there when she didn't protest. He turned her toward him, and she contemplated him with an expectant expression.

"Okay." He took in a deep breath, then exhaled. "Nat King Cole sings 'Stardust.'"

She didn't even take a beat before answering, "One of the single greatest songs of all time, bar none."

"Yes. I've always thought it was a shame it was a breakup song, because that means it wouldn't work at a wedding."

"Me too."

For the silence that ensued, the word *loaded* didn't even begin to cover the vibe. He almost resented the universe—not Victoria, just the universe—for this moment. She'd been there for close to two weeks, being bad at things but trying. Quietly delighting in the growth of kittens. And now, understanding about "Stardust." But he had so much change on his plate right now. And might be about to have even more, depending on the outcome of the *talk* Doc Taylor said he wanted to have on Monday, over pie at Minnie's. Dammit, he didn't have *time* for the most beautiful woman in the world to show up, at age twenty-two, and force him to choose between Frank Sinatra and Ella Fitzgerald singing Cole Porter. Which didn't explain why he was cupping her shoulder, flexing his fingers there, stroking the curve of the muscle until it relaxed under his touch. He dropped his hand, stuffing it back into his pocket and resuming the walk toward the barn.

"Um." He knew there were more things they should cover before the rope demo. They'd never worked together before. Hilltop was pretty stringent about safety. But his mind was full of stardust melodies and visions of Victoria, wound up in love knots. "Um. If you want to pick the music instead, that's fine."

"If you've been using that low-quality 1930s recording of Benny Goodman—although it's still one of the greats, no question, not about that—then trust me, whatever I pick will be an improvement. Can I play it from my phone or—?"

"Yeah, as long as you already have it loaded. We have one of those plug-in speaker things, but it doesn't do well if you're trying to stream stuff. The music freaks the lawyers out. We're kind of illegal right now, technically, since we don't have an ASCAP or BMI license to play it for customers. It's all under the radar, though, so . . . I thought you had to get a cheap phone."

She sucked in her cheeks. "Welp. Yeah, but it's still the same brand and it has the same kind of plug. It's just the old model that came with no upfront cost. It won't really do GPS or some other stuff. But I can still get all my music on it, including the songs I have in mind. Plus, y'all seem to have some pretty solid wi-fi here, at least near the big house, if I did need to add anything."

"Yeah, we do. I sorta made that job one. You aren't supposed to have your phone out at all during Giddyup, by the way."

Victoria chuckled. "Well, now I know that."

She'd probably known anyway; it was a pretty standard rule at kink events. But whatever; at least they'd have better music. Or . . . different music. He hoped it wouldn't ruin his flow.

Watching her walk into the barn, already flicking through her playlists, he was pretty sure his flow would be the furthest thing from his mind during the rope demonstration.

Chapter 9

"I've given you about seventeen minutes," Victoria said when she plugged her phone into the speaker on a shelf by the barn's tall, wide, open double doors. "Figured you might need a little extra time since we haven't worked together before."

"Perfect. You gonna tell me what's on it?" Ethan was talking over his shoulder, heading to a door on the opposite wall that appeared to lead to a utility closet.

"Nope. You have to be surprised. I think it'll be good surprises, though." She toed off her boots, leaving them next to the mat under the suspension frame, then shucked her shorts as she looked around the barn. It wasn't a double rank of stalls bordering a long hall, like the horse barn, but an open square with stalls and large lofts on two sides. Some stalls had been opened out and redesigned to create two long supports for bondage, flanking the central frame where she and Ethan would be playing. The back wall was bare except for a few storage cabinets, but she saw eye hooks and some chains hanging from the rafters. Plenty of room for more ambitious multiplayer scenes than the scaffolds would allow.

The whole space had a distinctly old-fashioned look, like a movie set. She'd only been in it once before and hadn't seen it at night; the charm of the setting was enhanced by the fairy lights strung from the lofts and the spotlights on the individual play spaces. As she looked around, the spots on the sides went out, leaving only a pool of light over the central mat and the glow of the fairy lights all around.

Ethan emerged from the utility closet carrying a long duffel bag. It made a heavy, clanking thunk when he dropped it on the mat.

When he unzipped it, Victoria could smell the rope, an instant hit to her senses that primed her body for what they were about to do.

She sat down close to the bag and started stretching, easing herself into things.

Her shoulders and hips were tight from days of unaccustomed physical labor. The stretches verged on painful and she had to slow down, backing away and reining in her eagerness. Pulling a muscle would spoil everything, and she wanted . . . *everything*. Everything in that bag, every part of her bound, wrapped in rope like the tightest hug in the world. Tight enough to hurt and strong enough that her entire body could literally depend on it. She wanted to fly.

And she wanted Ethan to send her soaring. His hands looked sure and capable as he laid out his ropes, which were color-coded with whipping at the ends. Most of them were undyed, she noted with approval, including one that appeared to be a fifty-footer. If he followed through and gave her all those, she'd have plenty to work with later. And for the demo, the natural hemp would look wonderful with the rich purple he appeared to have chosen as an accent color.

People started filtering into the barn, a few at a time. Some of them greeted Ethan, a few also nodding politely at Victoria. She didn't know any names, hadn't seen any familiar faces yet. It was an interesting feeling; there was a freedom in anonymity. For all anyone knew, she was a professional bondage model. She was whatever she appeared to be until people knew otherwise.

She reached for her shorts and pulled a hair elastic from one pocket, using it to put her hair back. Ethan glanced at her, then stepped over and held his hand toward her head, a question in his eyes. When she nodded, he wrapped one hand around the base of the ponytail.

"Probably need to move this up a few inches so when I wrap it and put tension on, it's not pulling at your neck instead of your head." He shifted his hand, pressing the spot he meant. He stroked the top of her head and then flipped his hand through the ponytail as he moved away.

She tried to ignore the shiver his touch had sent through her and wished the sports bra did more to hide the instant hardening of her nipples. The barn wasn't as cool as she'd expected—a few white ceramic heating panels were placed here and there—so she couldn't blame her body's reaction on the temperature. If she got any wetter, there would be no hiding that either, especially not once she was hanging in the vulnerable position he'd described.

She could tell herself all she liked that it was the smell of the hemp revving her up, that her body was so eager because she hadn't been tied up in months and needed the freedom and release she only found when she gave herself over to the rope. Those things were true, after all.

But those factors were nothing compared to the way Ethan had taken such care, since hearing about the coffee shop incident, to gain her eye contact and ensure he had her knowing consent before he laid a finger on her. And that was nothing compared to "Stardust."

Okay, so he wasn't her type. She wasn't into cowboys or boys next door or even semiblonds. But for whatever reason, she wanted him, plain and simple. Or complicated and involved, depending on what equipment they had handy. And any way in between. But he thought she was stupid, possibly, and he seemed to have issues with the way his life was going, even though things seemed to be going incredibly well for him. He was getting everything he wanted from what she could tell, but for some reason he wasn't that happy about it. Yes, he smiled and was goofy and seemed to have work he enjoyed. But when he thought nobody was looking, he brooded. She hadn't known him long enough to know whether that was his base state or not, but she'd dated a chronically unhappy guy once and knew better than to go there again.

There was nothing worse than wanting to make somebody happy whose natural frame of mind ran to dissatisfaction. Although as a fling . . . it could work. They could help take each other's minds off their various troubles. It could *only* be a fling anyway, because she wouldn't be here too much longer, right? She still told herself that, desperately needing to believe it, but every day it seemed less like the truth and more like a dream she'd once had and was beginning to forget.

The crowd had grown substantially while she stretched and mused. A few dozen people lined the central square on all sides now and more were trickling in. Ethan scanned the bundled ropes he'd laid out, nodded as if he were satisfied, then snagged a stool from the other edge of the mat and placed it directly under the center hardpoint of the scaffold, where a heavy ring was already suspended. Ethan's body radiated energy as usual, but it was focused now, intense. When he looked at her, his gaze was more serious than she'd seen since the day she arrived at Hilltop. At least when he thought anyone could see him.

"You ready to start?"

"Yeah. Let's do this."

He held out his hand and she took it, letting him pull her to her feet. "You'll need to start the music, unless you want to give somebody your passcode."

"Oh! Duh. Right." She jogged lightly to the shelf with a sheepish smile, tapped her phone screen, and started the playlist she'd created minutes earlier. The audience didn't react as Ella Fitzgerald's voice floated across the room, probably because most of them had never heard the opening lines of the song. But when Victoria turned, she saw Ethan grinning broadly. By the time she got back to the mat and Louis Armstrong had chimed in, the crowd was chuckling at "Let's Call the Whole Thing Off."

Ethan pointed at the stool with the bunch of rope he held in one hand. "Noice."

She took a seat, propping her feet on a rung. "Thanks. Not Cole Porter, but, you know. *Ella*."

"And I do love a Gershwin tune." He turned to the crowd, raising his voice only slightly. "Howdy, y'all, and welcome to the Bondage Barn. I'm Tigger the Rigger, and my lovely model this evening is . . . oh, crap." Sheepish, he turned to Victoria and stage-whispered behind his hand, "What's your scene name?"

She laughed out loud. "I can't believe neither of us thought of that. Would you believe Piglet?" She could tell by the look on his face that he didn't believe it for a second. "It's Velvet."

"Thank you." He turned back to the spectators. "My lovely victim this evening is Velvet, ladies and gentlemen. It's our first time working together. My usual partner couldn't make it and Velvet was kind enough to sub in on a moment's notice. Give her a big hand." After a short round of applause, Ethan brandished his fistful of rope. "We hope you enjoy the demonstration."

The scene had started and she'd given him blanket permission to touch her. He didn't hesitate but handled her with confidence now, quickly wrapping her chest in the snugly tied harness that would support most of her weight once she was in the air. He was almost done when the mellow strains of Ella and Louie ended and a rapid drumbeat began. A few of the crowd members started to snap along, and one couple broke out into a quick swing dance move in the corner.

Ethan paused, his head and shoulders moving in time with the music. "Gene Krupa?"

"Yeah." Her voice sounded lower, husky, almost sleepy. She was already getting happy and floaty from the rope, from being handled, from the process.

"I stand corrected. This is better. Scoot back so your butt's off the stool, then lean forward to counterbalance." He went back to work, moving with such rapid assurance as he wove the rope around her body that sometimes she could hardly see his hands moving for the blur. She knew the feeling. It was her getting-things-done song, her montage music. Before she knew it, she was roped into the position he'd described to her before the scene, her arms bound to her calves with a two-column tie, her wrists and ankles similarly bound.

Ethan was whipping suspension lines from the back of the chest harness up through the ring, then back down through a quick wrap around her extended ass and thighs. One more pass up, then he cupped her chin gently and tilted her head to the right angle, stroking her cheek a moment before he started the wrap around her hair.

When Gene Krupa was replaced with "Fly Me to the Moon," Ethan laughed, leaning against her for a moment. She felt his amusement through the motion of his hip against her flank and his hand on her neck.

"Oh my God. Too perfect. I . . . love this song. And perfect timing. This is the moment for Frank."

"Mmm." It was all the answer she could muster, from so deep inside her happy place.

The rope around her hair pulled taut; she assumed he'd passed it through the ring as well. He made a few more checks and adjustments, then pulled all the tension out of the suspension lines, ready for the dramatic moment.

When he pulled the stool out from under her, leaving her in midair like a magic trick, the audience clapped, and a few people whooped. Then, to Frank's accompaniment, Ethan tugged and adjusted further, pulling her ass higher and finally hoisting her entire body up several more inches.

Flying. Rocking gently. Not floating, because flight took effort, meant accepting some pain—the ropes pressed into her skin and squeezed her, and she could feel every ounce of her own weight where the lines rose from her body to the central ring. She closed her eyes and let her other senses take over, smelling the rope, hearing the gentle creak of it when she shifted slightly. Ethan wasn't touching her, but she knew he was holding her up. Probably tying the line off, if she bothered to look. But she didn't bother. He was *there*, as close as if he were the one wrapped around her.

Lust goggles. Had to be. Ethan could think of no other reasonable explanation for the way he seemed to be the only one to notice how Victoria, bound, was the most beautiful thing to ever happen at any kink event, ever. Or at any art museum, because she was definitely art.

Dude, she's a person, stop dehumanizing her. Objectification is not cool.

Objectification was a good word for it, though, because as he worked—played out the ropes, carefully wrapped and wove and manipulated Victoria's limbs into the exact pose he wanted—he felt almost as if he was standing outside himself, watching the scene unfold. And holding his breath. He and Victoria and the rope formed an endless loop of intent, agreement, consent.

Everybody hanging out in the repurposed old barn paid attention and clapped for the demo. For Victoria's brilliant music choices. They were enthusiastic. But it was clear to Ethan that he was the only one having a transcendent moment. Maybe Victoria was, too, but he was trying not to let himself think too hard about that. If she wasn't, that would be a bummer. If she was . . . how could it ever be a one-off?

He'd always felt more tolerant than understanding of the kinbaku masters who often performed at big BDSM events, with their silk robes and their models dressed in traditional Japanese undergarments. Quiet music, a sense of reverence and ritual. None of it had ever seemed to match his own experience of rigging, which was as physical as a sport to him. Ropes were cool, he was kind of a geek about the gear, and tying up women who liked to be tied was fun as fuck. If they also wanted to fuck, either during or after? Two thumbs up. But this, whatever was happening right now . . .

This was new.

Everything here was utterly familiar to him. The barn he'd played in since childhood, the beams and joists he'd inspected and reinforced by hand to ensure safe suspension, the rings and clips. His palms and fingers, oversensitive from all the recent scrubbing, felt every inch and tug of the handmade hemp rope—*this may be hurting me more than it hurts you*—but every movement was automatic, so engrained in muscle memory he hardly needed to think about it. Flow, groove, the zone . . . this was where he found his, and that was part of why he loved doing this. But tonight . . .

Tonight, everything was new because of her.

Or maybe because of Gene Krupa. The brisk music fit the mood so exactly it seemed to infuse him with lightning speed and uncanny deftness. It was almost dreamlike, the speed with which he bound her chest, her slim, soft arms and smooth legs. She seemed to hit sub-space almost immediately, barely making more than the occasional soft gasp as he pulled and tied and tightened. When he positioned her head for the hair tie, she looked completely blissed out, drugged by the rope. He found his hand lingering against her flushed cheek— *Velvet*—and he had to force himself to stop touching her face like a lovestruck idiot and concentrate on the tie.

Until the music changed, and he realized that either by instinct or luck, she'd timed it so "Fly Me to the Moon" started right before he was about to hoist her. He laughed, the breathless spell broken but in the most amazing way. He even commented, unable to resist stroking the fine hairs on the back of her neck, but she couldn't articulate her answer from wherever she was in her head. She hummed, smiling, sounding like sex.

Perfect timing for Frank Sinatra, worst possible timing for this woman to happen along. He knew it. But he was having trouble re-membering why he cared. *Too much other shit happening in my life to make a rational decision. The ranch is sucking me in. A girl who works at the ranch would only suck me in deeper. She's too young for me. I'm too young to be meeting somebody and instantly thinking that if we got together, we'd settle down and have babies. Run away, run away.*

Yeah, all that was still in his mind. None of it had changed. But . . . somewhere between their first conversation about minimalism and "Gene Krupa or GTFO," maybe *he* had changed. He considered that possibility as he pulled the suspension lines taut, adjusting the ten-sion to distribute Victoria's weight more evenly. Once her position-ing was perfect, he temporarily secured the line and pulled the stool out from under her with a slightly dramatic flourish. *Ta-da!* The crowd seemed to appreciate *that*, at least.

He whisper-crooned a few lines along with Frank as he made a few more minor adjustments to raise Victoria's hips so her back was parallel to the floor, her head tipped up the perfect amount. Then he pulled on the line near the tie-off again enough to lift her beyond the spit-roasting zone, so the audience could see her better. And so that he could clear his head of the imagery.

Once he'd tied the main line off to a hardpoint on one of the scaffold uprights, he turned and gave himself and the spectators a moment to simply appreciate the sight. To most of them, perhaps, it was just another demo, just another thing to try. The position was good for a lot of activities, actually, providing not only angles for sex but great exposure for paddling, caning, any sort of impact play on the ass and the backs of the sub's thighs. And it was fantastic for bastinado.

He wasn't into much of that, except in an occasional playful way. If he wanted to cause pain, he knew a hundred ways to do it with rope, and savored the marks left that way better than any impact bruise or welt. After tonight's session, Victoria's body would be covered with evidence of what they'd done. Stripes and knot spots, her skin's record of how the rope had embraced her. He wouldn't get to see most of it under her sports bra and yoga shorts, but it would be beautiful. Nearly as beautiful as the sight before him now.

He'd used purple rope for the chest harness, and the dark color was mostly lost against the black sports bra. More purple bound her wrists and ankles, and it showed up beautifully against her fair skin. The rest of the rope was undyed, and the soft tan color nearly disappeared against the backdrop of the barn walls. She almost looked like she was floating up there.

Frank was wrapping it up, so Ethan sauntered back to Victoria and ran a hand along her side, shoulder to hip, giving a slight push to send her into a slow spin. If he had longer, he would change up her position, keep her in the air and move her around like his personal, posable kinky rag doll. She seemed flexible and fearless, either a natural at suspension or very experienced or both. Where'd she learned it? From some art school Yankee?

Frowning and cocking his head, he crouched below her and wiggled his fingers; the audience could see what was about to happen, but Victoria couldn't. When he tickled her soles, she jolted up from fantasyland, trying to squirm away but helpless to do so.

"No, no, no fair. No!" She giggled frantically. "Stoooop."

He noted she didn't safe out, so he kept tickling. "I don't even get a please?"

"Pleeeeease stop."

He grinned and pressed the tickled area to soothe it, slowing her spin in the process. When he stood up, they were face to face; he put his hands on her shoulders to stop her turn completely. Then he made the mistake of looking into her smiling eyes as the music changed again.

The softly swelling violins seemed to take his heart along with them. As Nat King Cole started to sing, Ethan leaned forward, remembering at the last second that he couldn't kiss her. No sexual touching. Instead, he rested his forehead against hers.

"'Stardust'? Are you trying to woo me through song, Velvet?"

She smiled dreamily, then let her eyes drift closed and sighed as if she'd never been so content in all her life. "Why? Is it working?"

Ethan swallowed and straightened, pushed her into another spin, and stepped back to let the audience watch. When she slowed down, he walked around with her for one last rotation, then reluctantly left her side to release the main line. In slow, careful stages, he eased her down to the floor, shifting the ropes like a puppeteer so she would end up in a sitting position, feet out in front of her.

From there, it was the work of only a few minutes more to unbind her. Hair first, then hips, wrists and ankles, elbows and calves. He left the purple ropes binding her chest and helped her to her feet, where she wobbled a bit as they both took a quick bow to rousing applause.

"You need to sit back down for a minute?" He put an arm around her waist, steadying her.

"Yeah. That's a good idea." She let him hold her all the way down and then relaxed into the mat as if she might fall asleep. The dreamy smile was on her lips again. He had never wanted to kiss anyone as much as he wanted to kiss her.

"Hang on." He put a hand on her hip, allowing himself one last touch before the scene felt entirely over with. "I have a blanket in my bag."

It was fluffy and patterned with giraffe spots; Robert had given it to him for Christmas and he'd kept it in his bag ever since. He spread it over Victoria now, bending over to make sure she was all tucked in. She nestled deeper into the cozy warmth, murmuring a thank-you.

"Do you need anything else? Hugs? Water? You were amazing, by the way. You did such a good job." Okay. Maybe that last touch wasn't the *very* last one. He ran his hand over her hip again, then her waist, her shoulder. It was hardly sexual. She was like a cute, cuddly plush animal, a kitten or puppy, snuggled up with her eyes barely open. He didn't want to fuck her so much as spoon her to sleep.

"I'm good. Go ahead and clean up." Her words were still slurred a little but starting to clear, her eyes blinking back to normal as she reoriented herself to the world around her. But her mouth, the curve of her lips, held a hint of regret, of tension not yet relieved. Under the blanket her body was restless, her legs shifting against one another, her back arching slightly.

He took a wild guess and lowered his voice. "Do you need to go somewhere and . . . come?"

She squeezed her eyes closed, then opened them and shrugged. "Kinda, yeah."

"Okay. I'll clear this out and then we'll go, okay?"

"Okay. Thanks. You're wonderful . . ." Her voice trailed off again, her eyes drifting shut, but her body shivered.

Rope could work like magic on the right person, transporting them to places they could never go without being bound. But it was dark magic sometimes, exacting a price. Ethan gathered his ropes quickly, not stopping as he usually would to wrap and stow it carefully in his bag. He didn't want to leave Victoria hanging in this limbo, her body all revved up with no place to go. No harm would come to her if she didn't get off; she had almost certainly been tied up and not pleasured before now and would again. But he wanted her to get what she needed from the experience.

His brain and libido had been at war for some time, not just that evening but since meeting Victoria. The battle came to a crisis now as he fetched her phone from the speaker and collected her clothes. Did he help her to her cabin, usher her safely inside like the gentleman he knew himself to be, then hie himself off to his own tiny house to jerk off into a sock or dishrag? Did he linger just inside her cabin door, making it plain he was available for her use if she needed any assistance with her pesky arousal problem?

Or did he boldface lie to himself, tell himself he was playing it by ear, when all the while he was planning to work in a kiss at the earliest possible opportunity that wouldn't make him seem like a manipulative, using assface?

Yeah. Probably that last one. And he didn't lie to himself; he was honest. He was planning to go for it. He kind of wanted to figure her out, but he also *really* wanted to figure out her vagina with his penis, and he was over feeling weird about that. Yes, she was young, and yes, it was probably ill-advised to hook up with her. But she was over twenty-one, she was incredibly hot, and she had seemed to be flirting with him even before the scene. He had condoms in his gear bag, they were two healthy young animals with what seemed to be compatible sexualities, so . . . yeah. Obvious outcome. If he'd met her at a club and they'd done that scene, and she'd talked about his underwear and confessed that she needed to come, he'd already be plotting the fastest route home to get her into bed.

This wasn't a club, though. And he'd never met anybody quite like Velvet—Victoria—at a club. Or a kink convention. Or anywhere. She was the weirdest mix of perfect and the absolute worst, intelligent and completely lacking in what he thought of as common sense.

But it was more complicated than that, wasn't it? It was only common sense if you'd learned it growing up, if you'd seen and lived it and expected it to be part of your life. And the areas in which she was the worst were the same areas she was striving to change. When he took her hand to help her to her feet again, his other arm naturally found her waist like it was made to fit there. She was still a bit shaky, but they exited the mat gracefully, like the royalty of suspension bondage, because together they seemed to form a unit that worked better than either of them individually. *Fuck.* How was he supposed to resist that?

Chapter 10

Why hadn't he kissed her? His mouth had been right there; she'd been able to feel his breath on her lips. Though what he'd done instead had been almost more intimate. Putting his face against hers, whispering about the music they'd just found out they shared a taste for. She *hadn't* been trying to woo him through song—at least not consciously—but it had obviously worked. And once the idea was out there, her mind and body had latched onto it. Possibly the ropes had played a role.

Okay, more than possibly. Almost certainly. After months of deprivation—she hadn't really even dated anybody all year, and her last kink encounter had been a platonic one in December—doing a complicated suspension with a guy she found attractive and insisting on no sexual stuff during the scene had been naïve at best, stupid at worst. She was literally aching with need, her knees weak and her brain unable to clear itself. Even the pressure of Ethan's arm around her waist, the warmth of his body against hers through the heavy layer of blanket over her shoulders, was enough to keep her at a boil.

It hit her like a blinding flash when they stepped out of the barn: The scene was over. Right? They were just two people again, two consenting adults. When Ethan started to walk her back in the direction of the horse barn, and presumably from there back to the cabins, she balked and twirled out from under his arm, catching his hand at the end of her swing and pulling him the opposite way. The trail to the Bondage Barn kept going up the hill, past the stake lights. Within a few steps they were in shadow.

Ethan shifted his grip on her hand, following her with a nervous laugh. "What—where? Hey, where are you going? I thought you wanted some privacy."

"Shh."

He repeated himself in a whisper. "I thought you wanted some privacy."

"It's private up here. Nobody behind the barn. Nobody farther up the hill."

"Well. Except probably some snakes, maybe a scorpion or two. And you're barefoot right now."

Good point. "Did I leave my boots in there? Oh . . . where are my shorts?" She was still way too out of it.

"In my bag." Ethan slung it forward and unzipped it, digging for a moment and then pulling out her boots. She stomped her feet into them, grimacing at the lack of socks and the fine layer of grit. But probably she wouldn't have to do too much walking like that.

"There. All set."

"You're . . . Victoria, you have *got* to get some real boots. Look." He set down the bag and knelt beside it, then reached for one of her ankles, curving his fingers around it and sliding them up the back of her calf. "Your feet are sort of covered. But if a snake strikes, it won't just aim for your foot. If you walk past some thistles, they won't be on the ground. Even through jeans, your skin could take damage. And that would be a real shame." He reversed course, looping around the arch of her foot, then tracing the backs of his fingers up the inside of her leg.

By the time he got to her knee, she had to bite back a groan. "Okay. Point taken. I'll find some real boots."

"Promise?" He shifted his fingers a few inches higher, grazing her inner thigh and sending a hot shiver of need straight to her clit.

"Oh yeah."

Ethan tsked. "Victoria, I don't think you're really focused on this important safety issue right now." To her vast dismay, he pulled his hand away and stood up again, pulling the bag back onto his shoulder.

Her eyes had adjusted enough to the moonlight to see that he was smiling, though. A good sign. "I think maybe some altruistic cowboy should show me all the places a snake might get me if I'm not adequately protected. That'd probably learn me."

"Oh, I'm all about adequate protection." He patted the duffel. "Like a good Boy Scout."

"You probably really were a Boy Scout, weren't you?"

"I ditched it after Cub Scouts. That whole thing was more Logan's jam than mine."

She shifted her weight, making no effort to hide the fact that she was rubbing her thighs together. Pressure, damp and incessant, persisted where her legs met. She could deal with it alone, but that wasn't nearly as much fun as having help. And tonight she was definitely in the mood for help.

"My cabin," she pointed out, "is all the way across the main venue down there, past everybody you know. My boss . . . I guess your boss, too, now? Or however y'all work that out."

"Yeah, Logan's pretty much the boss."

"But this trail leads up the hill to your place, right?"

He literally dropped his jaw; it hadn't occurred to him. She could see it plain as day on his elastic face. *Cute.*

"My place." He tried to shift the subject. "I haven't heard anybody else call it that. I like it. *My place.* Yeah."

"Ethan?"

"Mmm?"

She stepped forward, framed his face with her hands, and kissed him. Warm lips, evening stubble, wintergreen, salt. No hesitation: he kissed her back as if he'd been anticipating it. As if they'd done it a thousand times before, but the repetition made it no less enjoyable.

His bag thunked to the ground again and still his hands found her hips, resting there without trying to pull her closer. She was close enough to feel his dick start to firm up against her belly. And she was horny enough to take full advantage, arching her back and letting her weight press into him. Almost like it was an accident, but she was under no illusions. He knew exactly what she was up to.

There were at least a dozen reasons this was a bad idea, but Victoria had been reconsidering her life choices for months and was all out of considerations. The spell of the rope and the night swirled through her veins, compelling her toward the nearest source of trustworthy touch—toward a means of safety and comfort, even if it was only a temporary fix. They were both single, Ethan didn't seem any more inclined to drama than she was, and they could work out any weirdness after the fact.

He kissed her slowly—not hesitantly, but thoroughly, really taking his time. When he finally moved his hands, exploring her spine and then down to the curve of her ass, he seemed thoughtful about that, too. Pondering, learning. Even under the warmth of the blanket she still wore like a shawl, she shivered when his fingers reached the tops of her thighs and he pressed her firmly against him, lifting her slightly.

The kiss ended gradually. They nipped and sucked and tasted away from each other, moving on to necks, ears. Victoria needed more but hadn't wanted that moment to end either.

Ethan murmured against her ear, raising every fine hair on her neck. "My place, huh?"

"Yeah. You have a sleeping bag up there, right? We have this extra blanket if it gets too cold."

"True." He rested his forehead against hers as he had during the scene, this time letting his nose brush the tip of hers. He was breathing hard, way less calm than he'd seemed during the kiss. "Are we just fooling around for fun or . . . I'm not in a place where I'm really ready to—"

Impatient, Victoria placed a finger over his lips. "If I'd wanted to find a man and settle down, I wouldn't be here in the first place. I'm not looking for a boyfriend. I'd just like to have sex because that's usually more fun than masturbating alone. And you . . ." She ran the finger down, toying with the vee of neckline his buttoned shirt exposed, then sliding her hand down to grab his belt. "You seem like you'd be a *lot* more fun than masturbating." She was debating whether to go the last few inches, cup his cock, *really* let him know how she felt, when he reached up and started echoing her movements.

The finger on her lips. Then playing around the top hem of her sports bra, which exposed a lot more than his shirt. When he turned his hand to move it farther down her body, he made sure to graze the inner curves of both breasts with his outspread fingers. He looped his fingers around the bottom wraps of the chest harness she still wore, pulling the rope tighter and higher for a second before releasing it. Then his hand crossed her bare stomach and she gasped. So close. So close to where she needed his touch.

She didn't have a belt on. He went for the hip-hugging waistband of her yoga shorts instead, gripping the fabric and twisting it in his hand as he had with the rope until it pulled up tight, squeezing her pussy and clit. "I want to tie you in a karada in the worst possible way."

"Maybe later." She pulled on his shirt, backing up along the trail, trying to ignore the flood of slick heat between her thighs. "Takes too long, and it's too hard to fuck around the crotch rope."

"Oh my God. You're . . ." He licked his lips, then let go of her, stepping back and picking up the dropped duffel bag.

"I'm what?"

"You're so right. This is gonna be much better than masturbating."

He grabbed her hand and pulled her in his wake, forging up the trail. She followed, holding the blanket around herself with one hand, trusting Ethan to lead her in the dark. And hopefully, if there were any snakes, they'd aim for Ethan's sturdy leather boots.

You're perfect. Ethan had been a split-second away from saying it. His mind fought for a compromise position, anything other than, *I'm falling for you in a big way; you may be the one*. It settled on *lemon meringue pie*.

Seemed almost too sweet at first, pure sugar and fluff. Then the heart of it hit you, still sweet but also so tart it made your mouth water. Your taste buds almost couldn't handle the complexity. A truly good lemon meringue took time to appreciate, and that was Ethan's experience with Victoria Woodcock. As innocent and sweet as she appeared, she had depth and bite, this woman, and the only thing he knew for sure as he led her up the dark hillside to his not-quite-finished tiny house was that he needed more time and more information to appreciate her properly.

Sweet Jesus, she had been fun to tie up. Perfect, in fact. He needed to let that simple truth into his calculation because it was undeniable. If nothing else was a factor, if his only consideration was how this woman rated as a rope bottom, Victoria was his ideal. And not just because of her looks, which he'd started to realize he wasn't objective about, not remotely. But because of the way she moved, the way she moved *with him*, the way she followed his cues, the things they didn't have to say to each other.

And it was the same even when it wasn't about rope. Cleaning a damn john. He could move his arm a certain way, say, *You know, under the . . .* and she would nod and shift the scrubber and angle it the way he meant. Or helping move hay. She wasn't strong enough—wasn't physically large enough—to use the hooks and pitch the hay, but she'd adapted into the flow of the activity anyway, helping to shift the pitched bales into line on the back of the trailer and speed things along as if they'd been working together for years.

Holy fuck, and the music thing, which he maybe should've expected. She was an art student of some sort, right? He should have asked more about that. He *would* ask more about that. After. After he'd filled her every need, finished the scene they were both pretending had ended but hadn't *really* ended yet. The scene that had shifted partway through, become something more. Because of fucking Gene Krupa and Nat King Cole and things they hadn't negotiated aloud because maybe neither of them had realized them until right that very minute.

"You okay?" he asked her, but didn't look back. He couldn't. If he did, he'd end up kissing her again, laying down the blanket that currently wrapped her shoulders, feeling for a condom in the dark in his bag, and nailing her under the stars among all the potential snakes and whatever, and he wouldn't exactly regret that if it happened, but it wasn't his first choice. He wouldn't regret the sex but would definitely regret a snake or scorpion.

"Yeah." It was a whisper in the dark. Husky, eager. Probably he was reading into that, but at this point his dick was so hard he didn't even care anymore because he knew she wanted to fuck as much as he did. She squeezed his hand, rubbing his palm with her thumb, and he almost whimpered at the pressure of his cock against the implacable barrier of his jeans. *Velvet*, that was what his dick kept saying, *Velvet*. Yes, his penis-driven brain had adopted Victoria's scene name wholeheartedly and seemed determined to pinpoint its accuracy in the one specific area it cared about.

"Almost there."

His eyes had adjusted to the dark, and he could make out the shape of the house ahead. Since Victoria had seen it last, the two lofts had been framed out and decked, and the windows, skylights, and door installed. The walls were still bare studs, awaiting more wiring and plumbing. Ethan hoped the place wasn't too small for Victoria's claustrophobia to handle. She hadn't been comfortable in the unfinished frame, visualizing all the walls with none of the windows.

She was obviously thinking along the same lines. "Okay. Do you have a blindfold in that bag?"

He pressed his fingers into hers, trying to convey reassurance with his touch. "I don't think you'll need it. But we can do that if we have to, sure."

He led her around the stakes that marked the outline of the future deck, then let her go first up the folding step stool that was temporarily acting as his front porch.

"It isn't locked."

She leaned to the left first, tapping the floor-to-ceiling window—a glass wall, really—next to the door, which was also single-paned glass. "Nice."

"Taking full advantage of the view." He was more interested in the view in front of him. She'd wrapped the blanket around her top half, but he was treated to the moonlit curves of her shapely ass in yoga shorts, just below eye level, as she turned the knob and opened the door.

He mounted the steps behind her and closed them in, debating whether to turn a light on. In the end he decided against it; their eyes had already adjusted and it wasn't much darker inside the structure than it had been outside. No lamps were installed yet anyway, so it would've been a harsh work light, not really the mood they were going for.

Victoria's silence as she peered around the shadowed space made Ethan anxious. He reacted as he often did, with unfortunate smart-assery.

"So . . . big enough for you?" His tone implied he wasn't talking about his house and her claustrophobia.

She turned around, the planes of her face catching the moonlight as she raised her eyebrows at him, looked very pointedly down at his crotch, and then deliberately reached out her hand to cup his cock through his jeans. She pursed her lips, tilted her head, and shrugged before releasing him. "Yeah, it's fine."

She'd out-smart-assed him. God help him for enjoying it so much.

He dropped the duffel and went for his sleeping bag, pulling out the double layer of mat he'd been using and laying the pieces side by side before unzipping the bag and snapping it out to float down on top of them.

Victoria dropped the fuzzy throw and put her hands on her hips. "Two mats, huh? Were you planning on company?"

Ethan shrugged as he stood up. "Yep. Little lady named Roxie usually gets a whole mat to herself when we're camping out. But for you I put it dog hair side down, 'cause I'm just thoughtful like that."

She laughed, letting her arms drop, then swinging them back up to finger the top of the rope harness. "I appreciate it. Mind if I make myself more comfortable?"

"Oh. Sure. I can untie it. I should've asked . . . oh."

She'd unhooked the back of her sports bra, and was pulling one of the straps out to work an arm free. Then the other arm. Finally, she yanked the whole thing loose, just like the magic trick girls did when they pulled a bra out from under a T-shirt.

Except it was a million times more magical when the bra disappeared and revealed perfect breasts, exquisitely framed by the rope he'd tied.

She stretched her arms over her head, then rolled her shoulders with a sigh. "Much better. Okay. Where were we?"

Chapter 11

Go big or go home. Victoria figured if she was going to jump into bed—or sleeping bag—with Ethan Hill, the best approach was brazen and dauntless. Even if, now that she'd pulled her bra stunt, she suddenly felt too exposed and like she'd gotten ahead of herself.

A lot of the rope high had worn off on the trek up the hill, and now uncertainty was creeping through the lust haze. What if he found her too forward? What if he'd wanted to take things slow, be romantic instead of going at it like rabid bunnies?

He took way too long to respond to her flippant, *Where were we?* Or possibly her anxiety stretched the time out because when he did answer, he didn't seem at all displeased.

He stepped toward her, right into her space, until his chest was almost brushing her nipples, and found one of her hands with his. "We were already here." He put her hand back over his cock, pressing his much larger one over it to shape her fingers around the curves. "Which surprised me, I won't lie, but I'm willing to roll with whatever pace you want to set."

God, he felt good. In her hand, in her air, in her head. She squeezed firmly, making him groan and rock his hips a little. "That's mighty big of you."

"Oh, God." He huffed out a laugh and put his hand on her cheek the way he had during the scene. This time he didn't let go but stroked his thumb across her lower lip. "The mouth on you."

She let him tease her lips open but couldn't resist answering back right before he moved in for a kiss. "It's remarkably like the mouth on you."

His lips landed on hers, and then things got frantic for a bit. Tongues and sucking and biting and hands all over, two buttons popping off Ethan's shirt, Victoria's finger scraping against an unwieldy jeans zipper, boots hitting the plywood. They wound up on the sleeping bag, still somehow joined at the lips, Victoria on her back and Ethan pinning her hands beside her head. His shirt was off, jeans open at the fly with his cock pressing out against the barrier of his underwear. Boxer briefs, presumably.

Victoria's feet were bare and her yoga shorts were shoved halfway down her thighs. She was stuck underneath Ethan's weight, unable to wriggle the shorts off the rest of the way so she could wrap her legs around him.

She struggled against the pressure of his hands, hoping he would take the hint. He broke the kiss and breathed for a moment, dipping down again for a lingering bite at her lower lip before speaking. "Tie you up a little?" He squeezed her wrists.

"Thought you'd never ask."

"Okay. Real quick. Ugh, don't wanna move." He flexed his hips, grinding against her a few times, then levered himself off first into a plank position, then springing to his feet. "Right, need a fifty. No, a thirty. Uh. . . . yeah, fifty just in case." He shuffled his jeans off as he went for his gear bag, hopping on one foot, then the other, to kick them away. Then he swore, reached for them, and pulled what looked like his phone out of the pocket. "Cover your eyes."

"What?" She covered them and was glad she had a moment later when she saw a glare of light around her fingers. "What're you doing?"

"Ow. Looking for a fifty. The whipping at the ends is color-coded by length. Blue, no. Black, no . . . Aha! Red. Okay, lights out again. Now I can't see shit. Hope I don't trip over you."

She peered through her fingers, watching his return to the sleeping bag, rope in hand. Yes, boxer briefs, some dark color that looked black in the scant moonlight. He held a wrapped bundle of rope and was already loosening it, playing it out to give himself some slack. He could apparently see well enough to kneel astride her waist without any trouble at all.

"Hands, please."

She held them out, wrists together, as she had by the rope walk a few days earlier. This time Ethan tied off the wrap, snugly securing her wrists together. He stood up and stepped over her head, holding the long tail of the rope, and fastened it to one of the wall studs behind her. She had enough slack to twist and watch him make the slipped half hitch: the binding was enough to let her feel secure but so quick-release she could easily get free if she cared to. She pulled against it, relaxing as the resistance pressed the rope into her skin. "Thank you."

"Aw, wow. No, beautiful, thank *you*. You . . ." He held up a finger, then returned to the sleeping bag and quickly tugged her yoga shorts off. "Ooh, commando." Then he yanked his boxer briefs out and over his erection, which bounced gently as he skimmed the underwear all the way off and tossed it, and the yoga shorts, over to where his jeans had landed. "Okay, better. *You* . . . are too lovely to be real. So now I have to figure out what I'm actually dealing with here." He knelt by her feet, wrapping one hand around each of her ankles.

"Eldritch horror in a human suit. Damn, you've guessed my secret." She lifted a foot to nudge at his thigh, then tried to stretch enough to pull him closer somehow.

Ethan laughed. "I was going such nice places with it. I was gonna be all wood nymph, fairy princess." He bent over, shifting his position and starting to work his way up the inside of her leg with a series of slow, almost tender bites that flirted with the edge of pain and set her nerve endings alight from toe to pussy. Then he lifted his mouth from her thigh long enough to start singing "Angel Flying Too Close to the Ground."

"You lure me in with Nat King Cole," she muttered, letting her eyes close as his teeth sank into the soft flesh a few inches below her pussy, "then you hit me with Willie once I'm tied up. Sneaky."

"Only a problem if you don't like Willie."

His hair tickled her labia as he worked his mouth. She spread her legs, arched her back, tried to scoot an inch closer. No use; he seemed keenly aware of the rope's exact limit and was using it to help him tease her. Oh, he was good.

She should have anticipated that by now. He was good at so many things. Until recently, she'd usually been the same. In her former sphere, she'd been confident and smooth and one of the acknowledged talents. People sought her out, asked her advice.

I can't get this jacquard to come out like the design. Jackie said you could help me set the loom?

I know your thing is handcrafting, but Annika said you're really good at CAD and I just don't understand this, do you have time . . . ?

But here, she was . . .

Ethan started down at her other ankle, drawing her back in, keeping her in the moment. The sweet cloud of subspace hadn't dissipated entirely, but he seemed to keep her right at the borderline. Like the line between dreams and waking, it sometimes brought confusion, but sometimes clarity.

"Ethan."

"Mmm?" He kept his teeth at her inner knee, scraping against the skin.

"Ethan. My major is basically hand-dying shit like in the old days. Not . . . I mean it's textile design, but that's what I'm sort of *known* for?"

Oh my God. Why was she telling him this now? *Back, go back words, rewind!* This was why she had so much trouble getting laid outside of kink. *Where is the motherfucking rewind button?*

"I . . . what?"

"I got my internship at Balenciaga because they wanted to do a season of lining fabrics with hand-dyed inspirations, and I'd just won this big competition and . . . so my block prints and batiks were on the linings of some of my mom's friends' couture leather bags this year, and it's ridiculous? Because mostly I spent the summer getting people coffee and snacks and wishing I could see more of Paris. Oh fucking hell, why am I still talking?" She tugged at the restraint, but it was too late. She had completely fallen back into the real world.

Ethan seemed to have frozen between her thighs. She gritted her teeth, then raised her head to look at him. His face was mostly in shadow—the glass door and window were behind him—but he didn't look freaked out, only startled, as far as she could tell. He had pushed himself up a bit to lean on his arms, and his erection was clearly visible. Still going strong.

"So . . ." He tipped his head from side to side, then used one hand to press his chin even farther up in one direction for more stretch. She didn't hear a pop, but he seemed satisfied with the result. "So that was unexpected. Let me ask you two things, m'kay?"

Only two? God, that seemed more than fair. "'Kay."

"One: So you're saying you can tell me how to dye the fucking hombre thing that I've been kicking my ass over for weeks now?"

"Yeah. You have to do a bath with the sodium carbonate *first*, then start with the lightest color and—"

"That's . . . that's okay. You can tell me how later. These are yes/no questions."

"Oh. Okay. Yes."

He reached into his lap and stroked his dick a few times thoughtfully, twisting his neck again. "Two . . . okay, three questions. Two, can you tell me how to get this shit off my damn hands?"

"No. Yes. Um. Not . . . I can tell you what to do next time, but this time it's too late. Sorry."

Ethan sighed and let go of his cock, then sat back and leaned in the other direction, crawling toward his duffel bag of many wonders. "Okay. Just tell me later what I should've done, please?"

"I will. Aside from wearing gloves, I mean. Yes."

He turned toward her, and even in the semidark she could see the *oh, really?* expression. "Do you want me to get a love glove out of this bag or not?"

"I do. Yes. Please. I really do. Is that still an option?" Because how could he still want to do this, after she'd babbled her weird brain garbage all over his unsuspecting face?

"Pfff. *Yeah.* I'm sorry, did we suddenly stop being unwisely attracted to each other in the last two minutes?"

She shook her head. "No. I still totally would like to do you." Somewhere in the middle of her statement, the headshake turned to a nod. Yes. Sex. Yes. Wet, hot, stupid, sleeping bag sex in the unfinished tiny house thing in the moonlight. Her whole body cried out for that, even as her brain threw up its hands in disbelief at the entire situation.

"Same," Ethan reassured her as he pulled a strip of foil-wrapped condoms from the depths of his bag. "That wasn't one of the original questions, by the way. Oh . . . these are polypro, is that okay? I know you don't, but I do actually have a latex allergy."

"That's fine." Her brain nagged at her, suddenly more alert than it had been in over an hour. "So was *that* the third question?"

"Not yet. I'm getting there." Ethan ripped the end packet open without separating it from the strip, pinched the tip, rolled the condom down over his cock, and then crawled the few feet back to their weird love nest. He pushed her thighs apart unceremoniously, propping himself over her on one arm and taking his dick in his free hand to position it. He started to seat himself at her opening, then shook his head and backed off a few feet, lowering himself and swiping at her cunt with his tongue.

Electricity shot up her spine, zipped down her thighs, escaped her throat in a long, strangled sigh. When he licked again, slipping his tongue, then a finger, between her folds, she groaned and yanked hard at the wrist restraints, wishing she had her hands free to grab his hair. Knowing, at the same time, she would somehow enjoy that less. The ropes were all the security she had in this strange place they occupied—the ropes, and Ethan's voice, somehow not hating her, somehow reassuring her that she hadn't ruined everything.

"Three," he finally said between a lick and a swirl that left her head spinning. "Have you been laughing at me this whole time?"

Ethan pushed his tongue into a point, finding Victoria's clit by feel and circling it slowly. He waited out her answer, knowing she was still more rope drunk than she realized. All her reaction times were affected and she tugged restlessly at the restraints, her body taut, her eyes closed as she sought a way back to the subspace she'd achieved during their scene. He probably should have just skipped the rope and gone straight to the sex; that would've been simpler. But given her unexpected revelations—holy fuck, how hadn't he realized when he saw her at the ropewalk, plus she'd given him *so* many hints about the dye—he was unscrupulous enough to enjoy the advantage he gained by keeping her hovering at the brink of spacing out and making her try to think.

She wasn't *really* out of it. She couldn't blame the scene or the rope later for anything she said or did. But she was influenced, and it made her vulnerable. More truthful, maybe, and more open to truths.

Finally, she answered his question. "No. I haven't been laughing the whole time, no. Maybe . . . thirty percent? Fifteen? I'm bad at math. I don't know. Some percent but not most. I could have told you earlier, but I knew it was too late for the ReDuRan, and—"

"The what?"

"ReDuRan. The stuff you use if you get dye on something, to remove it. It's safe for skin and most clothing fabrics. You have to use it right away, though. Um. Ohh . . ."

He'd slid his index finger inside her. Testing her wetness, which was considerably higher than it had been before he'd started licking her pussy. Score one for licking pussy.

Of course *always* score at least one for licking pussy. College had taught Ethan that, in addition to a great many other things. "Okay. I'll make a note. Talk about percentages some more, that's kinda hot."

"I'm the *last* person to go to for hot math talk."

He pushed his finger deeper, dipped his head again, suckled her clit between his lips. She whimpered, her hips moving immediately toward his mouth. She started attempting to talk about math. Hot math talk from an art nerd's perspective.

"Percents? I can't . . . *oh*. Um. Okay. The . . . jacquard loom. You know, jacquard? It's when the fabric . . . oh . . . it's patterns woven in. And the guy, B-Babbage? You know, the computer guy?" She gasped, arching into his mouth as he started flicking his tongue across her clit in a rapid pattern.

Babbage. His brain wouldn't let that one go. He raised his head, ignoring Victoria's immediate wail of discontent. "You mean the difference engine guy?"

"Ngh . . . what? Um. Yeah. One of his . . . oh my God. Could you go back to . . . one of his influences was jacquard looms. They had these punch cards for the patterns, and . . ."

She smelled good, and he couldn't resist sucking her clit in again, relishing her grateful *aaah* as he flicked his tongue over the sensitive bundle of flesh. Back and forth, back and forth, following the rhythm of his finger sliding in and out of her pussy, until she arched and cried out, her breath hitching, her thighs clenching by his cheeks, her body taut against the pull of the rope and the grip of his hands around her thighs.

He could have seen it through, but he was selfish. Her body still formed a perfect arc of tension from wrist to hip when he shifted up a few feet, angled his dick with one hand, and slipped inside her clenching heat.

Victoria locked her legs around his hips, arching again and crying out against her own arm as she rode out her orgasm's second crest.

Or a really great fake. Ethan always wondered, but he'd given up trying to know for sure. He did what he could, and he genuinely believed he was doing right by his partners. Without a mind-meld, there was no way to know for certain. *Holy mother of God it's good* was all he knew at that moment, and he hoped with every brain cell available that Victoria felt the same way, and if so it was at least in part because of his efforts.

He pulled out and thrust in again, relishing the enveloping warmth of Victoria's body. Her body moved with his, responsive, receptive, *right*. And her face . . . the way her lips parted, the glance of moonlight off her cheekbone, the tumble of hair that had now mostly fallen out of its ponytail. Even her imperfections seemed perfect.

The ponytail holder was caught under her raised arm, and Ethan saw that a few strands of hair were pulled too tight. Her eyelashes fluttered and she winced as she twisted her head, apparently startled by the sudden, unexpected pain.

Ethan lowered himself to his elbows and carefully unraveled the elastic, freeing it from the strands and setting it on the floor. By the time he was done, Victoria had opened her eyes. She watched him, a sleepy smile on her lips. "Thank you."

"It looked uncomfortable." He stroked a lock of hair, twisting it around his fingers, then releasing it and moving his attention to her face. Her cheek was soft and the slightest bit damp, either with sweat or humidity. When he moved his fingertips to her temple to smooth back a final loose tress, Victoria blinked, and he felt the muscles jump under her skin. He worked his hips again, unable to resist the impulse to move, and she blinked again, then hummed in pleasure as she let her eyes close.

Ethan kissed her softly, wishing he could freeze time, knowing his body was already too far along to prolong things anymore. He sped up, so primed he was there within moments. He released her lips and gasped as the climax took him, flooding his body with sensation even as he emptied himself. Spiking thrills of pleasure chased after each other, lancing through his balls and belly, pulling a grunt from his lips as the orgasm wrung him dry.

"Mmm." Victoria pressed her lips to his cheek, his ear, his neck. "S'good."

"Yeah."

He meant a lot by that *yeah*. But words weren't forming, not in his brain, not in his mouth. The orgasm had melted his brain, even more so than he was used to. He had just enough awareness and willpower left to lift himself up, holding the condom safely in place while he slid out of her body. She whined an inarticulate complaint, and he knew what she meant because separating their bodies—like, ever again—seemed like the worst possible thing. Covering her gorgeous form with the fluffy throw, while the chivalrous thing to do, made him even sadder.

Also, he didn't have a damn trash can.

He had to settle for tying off the used condom, wrapping it in a few of the workshop-style paper towels he had by his toolbox, and stuffing it into an outside pocket of his duffel bag. He'd have to chuck it tomorrow.

Hope and realism set in; he brought over the paper towel roll and set it on the floor by his bag, because if he had any say in the matter, there would definitely be a round two at some point.

Next, he set to untying the rope, first from the wall stud and then from Victoria's wrists. She was limp, languid, practically purring. When he'd freed her hands and tossed the rope aside, she reached for him and pulled him down, tugging the throw aside, then flipping it back over both of them.

Of course he kissed her—softly, sweetly, sharing sighs of contentment and laughing gently when she yawned halfway through. He rolled to his side, coaxing her to roll as well so her back was snuggled against his chest. He couldn't remember the last time he'd spooned. He couldn't remember ever wanting to cuddle somebody to sleep either. This didn't even feel so much like wanting, though, as it did like . . . simply the way things would be.

Fate. This whole past year . . . Buying into the ranch. The sudden, game-changing success of Giddyup. Finally getting to build the house. The timely arrival of Marguerite so he didn't even have to feel guilty about leaving his old practice in the lurch. And now . . . Victoria. Appearing as if by magic, through an improbable string of circumstances, presented to him by the universe as the obvious next step in his year of things going spectacularly well.

Ethan didn't believe in fate. He didn't think the universe granted you wishes or handed you people like prizes. When everything seemed too good to be true, you were probably missing something important, in his experience. It was time to be cautious, not complacent. Which made absolutely no difference to the overwhelming amount he wanted to wrap himself around Victoria, entwine himself with her. Not just fuck her but get inside her.

He had no idea if she was anywhere close to feeling the same way—she seemed pretty casual about the whole encounter—and he knew he should probably be concerned with that. But his brain was too fried to get into the possible implications. And his body was too relaxed for him to stress out about it.

He only needed one thing, and he had it: his arms around Victoria as she nestled, trusting and sated, against him.

Chapter 12

Victoria liked to think her own priorities regarding what to install in the tiny house first would have been a bit different. Whatever else went in there, in whatever order, the toilet should have come *first*. Especially since, as a composting or possibly incinerating model, it would probably be self-contained rather than relying on a plumbing hookup.

Of course with no finished interior walls or doors, she would have had *less* privacy peeing that way than in her current situation—a few yards downhill from the house, behind some scrub, wearing only her boots and Ethan's shirt and hoping like hell nothing climbed up her leg or bit her ass before she was through. She felt the odds worsen as she waited enough time to feel mostly air-dried. Any second, a snake or scorpion or even just a scary possum would happen by, and she'd scream, and then Ethan would come running and see her squatting ignominiously among the bushes, and she'd probably feel compelled to make some anxious, nervous joke about golden showers and everything would be horrible forever.

A minute or so passed without incident or animal involvement, and Victoria finally stood up, wrapping her arms around herself and shivering as she headed back toward the house.

A few steps later she was distracted by the view, which drew her gaze down the hillside and out across the vista of the starlit landscape. A few lights twinkled here and there below—the inevitable signs of civilization—but for the most part the hills were dark sweeps of black-on-blacker, only the faintest contours visible.

The sky, though . . . was breathtaking. Clear, sparkling stars on a field of midnight blue, like a childhood memory of an impossibly beautiful night sky. She imagined it as a field of dark silk, shot through with silver, and then chuckled at the idea of how many artists must have stood under night skies contemplating how to capture the feeling of awe at this unearthly beauty. How to represent it without reducing it. Impossible, maybe, but she knew she would have to try at some point. The idea was already taking root.

The door squeaked behind her, but she didn't bother to look around. A few seconds later, Ethan's solid chest pressed into her back, and his firm arms wrapped the fluffy blanket around them both. She tucked her hands around his forearms, warming her fingers. Stepping back into the embrace, she could feel the waistband of his jeans, the knock of his boot against hers. At least he wasn't naked. She might have giggled at the idea of him strolling around in the dark in only his cowboy boots.

When he pressed his lips to her temple, she leaned into the kiss, trying not to think about whether all this affection was only for tonight. She could get used to it far too easily. And then what? Stick around cleaning up horse shit and making cakes because of a guy?

Her mind was full of stars and her fingers knew ways to weave them into lasting artifacts. At her best, she really could capture a feeling and share it with others. She wasn't too good for the work she was doing—she even enjoyed a lot of it, in a way—but if she didn't make art, design things, *create*, she wouldn't be herself anymore.

Still . . . tonight, a few nights, a few weeks. There was nothing wrong with enjoying this while she was here. If it seemed perfect, too good to be true, all the better, right? She would enjoy it even more. It didn't have to change who she was or who she wanted to be.

"Amazing view," she finally whispered.

"I picked this spot for a reason." He tilted his head to rest it against hers. "I like to be starstruck sometimes."

"Good choice." The hillside even blocked most of the firelight and other light sources from the event in front of the main house, though an occasional voice or whipcrack still reached them on the breeze. "Have you been to the Round Top music festival? Or Shakespeare at Winedale? When you get away from the buildings, the sky there . . ."

"Yeah. I love both of them. I go most years, when I can. One of my friends from college did a summer at Winedale."

"That's cool. I wish I could get back to both. I've only been a few times. I love how . . . subversive the whole thing is. I wish more people outside the state knew about stuff like that. It would give them a completely different view of Texas." Both the music festival institute and the Shakespeare program at Winedale had a great deal of fun with the contrast between the small-town Texas setting and the stereotypically highbrow cultural entertainment being presented. World-class string quartets playing in a lush old-fashioned music hall with carved Texas lone stars set in the ceiling. A group of college students from all over the country performing various Shakespeare plays in a converted nineteenth-century barn.

"Of course you'd love them both," Ethan murmured with a soft snort against her hair. "Such a good fit . . ."

"What?"

"Nothing. Nothing. Um, if you like stargazing, the McDonald Observatory's worth a visit, too. Bit of a drive but very cool." He tucked the blanket around them more snugly.

Victoria nestled into his chest, grateful for the warmth. She was getting drowsy again, now that the pressing call of nature had been answered. "I do want to go there. It's on my list. I have a . . . I guess a bucket list of places to go and natural phenomena to see. I saw a few on the drive from Rhode Island, actually. Cardinal tracks in fresh snow. At least I *think* it was a cardinal. And a true, live, unfiltered golden hour. I use a lot of natural influences in my work."

His chest bounced against her back as he chuckled. "Your work. Man, I was an idiot."

"Eh." She shrugged. "You had no way to know. By the way, I have a portable spinning wheel in my cabin if you want to learn to spin your own yarn from fibers."

"You're shitting me."

"Nope. It was one of the few things I didn't sell. I couldn't bear to. For one thing, I do actually use it, and for another . . ."

He gathered up her hair in one hand, scooping it to one side of her neck. The draft sent a chill through her, but it wasn't entirely unpleasant.

"For another?"

"It makes me feel like Sleeping Beauty. The whole bit with the spindle, you know."

Breath warmed her exposed skin, then heat descended in the form of lips and a scrape of stubble below her ear. "Jesus. You really are a freaking Disney Princess."

It sounded like he'd had this thought before, even without knowing about the spinning. She wasn't sure whether to be flattered or irritated. The things he was doing with his tongue along the muscles of her neck, and the stealthy way he'd managed to unbutton the purloined shirt she wore, argued in favor of flattery. "Are you implying you're Prince Charming?"

"Nah. Logan's more the type. So this list . . . that's a weird assortment. Stars and bird prints and the golden hour. What's the theme, there?"

It was getting harder to concentrate with his teeth scraping on spots he'd missed in their earlier session. "Oh, well . . . mmm. They're all visual influences, I guess. But either with texture or particular light qualities, and . . . God, could you just bite me like that but *everywhere*, that'd be great? And like . . . shapes that nature gives you and you see nowhere else, like the four-pronged angles of a bird's foot, or the way a cloven-hoofed animal's footprint has deep and shallow imprints in the mud and it's . . . aaah."

He had bitten into the meat of her neck, below her ear, and whatever she'd had to say about animal tracks disappeared into the growing aura of lust that encircled both of them. He whispered into her ear: "The aurora borealis."

"Mmm." She reached back, finding his hips, clutching at his jeans in an effort to leverage herself more tightly against him. "Man, you're good at dirty talk."

He cracked up, obviously caught off guard, and Victoria turned around in his arms with an unrepentant smirk that quickly turned to a giggle. She patted his chest, then nodded past his shoulder at the house.

"I'm heading back inside."

Halfway to the door, she heard the all-too-familiar buzz of her phone. When she got inside and found it—it was lighting up the outside pocket of Ethan's bag—she discovered a string of new text message notifications on her screen.

All from Alexandra, who seemed to have sent them one after the other within the past minute or so. A chill went up Victoria's spine as she poked the screen with a shaking finger, navigating to the text app to read all of them in order.

Vic call me ASAP 911

nvm Piper fell asleep in here watching a movie w/me so can't talk anyway, reply to text plz URGENT

OK I gotta just tell you bc I hv to get her upstairs. You nd to get away from Hilltop this weekend—hope it isn't too late. I'm so so so so sorry. Just found out the private party is some weird sex thing. SO SORRY. I DIDN'T KNOW.

Please get in touch. Hope you are safe and not up there for that. Love you.

"Are you okay?" Ethan stepped up behind her, touching her shoulders lightly.

Victoria showed him the screen. "Well. I need to figure out how to answer *this*. Other than that, Mrs. Lincoln, how did you enjoy the show . . . ?"

"Oh, fuuuuuck." His grip tightened, then he pulled her into a backward hug.

A new text slid onto the screen, and they both drew a sharp breath as they read.

Started to call the cops about it then realized if you're still there u cd be implicated in anything illegal. Plz let me know when you are away and safe. Take ur things and get a motel if u want, I will cover the charges. Will be there tomorrow to pick up. So sorry Vic. Especially after what happened in RI, this is last thing u needed to be faced with. Plz reply.

Victoria's gut clenched at the words *call the cops*, undoing most of the relaxation she'd achieved through ropework and orgasms. "Shiiiiit."

"At least she *didn't* call the cops." Ethan squeezed her tighter. "Of course if she had, this would've been the best night, because Chet's working tonight and the call would go to the sheriff's office because the ranch is outside the city limits. And most of the deputies either know what's going on and are cool with it or know that Chet doesn't want them asking questions about the supersecret party at his family's place. But the call would've been documented through the dispatcher, so it still could've been bad."

Chet Garcia, Ethan and Logan's cousin, was the sheriff of Bolero County . . . and one of the co-owners of Hilltop Ranch. He was also, as Victoria understood it, a frequent participant at Giddyup. Kink seemed to run in the boys' family. And in this case, the connection made things a lot safer for Giddyup.

The question still remained. "How do I answer? I have to keep her from driving up here."

"I gather you're not out as kinky to your family. So . . . do you wanna be?" He leaned over her shoulder and gave her a slightly maniacal grin. The effect was enhanced by the under lighting from the phone's screen. "If so, now's your chance."

"Have you lost your only mind?"

"I guess that's a nope."

"I need something quick. She's freaking out. Um . . ." Partial truths. She started texting.

I'm fine. In cabin for the night.

Ethan nodded his head, bumping his chin on her shoulder. "Smart. Doesn't say *whose* cabin."

Don't come here. U won't get on to property anyway. Private club members only.

She paused before hitting Send. "Um . . . what next . . . ? I need to make it sound like whatever she read may be true but it's not a big deal. *Oh!*" For this one, she could tell nearly the whole truth.

Also nothing to be sorry for. No need to pick me up. If ur worried about the kink it doesn't bother me. I'm an artist, remember? I had friends in RI who were into much harder stuff than I've seen tonight. And if you come here I'll lose my job and not have money to pay my bills. Please don't screw this up for me. I am safe and comfortable here. Love you, too.

She read it over and then sent it, hoping against hope it was enough to deflect Alexandra.

Enough time passed before the brief reply that Victoria suspected her sister had either written and deleted several attempted responses or had been so stunned that she couldn't even formulate words right away.

OK. Won't come. Will call or text you tomorrow.

Ethan was still reading over her shoulder. "Well, that doesn't seem ominous at all."

"Nope," Victoria answered. "No sense of foreboding coming right through the screen or anything."

"What do you think she's gonna do?"

She gathered the blanket around herself again and stepped reluctantly away from him to place the phone on the floor by his gear bag. "No idea."

"I should probably warn Logan." Ethan bent to touch the phone, lighting up the home screen. "It's only eleven. Tell you what, you stay here. I'm going down the hill to give him a heads-up. I'll grab some snacks and drinks and stuff while I'm down there, and maybe some extra blankets or something from the big house so we won't wake up in the morning with splinters in our asses. Sound good?"

He wanted her to spend the night? *And* there would be snacks? "That sounds amazing."

Victoria woke to the sun in her eyes and the all-too-familiar buzz of a cell phone against plywood.

"Fuck." She struggled out from under Ethan's arm, ignoring his mumbled protest, and grabbed the phone. "It's another text from Alex."

"Mmm? What time is it?"

"It's . . . eight o'clock."

"Hmm."

I know you're an adult and can make your own choices. I am try-ing really hard to respect that. But I love you and I can't let you stay in a situation I don't think is safe—

Jesus, and Alex thought the vanilla world was any safer? True, there were abusers in the BDSM world just like anywhere else. And plenty of assholes. But there were also built-in protections, negotia-tions, safewords. Honestly, she felt like it evened out . . . and she felt infinitely safer and more respected at Giddyup than she'd ever felt at the few frat parties she'd attended with friends from Brown.

—so I'm going to have to do *something* if you don't get out of there. If you're making money helping out this weekend, do that. But you need to get your résumés out there and find some other job be-fore the next one of these Giddyup things—

Damn, she'd named it. Heaven only knew what she'd found on-line about it.

—or I'm going to have to at least tell Mom and Dad what's going on. They're worried enough as it is, so I really don't want to do that.

"Fuck me." Victoria started typing a reply.

Ethan hummed from over in the nest of comforters and blankets they'd bedded down in. "Mmm. 'Kay. Come closer first. Don' wanna get up yet."

"Ha."

"Is that your sister?"

"Yeah. Hang on."

I've already been looking for a job, but my field is competitive, I don't have a degree, and I can't afford to fly anywhere for in-person interviews. So I can't make any promises about the time frame. Mom and Dad don't need to worry. I'm fine. You trusted Mindy before you knew about Giddyup. That doesn't need to change. Her sex life is her business—

Victoria deleted the last sentence, realizing how wrong it would be if Alexandra took it literally, and sent the text. Alex replied quickly; she could thumb type like the wind.

Not going there with you. That's between me and her. Please call our parents. They're worried and you're crossing over into asshole or crazy territory about ignoring them. About everything. None of us think you're behaving rationally anymore. Agreeing to work on a dude ranch, then staying when it turns out to be the new Chicken Ranch isn't helping with that.

Fingers shaking, Victoria exhaled and typed her response as fast as she could, her fingers making audible pats against the screen.

No money is exchanged for sex here. It's all consenting adults doing things that are nobody's business but their own. The only one trying to do any harm here is you, threatening to out them and... idk, what are you saying, that you'll try to have me committed because I dropped out of college, accepted a job you got me then took a dislike to, and neglected to call my parents for... what, a few weeks? Seriously? This isn't the 1800s. I'll call them when I'm ready. In the meantime, kindly back the fuck off.

She stabbed a finger at the screen to send the text, then heard a swishing noise. Looking toward the makeshift bed, she saw Ethan sit halfway up and pull the bag of food toward himself. He pawed through the selections, looking delightfully mussed and heavy-eyed.

"Banana or orange? Ham sandwich? Potato chips?"

Victoria suddenly realized she was starving. "Yes, please."

"Attagirl. Keep your strength up. There's another play party tonight, after all."

"Do you have a way to make coffee up here?"

The phone buzzed in her hand and she sighed before lifting it to read Alex's reply.

Please get out of there before the next whatever weekend sex freak thing. I'm not sorry for trying to protect you. I love you, baby sis.

She honestly had no idea how to respond. She typed and sent *Love you, too* without addressing anything else. It was too early and she was too hungry and uncaffeinated to think about all that.

Unfortunately, Ethan didn't feel the same limitation. "What'd she say this time?"

"Ugh. Basically that if I don't find another job and leave here before the next Giddyup, she'll tattle on me to our parents." She sat down beside him with a flump, crossing her legs and leaning her chin on her hands like the child Alexandra clearly thought she was. "She also called Hilltop the Chicken Ranch and implied that if I stayed, the family might try to have me committed."

Ethan sat all the way up, agape. "This isn't the fucking Victorian era."

"That's what I said!"

"Can people still *do* that? Well, I guess they must be able to, come to think of it. People are always having relatives taken to rehab . . ."

"But kink is my antidrug."

He laughed out loud, the sound filling the small, mostly empty space. Roxie roused herself from under the edge of a blanket, giving Ethan a curious look. Then she stood, shook herself vigorously, and trotted over to scratch the door.

He groaned and stood, stretching, then strolled naked to the door to let her out. "I really should have a doggie door."

"Why don't you?" Victoria hadn't had much chance to admire the view last night in the dark; by daylight, it turned out, Ethan had a surprisingly muscular butt and thighs. Or perhaps not that surprising, given how much time he spent on horseback and walking around among herds of cattle or sheep. In any case, it was a lovely surprise.

"Electronic ones are hella expensive. Regular ones are cheap, but then anything could come wandering in. Possum, raccoon, cats from the barn. A really motivated coyote."

"Motivated Coyote is my new grunge band name." She pulled one of the ham sandwiches from its zipper bag and dug in, momentarily forgetting the need for coffee as hunger took over.

"Heh. Hey . . ." He turned from the door suddenly, as if he had just thought of something; the view remained pleasant. "What time did you say it was, before?"

"Eight," Victoria mumbled around the sandwich, putting a hand in front of her mouth to block the sight.

"Crap. I have that suspension class at ten. I need to get to the main house so I can shower and then help with the setup." He started racing around the place, finding and yanking on clothes as he went.

"Mmph." She swallowed, then put the sandwich down and began the hunt for her underwear. "Me too. I think I'm supposed to be helping with setup. Uh . . . I have to go to my cabin for clothes anyway, so I guess I'll just shower there. You could . . . I mean if it's easier, you can just use my shower. Or if there's more hot water at the main house or something, or if you'd rather not go there and have everyone see us together, I understand. Whatever . . ."

He stopped, eyeing her pointedly and stepping over to put his hands on her shoulders. "I didn't even think about that. Of course I can shower at your place. Hell, I'll carry you there piggyback in front of God and everybody if you want."

Warmth filled her, not the heat of the night before but something new. Entirely new. "I don't think that'll be necessary. Walking will be fine." Her voice didn't betray her sudden tension, but all she could think was that she was in trouble here.

"We could hold hands," he offered solemnly.

She nodded back, forcing her face into a serious expression despite the sudden giddy urge to laugh. Or possibly cry. "Deal."

Chapter 13

After eight hours of selling snacks and soft drinks, going on "water patrol," and directing new Giddyup visitors to the various venues around the ranch, Victoria was almost as exhausted as she had been after her first shift of mucking out the stables. But for all her physical fatigue, her mind was on overdrive by the time she was finally free to shuck her Staff t-shirt Saturday night and blend in with the participants. Giddyup was like a kink convention, a school carnival, and a rodeo all rolled into one big, enthusiastic, fast-paced bundle of events. There was always something happening, and she'd gotten to see nearly all of it in bits and pieces.

She kept mental-noting things she'd like to explore in more depth next time—and then remembering there would be no next time. Alexandra would see to that. So this play party was her last hurrah, and she knew she should make the most of it. After a bite to eat and the world's fastest shower, she stopped long enough at her computer to re-read the email she'd spent far too much time drafting and re-drafting. She'd finally started deleting things, and now it was down to a few short paragraphs. Telling her parents she was okay, that she had a job at a very nice family-friendly place called Hilltop Ranch, that she was looking for work in her field. That she thanked them for all their support and was sorry she hadn't been upfront about her reasons for pulling away, but she would make arrangements to see them soon and discuss all that once she felt up to it.

She started to make more tweaks, then forced herself to stop and, before she could reconsider, hit Send. The world didn't come to an end, and after a moment she let herself enjoy the sense of relief over finally having done it. No matter what happened as a result, at least she'd taken that step.

It was one less thing on her mind to worry about, so she could simply enjoy the evening. She pulled the towel from her still-wet hair, ran a brush through it, then left it to air-dry. Then she put on a purple sports bra, another pair of yoga shorts . . . and, after a little consideration, some jeans and a well-worn black hoodie.

She'd had some offers from rope tops interested in tying her up. Diego had suggested she could be his "calf" for the lariat demo he'd be doing at eight o'clock to kick the evening's festivities off. But even with all those possibilities on the table, Victoria had only ever had one destination in mind. It wouldn't help her make the most of Giddyup, maybe, but it was the only place she really wanted to be.

Even in the low, warm, flickering light of the outdoor heaters and scattered strands of fairy lights, it was easy enough to spot a safety orange vest across the front yard of the main house. Ethan had the shift Logan had taken the night before: head dungeon master from eight at night until one in the morning and head of the cleanup crew for an hour after that. When Victoria spotted him, he was conferring with another few orange-vested types near the fire pit. She kept an eye on him while she snuck behind the concession counter, giving Robert a quick smile and wave when he shot her a questioning look from the point-of-sale tablet.

"Just getting some coffee for the DM. One sugar, right?"

"Hang on." He tapped an icon on the screen, attention back on the leather-hooded gentleman in front of him. "Okay, sir, got it on your tab. Straws are at the end of the counter. Enjoy the party!"

The guy was already unzipping the opening over his mouth. "Thanks, man."

Robert turned to Victoria and pointed to his side, where a curtained-off set of shelves stored some extra supplies. "There are bigger Styrofoam cups behind curtain number one. It'll screw the environment but save you a refill trip later. Two sugars for those babies."

She grabbed the larger, less ecologically sound cup, thanking Robert and basking in the warm glow of his obvious approval. It was nice to have, especially as she was being pretty obvious herself. In a way, playing the part of Ethan's . . . person-who-would-bring-him-coffee-for-his-DM-shift . . . really was making the most of her last play party at Giddyup. It made her feel even more a part of things. And *damn*, it felt good to be a part of this. She couldn't believe she was going to have to give it up after she'd just found it. Even if she wasn't playing tonight, the freedom of walking through the crowd, surrounded by people practicing their kink in the open, knowing that part of her was fully accepted, was like nothing she'd ever known.

Silly to get choked up about it, though. It was a fantasy world, and crying over having to leave was akin to a child crying because they couldn't live at Disneyland.

The dungeon master confab was just breaking up when she arrived at Ethan's side with the large cup of coffee. He took it with a look of grateful wonder.

"You're the *best*. Thank you, this is perfect. You're awesome." He dropped a swift kiss on her lips, not quite enough to satisfy her sudden longing to touch him.

"You're welcome. Can you use some company tonight?" Hands in her pockets, booted toe scraping a half circle in the dirt from the pivot point of her heel, she glanced around at the reveling kinksters as if Ethan's answer wasn't a big deal either way.

"Hey." He brushed her cheek with a thumb, drawing her attention back instantly. "I'd love that. Are you sure you wouldn't rather play, though? I can recommend some great riggers. There's a guy here tonight who does really beautiful, very traditional kinbaku. He's trained all over the world. Amazing stuff."

Tempting. She'd be lying to herself if she said it wasn't. But . . . "Eh. I think I'd rather just soak up the atmosphere for a while."

Ethan let his hand linger on her face, then drew her closer. He lowered his lips to hers, barely brushing against her skin. She closed her eyes, shutting out everything but the sensation of his breath mingling with hers, the faint prickle of his five-o'clock shadow, and finally the pressure of his mouth and the sweet intrusion of his tongue.

Only for a moment, but it was enough to set off sparks from her toes to her chest, as if he'd been ever so slightly electrified. After a second she fluttered her eyes open again to contemplate his face, wondering how she could have ever thought he wasn't leading-man material. He was one of the best kind. The kind who made millions and spawned copycat male models for years, none of whom ever quite captured the spark of the original because the whole point was that he was *different*.

And he had the whole fucking world in his eyes.

That's just the firelight. She had to believe so, otherwise her heart would break. She would be losing too much by leaving here before another month had passed.

Ethan pulled away, seeming reluctant but determined. "Enough of that, or I'll end up oblivious while something awful is happening right in front of me."

Was he already oblivious? Did he have any idea how awful she felt, feeling this wonderful and knowing how soon it all had to end? "Yeah, I know. You have a job to do."

Maybe he didn't feel as wonderful; maybe she was just the flavor of the month, and that was fine. It had to be. She'd already sent out so many résumés, placed so many calls, fired off a slew of hopeful emails about jobs she knew she wasn't *quite* qualified for. Slim though the chance might be, it was possible some of those efforts might pay off at any moment, even before she had a chance to re-search no-degree-required jobs in Dallas that would get her out of Hilltop and Alexandra off her back. But one way or another, she'd be gone soon.

Which meant she should have gone and found another rigger in-stead of staying by Ethan's side all night, helping him keep an eye on the players. Bringing him snacks. Talking, laughing. Telling each other their stories. Most embarrassing moments, dumbest decisions, greatest achievements. Victoria's becoming the youngest winner, and one of the few student winners ever, of a prestigious textile design award. Ethan's months at the Royal Veterinary College in London. The time she tried to install a massive self-designed wall hanging in her dorm room and it fell down on her in the middle of the night, taking two huge chunks of plaster out of the wall to boot. The time he actually swallowed a goldfish whole on a bet, then stayed up most of the night drunk crying because he'd swallowed it live and he was guilt-ridden that he'd killed it with a stomach-acid bath.

At one point, Mindy wandered over to the heater to warm up and joined in their chat. She was naked, wearing only the leather thong and name tag she always had around her neck. Her butt was striped with welts from a caning earlier, but she'd rested for a bit, recovered, and was now taking in the sights while Logan fixed a wobbly spank-ing horse.

"Not really what I'd planned for our evening off, but ..." She shrugged, turning her front to the heat and rubbing her hands together. "I guess I ought to just go put clothes on."

Ethan tilted his head as though he were considering the pros and cons. "Well, you know. Clothes are awfully constricting. I mean, it's up to you, but don't feel like you have to be in any rush."

Mindy snorted. "Oh my God. Perv. Don't be admiring my nakedness. I'm going to be your sister-in-law next year."

Victoria's heart flipped in her chest. "Really? Congratulations, that's wonderful." People's love stories came true sometimes; things worked out. She wanted that to happen to her someday, but tonight the longing struck her more keenly than it ever had before.

"Thank you! I always forget people don't know—I never wear the ring. It was their grandmother's. It's absolutely beautiful and I'm such a klutz. I'm terrified I'm going to pop a diamond out into some horse apples or lose it on a trail or something."

Ethan chuckled. "I don't think Memaw's ever worn it either. I've only seen a plain gold band on her finger for as long as I remember."

Victoria cast her mind back, trying to recall details Ethan had mentioned about his relatives. "Is that the grandmother who used to live here?"

"Yeah. Probably didn't wear the ring for the same reason as Mindy. Didn't want to lose it in a haystack or drop it down the well. Figuratively, I mean. There was a pump house back then, too. They weren't cavepeople."

So much history in this family. So much love built into each structure on the ranch, soaked into the stones and beams and the very ground of the place. Mindy seemed to belong here now, just as Logan and Ethan did. Victoria had never had a very strong sense of home, but Hilltop had that quality in excess. It seemed to draw people in, make them comfortable, keep them there. Probably Ethan would never leave, or at least not for long. He'd find a woman who wanted to settle down at the ranch; they'd take occasional trips with the tiny house, but their home base would never have to change.

That was a hypothetical woman in a future that might never come to pass, so it made no sense for Victoria to envy her. It made no sense, at two in the morning after cleanup was finished, for Victoria to push Ethan up against the wall of the Bondage Barn on the way back to his place and kiss him as if she could punish him like an old-school romance hero punishing a wayward debutante for being too irresistibly beautiful and headstrong.

He seemed to interpret her fervor as pent-up longing and gave back as good as he got.

"Wanna tie you up," he freed his mouth long enough to mutter at one point. She nodded and went right back to kissing him. It was a wonder they made it all the way up the hill to his tiny house—although it was a necessity since all his rope was up there.

When they finally crashed through the door, stumbling in their haste to get the lights on, tear their clothes off, and get entwined again, Victoria saw that Ethan's rope plans were more specific than she'd realized. He'd been busy that day, it seemed, installing certain small but useful details to the frame of the open area under the loft.

Eventually that space would serve as a living room, with a couch and an entertainment center; Ethan had designed the loft high enough to give him walking clearance underneath . . . by about an inch and a half. He'd confessed to a certain amount of glee upon realizing that Logan, who was six foot one, would either have to duck or hit his head *every damn time* he came over to watch a game.

For the moment, however, only Ethan and Victoria's height mattered, and nobody would be banging their head on the frame that night—which was good because the frame was now armored with a series of cleats and ring bolts that looked sturdy enough to secure a raging stallion, much less one medium-sized and extremely compliant rope bottom. The tools he'd obviously been using were pushed to one side, and the fluffy gray blanket was spread out beneath the arch to protect their feet from the unfinished floor.

With only her top, bra, and shoes off, Victoria couldn't resist dashing to the frame and testing the strength of the cleats, grabbing one of the highest ones and hooking two fingers through the closest of the top rings, then lifting her feet from the floor. "Oh my God! This is amazing, Ethan!"

In his *house*. Not only had he managed a bondage frame in his own house, he'd managed it in a house that was barely over two hundred square feet . . . and to any vanilla visitor, it would probably just look like decorative touches to make the place look more like a barn or a boat or wherever one found metal cleats suitable for attaching ropes.

"I know, right?" He pulled off his jeans, then joined her, naked, to help her shuck hers the rest of the way off. The yoga shorts came with them. "I mean, the kitchen is supposed to be the heart of the home, but fuck that noise. This thing is the real deal. As long as I don't want to tie up anybody taller than me. And you, you're . . ." He put his hand on top of her head, then slid it off, level, to the tip of his own nose. "You're perfect."

That flutter in her chest again, that faint tightening of her throat. *Not that, anything but calling me perfect.* "I'll fit okay, at least. So what's first?"

"Oh, right. Uh . . . karada!"

She giggled and started to sing before she could stop herself. "Oh, you say ka-RAY-da, and I say ka-RAH-da."

Ethan picked it right up on the way to his gear bag, but said *po-TAY-ta* and *po-TAH-ta* for the next line to keep the rhyme consistent.

Victoria called him on it. "Okay, but nobody actually says *po-tah-ta.*"

"Shh, I'm choosing a color."

She swung from the cleat and ring again, ignoring the pain in her fingers. "I hear dark red ombre is all the rage this year."

"Don't *make* me call this whole thing off." He came up with royal blue instead, a hefty hank of it, and approached her with a gleam in his eye.

"As if."

"Hey. C'mere. I got something for you."

She glanced down at his cock, which was semihard. "Mmm."

He swished up the bundle of rope, then smacked it into his other hand, obscuring her leering view. "On second thought . . . turn around. Yeah, just put your hands back up there and grab on again."

Skin tingling, pussy warming in anticipation, she did as he said. She wasn't surprised when the end of the rope whipped across her ass, but the sting pulled a gasp from her lips anyway. Ethan paused, and she was about to glance back to see what he was doing when another whipping blow came, thuddier than the first; he'd looped the rope.

By ten or twelve strokes in, she was hanging on to the support in earnest, whimpering at each pause. Then he switched to the single piece again, bringing more sting with more power behind it, and tears sprang to her eyes . . . but she felt herself getting wet, her clit throbbing with her rising heartbeat. She wouldn't have welts like

Mindy's—she wouldn't *want* welts like Mindy's; canes scared the fuck out of her and she didn't usually get off on extreme pain—but she knew Ethan was leaving marks that would last the night. On her butt, her back, the backs of her thighs. A ladder of stripes to commemorate the occasion.

The pain had started her on the climb into subspace by the time he stopped, and the first lingering touch of the rope on her skin took her higher still. Neither of them said a word as he started to loop and tug, arranging the rope into an intricate harness from her neck to her thighs. Victoria stayed wherever he put her, floating along with his unspoken directions, leaning against his warm body whenever she got the chance. Tasting whatever bit of skin passed near enough for her mouth to reach.

Eyes closed, relaxing into the rope as it encircled her, she put all her trust in Ethan. She would have said it was more emotional than sexual—except that when he finished the karada and slid one hand from her breast all the way down to her rope-framed pussy, then pushed two fingers past the rope and into her wet cunt, she nearly came on his hand. Her legs trembled, she exhaled, she pulled back from the wave of pleasure—and she opened her eyes to see him staring at her with wonder and longing and unmistakable sadness.

She shut her eyes again because she couldn't see all that and keep it together. "What next?"

"I wish I knew . . . oh. Don't move." He stepped away, and she heard a muffled curse, then the rustling of the gear bag.

When he returned, a whump by her feet suggested he'd dropped more rope. But before he used any more of it, he kissed her lightly, then tapped one of her temples.

"Hey. Can I put this on you?"

She braved a glance. He was holding out a blindfold—a nice one, silk or something like it, with a plush lining. *Yes.* "Please." Because neither of them needed to gaze into the other's eyes at the moment. It was too much; she was relieved he apparently felt the same way.

Bathed in warm, fuzzy darkness, she no longer had to decide whether to peek. She had to let herself go, let Ethan move her into position under the scaffold. He worked his way from one side to the other, top to bottom, weaving ropes through the karada and securing her to the frame. Victoria tried to picture what it must look like, the blue ropes around her body, the black ones he'd chosen for the web that held her ever more firmly in place. She was caught dead center, the focal point, unable to move even if she'd wanted to.

Victoria told herself that she would want to when it became important enough. But at the moment she couldn't think of anyplace she'd ever felt more inclined to stay.

Ethan had been almost unable to plan for that night—not because he couldn't think up anything to do with Victoria, a bondage frame, and a fuckton of nice rope, but because he couldn't narrow it down. He wanted to do *everything* to this woman, everything he knew. He wanted to learn *new* things just so he could do them to her. He wanted to hear her reaction, find out which things she liked the best, so he could better woo her by becoming awesome at those things.

Yes to the sounds she made when he whipped her with the tail of the rope he was about to bind her with . . . and probably yes to flogging. He needed to bring his up from the main house some night.

Some night soon, before she left.

No to that. He couldn't think about that right now.

Yes to the way her body looked, framed by rope. But mostly to the way she moved to his slightest touch, as if she could read his mind and simply knew what he wanted her to do next. He wanted to sink into her and stay there. That was all. And he couldn't have that.

When she opened her eyes, he couldn't bear the truth he read in them. He blindfolded her to spare himself, and told himself he'd seen only what he wanted to see. But that didn't make it any less perfect when he continued the ropework, lacing her into the frame he'd created below the loft. He was hard, aching now, and he worked quickly because he had to see her like this, but he also had to free her enough from the binding to fuck her soon.

When it was done—all the ropes woven into a web around Victoria, holding her into place in the middle of his still-unfinished home—he took a step back to appreciate his handiwork. Instead, he saw her lips part slightly, her head turn as if she was following his movement even though she couldn't see him, and then the words to a dozen old standards jumbled through his mind all at once. Because it had to be her, and she was too beautiful, and they couldn't take that away from him, the way she looked tonight.

He brought his hand to his mouth, tasting her, filling every sense he could with her. Even at a distance she overwhelmed him. The *fact* of her. The way she was so much more present than just about anyone he'd ever met, but would be gone in such a short time. It seemed impossible that he wouldn't continue to see her. There had to be a way.

"Ethan?" she whispered, sounding uncertain.

He'd been standing and staring too long, getting lost in his own head. "Be there in a second." It took a few seconds, actually, to open up a packet and roll on a condom, then start to unbind Victoria. Ethan started at her feet this time and worked his way up.

He could see how wet she still was, smell her arousal, hear it in her tiny gasps and moans as the rope and his hands passed over her skin. Once her legs and waist were unbound from the webbing, Ethan spread his legs wide enough to accommodate the height difference, hooked one of her knees over his arm, and used his other hand to push the rope at her crotch aside enough to make room for his cock to enter her.

The angle was awkward. His legs were shaky. But both of them sighed when he was fully sheathed, as though it was perfect.

"I won't last," Victoria said almost instantly. More to be polite, he thought, than in any way apologetically.

"I don't want you to." He pulled halfway out, then thrust in again. Not too hard, but enough to make Victoria groan and tighten her legs around his waist.

"Again," she begged.

He obliged her, repeating the motion as precisely as he could. Then again, and again, and again, and she stopped breathing, her entire body turning to warm marble in his arms, pulling tight against the ropes as she came.

Too much. She was too amazing, and his leg was cramping, and he needed something he couldn't get in this position. When Victoria came down from her orgasm, sighing and trembling, he let himself slip out of her—disappointing to them both, from the sound of it—and rapidly unwound the rest of the rope web, hoping her legs would hold her up.

When she was finally untied, he used the karada to haul her into his arms and lift her feet clear of the ground, then walked her over to the pile of blankets with the sleeping bag on top of it. When she collapsed gratefully onto the heap, she pulled him down with her. Then she surprised him by slipping off the blindfold but rolling to her stomach and lifting her hips enough to slip a pillow under them.

He didn't need an engraved invitation. He knelt between her thighs, gripped the ropes covering her hips, and buried himself inside her again, covering her like a stallion. This time he held nothing back—he took her fast and hard, grunting at each stroke while she groaned her pleasure into the blankets. It was raw and basic, and they might as well have been two animals rutting in the night.

Except for the way he found her hands with his when she came again, and then he came a moment later, and they laced their fingers together tightly and he never wanted to let go.

Chapter 14

It had been a weird Giddyup for Ethan.

It was the best of Giddyups, it was the worst of Giddyups . . .

He watched Victoria on yet another phone call Monday morning and thought about the weekend they'd just spent. Mostly joined at the hip, at least figuratively—sometimes literally—except when their work required otherwise.

They'd slept like logs after the previous night's play party and subsequent shenanigans, and he hadn't set an alarm; Roxie's door-scratching and insistent face-licking had roused him at eight-thirty. He'd gone outside with her—*really gotta get that bathroom walled in and the toilet set up*—and returned to find Victoria awake and attempting to take rope-and-lash-mark selfies.

"I don't post them anywhere," she reassured him. "They're just for me, or to show friends sometimes for bragging rights."

"Oh, I understand. Would it be easier to let me take the pictures?"

"I thought you'd never ask."

He couldn't remember a more entertaining Sunday morning. Or a more entertaining, easy, enjoyable . . . *any* time. Not just the best Giddyup but the best weekend-long date, because that was essentially what it had turned into. And within another few weeks she would be gone. Which made it the worst of times.

Maybe even sooner, the way her phone was lighting up now. Apparently, the round of résumés she'd sent out the previous week—even before Alex's ultimatum—had been aimed at exactly the right targets. It was an hour later in New York, and the first call had come in at eight that morning Texas time. Some clothing store company she'd apparently interned with wanted to set up a Skype interview that afternoon. Then one of her former teachers, who was apparently now some design company's director of textile-something-merchandising-stuff, called because he wanted to talk to the vice president of something *else* about interviewing Victoria for a position other than the one she'd applied for, but that she might be perfect for, if she was interested.

Or . . . something like that. He couldn't quite make it all out, and a lot of the terminology flew right past him. Victoria talked fast when she was excited, and each time she got off the phone she was very, very excited. She kept her cool admirably *during* the calls, though; her voice never wavered, even when she did the "Scream" face at Ethan or mouthed *Oh my God oh my Goooooooddddd* while bouncing around the room.

She was more composed, apparently, when she switched to French—which happened during this, her third phone call of the morning; she'd actually made this one herself, in response to an email she'd received while they were sleeping. To Ethan's ear she sounded fluent in the other language, but probably she had to stop and actually think about what she was saying a bit more, and that seemed to slow her down a tad.

He could tell one thing was the same, though. In English, in French, it didn't matter—the woman clearly knew her shit. Whatever she was talking about, she knew the stuff inside and out; she was an expert in her field and was passionate and confident about it.

Ethan hadn't considered that the whole time he'd known her—except for during the kink and sex—she had been completely out of her element. Honestly, she'd managed pretty well. Within the last week or so, she'd started to get faster at the housekeeping and barn chores and begun figuring out more and more things for herself. She wasn't fast enough to keep up with Robert, but then, nobody was.

Now, though, she was on her own playing field. And the difference was as noticeable as bringing a blurry picture into sudden, sharp focus with one push of a button or twist of a knob. *This* was Victoria Woodcock, this brilliant woman who seemed to know everything about anything to do with fabric. How to make it, what to use it for, ways to make it cheaply enough to profit, ways to make it more environmentally friendly, ideas about marketing it. Listening to her, watching her body language and expressions, even when he didn't know what she was saying, Ethan could see that she belonged in the world of whoever it was on the phone.

That knowledge shouldn't have made him ache from his temples clear down to his gut because, despite last night's passion-fueled festival of emotions, he'd only known her a few weeks and she'd never planned to stay long at Hilltop. But it did.

So did the obvious relief on her face the next time she caught his eye. She smiled at him, made a silent, exaggerated *phew* shape with her mouth while swiping her hand across her forehead. Then pointed at the phone, shook her head, shrugged, pouted. He had no idea what she was trying to convey there.

A few minutes later she hung up and tossed the phone lightly onto the blanket next to her.

"Oh. My. God."

"I take it that was a good French call?" Ethan pushed her cooling coffee mug toward her. He'd stolen his brother's Chemex and electric kettle along with a bag of freshly ground coffee the day before and was starting to think maybe hipster coffee wasn't such a bad idea after all.

"That was a good French call." She sipped the coffee, then waggled her hand. "Well, it was an encouraging French call. Balenciaga has already filled the position I applied for. *But.* I was applying for it because it was the only thing they had open. I never in a million years thought I actually had a shot at it. Apparently they got my résumé after they'd already made a decision or I would have been in consideration. Pascaline Girard, who I worked for last summer, was calling to tell me she would be keeping my CV handy in case anything new came up. It's like midnight there or something, I think, but she keeps really odd hours. Anyway."

Ethan nodded. He'd gotten that it wasn't a job, but was still a good sign. "So that's one interview, one maybe, and one you're-on-the-short-list-for-next-time. Just from the first round of applications. You're . . . kind of a badass, I gather."

"Well." She shrugged, scrunching her face. "I think I just . . . overestimated the importance of the actual degree and underestimated the value of my internships. I was so freaked about not having finished the BFA that I was really only trying for jobs I *knew* didn't require it. When I send out more résumés this week, I guess I need to go ahead and apply for even the long-shot jobs. Pascaline just laughed about it. Said I'd finish *un des ces jours.*" She waved a hand airily. "Someday. If I wanted to. Not that I'll ever be able to afford it on what I'll make in an entry-level job in the fashion *or* commercial design biz. I'd need something in industry to start higher, and I suspect I couldn't get away without the degree there. But still, these results are definitely encouraging."

"Industry . . . Isn't fashion a commercial industry? Or . . ." He knew the words, but she obviously meant something particular that he wasn't grasping.

Victoria half smiled, indulgent. "So, there are things like . . . tarps. Or the mesh fabric that covers speakers. Or carpets specifically designed for places like hotels and office buildings. Let's see, what else . . . The fabric on the chairs in your doctor's office. The breathable fiber webbing covering the backrest on Logan's office chair. Somebody had to design all those, and somebody had to design or program the machines that weave them. Figure out what materials would work best. Where to source that material for a price that will still enable the manufacturer to profit. And a million other decisions. So on one end you have textile manufacturers who are focused on industrial applications, like the factory-made chair fabrics, or your Tyvek house wrap." She pointed at the nearest wall. "On the other you have high fashion, which is . . . oh, like small batch high-end or couture applications, or one-of-a-kind custom stuff. Which is sometimes prototype work for the next season's ready-to-wear. And everything in between is more or less the commercial stuff, like mass-produced clothes, home furnishings, things you can walk into a box store and buy. And those are all *jobs*."

Ethan blinked a few times, then looked around the tiny house slowly, suddenly aware of how many different textiles surrounded them. The blankets and pillows, the sleeping bag, the waterproof tarp and canvas drop cloth folded in one corner. Their clothes. The house wrap. Roxie's collar.

"Holy shit."

"Mm-hmm." Victoria nodded, as if she'd seen the reaction before. "It's invisible, right? Nobody thinks about it. But once you do . . ." She grinned and began to sing, in a pleasantly tuneful voice, "A Whole New World."

"And she sings, too."

She chuckled. "I'm a Disney Princess, remember? Hey . . . it's almost nine. Aren't you supposed to be somewhere at ten?"

Ethan groaned and flopped backward on the pile of blankets that had become his new happy place. Then he had to ward off Roxie's lick attack before he could address Victoria's question. She leaned on his chest, chin on her hands, all attention. It was a view he could all too easily get used to.

"I am," he said reluctantly. "Minnie's diner in town. I'm meeting Doc Taylor..."

"He's the vet here in town, right? The one you're supposed to take over for?"

He chuckled ruefully, relishing the feel of her welcome weight pushing back against the motion of his breathing. "Even you've heard about that? Must be fate, then."

She shifted to rest on one hand, freeing up a forefinger to trace his lower lip. "You don't seem very happy about it. Are you sure you believe in fate?"

Ethan kissed her fingertip in passing and considered her words. She wasn't wrong; he wasn't especially happy about the idea. But he wasn't particularly unhappy either. He felt oddly neutral about it. There was none of his old excitement for the plan, but he still couldn't imagine a life where he didn't follow through with it. He *wanted* that life. Eventually.

That didn't seem like an answer to her question, though. "I haven't decided yet. I'm just going through some stuff, I guess. Not really ready to make a big decision that'll keep me in one place forever. If we talk about anything today, though, it'll probably just be Doc feeling me out about the whole thing." He ran his fingers up into her hair, working through the fine, warm strands until he could cup the back of her head and pull her down for a kiss.

It was a great kiss, which didn't help Ethan sort through his conflicting thoughts. Because it was clear Victoria had no intention of sticking around, and the more he let himself forget that, the harder it would be when she left... but he couldn't seem to help himself when he was actually *with* her. He had imagined this whole bachelor experience, traveling around, spending a few weeks or months in one place and then moving on to a new landscape. Now he kept seeing Victoria there with him. Worse yet, he kept seeing her *here*, at Hilltop. The tiny house complete and surrounded by hardscaping, a garden of herbs and flowers blooming, and Victoria sketching the blossoms in springtime.

She shifted away from his mouth, dipping lower to nibble on his ear, and he spoke without thinking. "If you don't find another job, you could always stay here and make rope with me. Help me travel around and sell it. That's all working with textiles, right?"

Victoria's body froze, every muscle tensing under his hands.

Oh sweet Jesus, what just came out of my damn-fool mouth?

When she sat up, he was doing his best to smile wryly, as if he'd been making a joke that he knew wasn't that funny. "It's always good to have a backup plan, just in case," he added.

"Just in case," she echoed, eyeing him uncertainly. "It has been fun to work with the dyes, I admit. I can write all the steps down for you before I leave. Find some good links about techniques you can try." She patted his chest, then stood up and swung away from him. "I need to meet Robert in the kitchen in fifteen minutes to help him take inventory before his shopping trip. You need to head out, too, if you're gonna fit in a shower before you go into town."

He needed one too badly to skip it, so he got up and tugged on his previous day's clothes, pulling some fresh ones from the plastic tub he was currently using as a dresser.

They held hands most of the way to the main house, whenever the trail conditions allowed for it. Ethan told himself he should pull back, but every time he tried, it didn't work. It felt so natural to gravitate toward her, instead of away from her, that he'd find himself right back at her side or reaching for her hand before he even realized he was doing it.

Fuck.

An incredibly beautiful, show-tune-and-big-band-loving rope bottom who seemed fine with a no-strings-attached relationship. Probably his dream job waiting for him in town, complete with a side of Minnie's pie of the day. And Giddyup doing better than any of them had ever imagined possible.

How could everything be going so well . . . but feel so unsatisfying?

Victoria's mind kept drifting whenever Robert stopped talking long enough to count. She wouldn't have minded it drifting to her job search; she was already making a list of additional places to apply, different avenues she might take if she ignored *bachelor's degree required*. Instead, her thoughts were less legitimately tempted from the inventory work by memories of the weekend, and she kept trying to puzzle out exactly what she was doing with Ethan Hill.

He was nothing like her usual type. He was outdoorsy, insanely practical, not that into art as far as she could tell. He lived in—and was possibly about to buy into a *second* business in—a small rural town in a state she had left as soon as possible for all kinds of reasons. And yet . . .

On paper, Ethan was all wrong. In person, however, he seemed to fill some need she hadn't ever realized she had. Fireworks and drama she could have understood; anybody might go for a short, hot, ill-advised fling with a ruggedly handsome cowboy rigger. This wasn't that, though.

This was *easy*. It felt natural; it felt obvious. As if they'd been to-gether forever, and she had a groove in her soul that Ethan fit into perfectly. She kept forgetting they weren't really together at all, and that a long-term arrangement simply wasn't feasible.

Thinking in the long term about *anything* was hard right now. When she'd finally emailed her parents the previous afternoon, she'd struggled to find a way to express her goals, to tell them how she saw her life working out from this point forward. She wanted to ease their minds, not just by saying they shouldn't worry but by showing them she was confident and had a clear plan. Instead, she'd ended up with a lot of vague statements like *exploring the available opportunities* and *depends on what happens down the line*. Still . . . at least she'd sent it. She dreaded checking her email again and seeing the in-evitable reply; the last thing she'd read had been from Pascaline, and that had been so wonderful she hadn't wanted to spoil her mood by reading anything else.

"Did you get that?"

Victoria snapped back to the present with a sheepish smile. "Sorry. I zoned out. Could you repeat it? The last thing I had was ten pounds of onions. Wow, that seems like a lot of onions. Was that right?"

"Yes, that's right. Somebody overdid it a little at her first Gid-dyup, though." Robert tsked and shook his head. "Forty pounds of Yukon Gold potatoes and a big bag of new potatoes."

"Got it." She noted it on the pad she was holding. "Yeah, it was kind of intense. So much fun, though."

"Gotta learn to pace yourself. Or not, I guess, if you'll be gone by next time."

"Oh." She was surprised he knew. "Did Mindy and Logan . . . what did they tell you?" That she'd put the whole enterprise in dan-ger of outing because she hadn't foreseen that her sister—an attorney and well-known nosy person—would go digging around and discover that Hilltop Ranch was also the home of the largest monthly kink gathering in the Southwest?

Robert tilted his head and pursed his lips; he looked as though he was considering whether to tease her or not, then seemed to decide against it. "Just that you had stepped up your job hunt and were planning to clear out within a few weeks. They told me so I could help them find a replacement; having you here made us all realize how much we needed another hand, at least part-time. But it's hard to find somebody who can *also* help during Giddyup, so it may take a while. We can't just hire some teenager from town who needs an after-school and weekend gig."

Under the relief, Victoria was weirdly flattered. Nothing she'd done at Hilltop, with the possible exception of the rope making, which wasn't part of the actual job, had been particularly skilled work. It wasn't difficult to learn, just labor-intensive. But she'd made an effort to do it well, and she'd come a long way in a short time. It felt good to know she'd been at least some help after all.

"Was it supposed to be a secret?" Robert asked.

"No, no. I'm just sorry to be leaving you short-staffed."

He shrugged and turned back to the pantry shelf, moving the potatoes to one side and consulting his menu plan. "Well, you're giving us plenty of notice. You didn't just dash off in the night on a stolen horse or something. You'll get to stay on the list of cool people we like around here and would like to see again."

"I'm honored to be on that list."

If Victoria had wanted to abscond at night on horseback, Mindy and Logan might very well have helped her find a horse for that purpose. They'd been unbelievably kind and generous from the start and had immediately expressed outrage on her behalf at Alex's reaction to finding out about Giddyup. Of course they were also frightened and angry at the notion of somebody threatening to out them and their customers . . . their friends. They could do little in response other than warn Chet and try to help Victoria find a job if they could. But they'd given Victoria so much reassurance, shown so much concern, that she still choked up thinking about it.

Sweet and thoughtful and willing to help even a relative stranger in a time of need—those were the *perverts*. And the one who thought they deserved public exposure and humiliation—that was the *moral* person. Victoria marveled at the irony every time she thought of it, but she was as helpless as Mindy and Logan in this situation. The best she could do was intensify her job search and cross her fingers harder than ever before that one of her prospects would work out in time.

And then . . . she'd have to leave.

Chapter 15

There was lemon meringue that day. In his mind, Ethan knew that was because it was a Monday. In his heart, he felt it had to be a sign, even though he didn't believe in signs, any more than he believed in fate. All the sweet, fluffy goodness of the meringue, then the tang of the lemon hit your taste buds and for a second or two you wondered what you'd just bit into. Then everything blended together perfectly and it all just . . . worked. Sweet, sour, then the perfect mingling of both.

Minnie's lemon meringue recipe was a closely guarded secret and it was genius. Ethan wasn't as confident about the proposed ownership agreement Doc had brought along for his consideration. He couldn't read Doc's expression, so Ethan had no idea whether his soon-to-be boss/partner was apprehensive or excited or what. He did know he never wanted to play poker against the old guy.

"I had 'em leave all the dates blank," Doc explained, pointing to one of the carefully flagged pages. There were a lot of those. *Sign here. Initial here.* "Gives you some time to take it to a lawyer of your own if you want. Get the finance part checked out and all. It's kind of a custom job, but if you need some changes I'm sure the lawyers can figure it out." He passed a hand over his freckled scalp, scratching lightly on the very top, where no hair had existed for decades. "You can start whenever you like in the meantime if you need to. We could work out something, maybe prorate some compensation at the relief rate. I heard you already left Winston's place."

Technically, Ethan's last day had been over a week ago. Even though his lease had ended in San Antonio—along with his various utility bills—and his stuff was safely stored at Hilltop for free, he felt like he *ought* to be jumping right into the new job. That would be the responsible thing to do. It was his plan, after all.

"Yeah," he said, sliding the papers closer and flipping through them as if he had a clue what he was reading. "Probably a good idea to get it checked out. I'll give you a call later about a start date, if that's okay. I'm trying to take care of some stuff up at the ranch while I've got the time off."

"A'ight. Take your time." Doc cleared the last bite of pie from his plate, taking a moment to savor it before speaking again. "Damn, I love Monday pie." He picked up his hat from the vinyl bench beside him, rolling the brim between his fingers before stretching out one hand to Ethan.

Ethan stood up and shook Doc's hand, smiling and nodding and generally trying to give the impression he was pleased with the situation. Before Doc let go, he donned his hat and clapped Ethan on the shoulder with his free hand, squeezing for a second before releasing him.

"I know it's a big step. And I want you to be sure before we sign off on anything. But I have to say, Son . . . I couldn't be prouder if you were my own." Then he cleared his throat and clomped out with a nod to the young woman behind the counter.

Ethan could've sworn he saw Doc's eyes glimmering with tears. So much for poker face.

He was choked up himself as he sat back down, and he wanted it to be because his life was turning out almost exactly as he'd always wanted. Or rather, he wanted to be rejoicing in that, instead of feeling like his stomach was about to toss the pie out on its ear.

Doc wanted him to be sure? How could he be anything else?

Since the age of eight or so, when he'd first met Doc Taylor over the heaving flank of a birthing mare, Ethan had known what he wanted to do with his life. From that time forward, he'd done everything with a single motivation: to join Doc's practice. Once he was old enough to realize Doc had to retire sometime, he'd dreamed of taking over the practice. He was the most capable unlicensed vet tech imaginable once he was old enough to work with Doc as a teenager. He'd pushed himself to excel in science and math, then flouted the family tradition to get his undergraduate education at Texas A&M instead of the Hill family alma mater, The University of Texas at Austin. But he'd aimed even higher, finally earning his DVM at UC

Davis. Back to A&M for a year-long large animal internship, a once-in-a-lifetime practicum at the Royal Veterinary College in London, then an associate spot at a practice near San Antonio. Always in the back of his mind was the certainty that he would end up back here in Bolero, prepared to take the reins from Doc Taylor.

Eight-year-olds from small rural towns don't know much. But Ethan wasn't a wide-eyed kid anymore, and he knew the world was a lot wider than Bolero, Texas. Maybe he should have questioned himself sooner, let his dream evolve along with his perspective.

Toying with the crust of his pie, Ethan thought about Victoria. How she'd thrown caution and her plans to the wind, given up just about everything she'd known, and rebooted her life from scratch with practically no safety net. It had been hard for her at first, but she'd taken what came along and worked with it. Refused to stay in unacceptable situations and worked hard to make the best of the acceptable ones. Figured out how to handle things, mostly. And it hadn't turned out so disastrous after all—she'd trusted her instincts, and now her risk seemed to be paying off in ways she'd never anticipated. When he'd left that morning, she was talking about applying for jobs she might not have even considered *with* a degree before. Jobs that paid better, jobs in a wider range of industries.

Maybe he needed to do that for a while, to broaden his horizons. Roll with the flow and see what happened. Be afraid of the unknown but willing to take what came.

That had never been his jam, either in kink or in the vanilla world. But maybe . . . maybe he *should* think long and hard before putting down even deeper roots in Bolero. That was definitely a factor he hadn't considered as a kid, but now he saw the town through adult eyes. He'd seen other places now, met other kinds of people.

Bolero was home and he loved it. He even recognized its strengths . . . But damn, was it *small*. Provincial. Backward, even. Returning to Texas after living in California had been a serious culture shock, and Bolero sometimes seemed like the epicenter of all that was problematic about Texas. It was that old uncle at a family reunion who seems like the most charming guy in the world until he suddenly makes a racist joke. He doesn't seem that bad when you're a little kid, but when you grow up and learn some things, you cringe whenever he comes over because you know that stuff is just *not okay*.

On the other hand . . . Ethan studied the contract Doc Taylor had left with him, a graduated buyout over five years, at the end of which time Doc would retire outright and Ethan would own the practice. To allow Ethan more time at Hilltop in the first few years, he'd be working a smaller percentage of time proportional to the percentage of his ownership interest, with compensation similarly aligned; then the workload and compensation would shift during the third year to allow Doc to ease into retirement in stages. It was the only contract of its kind he'd ever seen or even heard of, and it seemed incredibly thorough. The cover page included the name of the lawyer who'd apparently drawn it up, from a big-name firm in San Antonio.

"More coffee, hon?" Doreen swung the pot near his cup, waiting for an okay to pour.

He nodded, watching the dark roast fill the white enamel as if he could divine answers in the swirling depths.

Doreen lingered after the cup was full, her weight on one hip, her head tipped to the other side. "Everything okay? You and Doc T. looked like things were gettin' pretty serious over here."

Ethan shook his head with a rueful smile. He'd tell it here and by morning everyone in Bolero would know. "Doc finally asked if I want to buy my way into his practice, Reenie. Become the new vet at Creekside Large Animal Clinic."

"Oh, congratulations!" She put the pot on the table and bent down to give Ethan an enthusiastic hug, leaving him awash in a cloud of rosy perfume, spray starch, and eau du deep fryer. "I can't believe you're coming back for good! First Logan, then Mindy Valek, now you. Who's next?" She might have *said* she couldn't believe it, but apparently it never occurred to her Ethan might do anything but accept Doc's offer.

"Good question." *A whole lot of kinksters*, he thought but didn't say. Of course those were only temporary visitors. Not permanent residents, like he would be. "I haven't signed anything yet, by the way. Have to think about some things first."

"Well, I'll leave you to look over your papers, then. But congratulations again! That's such excitin' news."

She sauntered down the aisle to the corner booth, where a handful of teenagers had trundled in and ordered a ridiculous quantity of food. FFA kids, judging by their caps, jackets, and boots. They were obviously taking advantage of the period they should be spending in the barn to grab an early lunch; Ethan had done the same thing in high school. For the juniors and seniors, the ag teacher and the constabulary always turned a blind eye as long as the privilege wasn't abused and nobody got into trouble in town.

If he started working with Doc, he'd probably get to know all their names before the school year was out; they'd be gearing up to show their steers or goats or hogs, worrying about how to get those last few pounds on their animals. At his practice in San Antonio, he had never had to deal with poultry and rabbits, but he would see all those animals and more working with Doc Taylor. Even a few farm dogs and barn cats. It would make for some nice variety.

One of the boys shoved half a double-sized burger into his mouth, and Ethan looked back down at his coffee to avoid seeing any more horrors. His foot started to bounce, his body signaling it was ready to *go*, to *do*, to *act*. He ignored it and picked up a straw wrapper instead, smoothing the thin paper and then carefully folding and looping it back on itself to form an intricate woven knot. Something that might look perfect centered over a breastbone or as the central waist piece of a karada. Maybe at the next Giddyup weekend he would find a willing rope bunny and try it out. He never had a shortage of volunteers, it seemed.

"Sign me up," Ethan murmured. He tugged too hard on one end of the wrapper, tearing the paper and ruining the symmetry of the knot. "Crap." There was only one volunteer who interested him, and she would be gone before the next Giddyup.

Just like the poem. "Nothing Gold Can Stay."

He started whistling softly as a cover, in case anyone had noticed him talking aloud to himself. "Don't Fence Me In." Couldn't go wrong with the standards. Except the song's antihero, Wildcat Kelly, always made him think of his brother, whose scene name was Wildcat. Perhaps a different selection from the Cole Porter songbook was called for.

His leg was on a mission to escape from tedium. Ethan reluctantly picked up the sheaf of papers and scooped his hat from the seat beside him. He slid from the stall and started to drop a ten on the table but, after eyeing the goofy FFA crowd, decided to walk it over to the counter instead and hand it to Doreen directly. She headed his way after dropping off more slices of pie for two women at the far end of the counter.

"Thanks, sugar. And congrats again!"

He nodded and spun on his heel, but even before he was out the door he could hear the women asking her what the congratulations were about. Yep, the grapevine was already in action.

Let them spread the news if they liked. The grapevine was wrong as often as it was right, and Ethan still hadn't put his signature on Doc's contract.

Compared to a hotel maid, Victoria knew she had it easy. A dozen cabins, plenty of time to clean them thoroughly, and two people to divide the work between. It was still hard work, though, and two cabins' worth of guests hadn't left until that morning, so she would need to do another round of laundry that afternoon in order to get everything ready for the handful of folks expected on Tuesday.

As she finished up the bathroom of the last cabin, Victoria patted herself on the back for one thing: If nothing else, by God, she knew how to clean a toilet now. And if she could ever afford to stay in a hotel or motel again in her life, she planned to tip the hell out of the cleaning staff, because they deserved it.

That old privilege was creeping in again, though. She'd realized it that morning while working and thinking about how to prepare for the Skype interview in the afternoon. All the jobs she was looking at—even the ones in fashion that paid "nothing"—paid more than most hotel housekeepers made. For that matter, Logan and Mindy were paying her more than that hourly right now. Her *least* promising options were better than somebody who really did this work as a long-term job, but she was already eyeing some openings askance because the salary or benefits package didn't look great, or she wasn't sure she'd like the commute to work from wherever she was most likely to live in a given area.

And she hadn't done anything in particular to deserve any of that opportunity, other than be born into the right family at the right time.

"I should volunteer somewhere," she muttered to herself.

A spider scuttled from behind the commode, and Victoria rose from her knees enough to free one foot and squash it. A quick spritz of disinfectant and a wipe later, the scene of the crime was spotless again. Just like the rest of the cabin. It was a rewarding feeling—a very specific set of tasks, for a very specific and useful purpose, accomplished in a reasonable amount of time and checked off the list. It had a clearly defined beginning and end. She would probably miss that when she found a job in her chosen field, where often the only hard-and-fast thing was a deadline.

Victoria lugged the cleaning supply caddy and mop bucket back out to the UTV and hoisted them onto the bed, then climbed into the driver's seat and steered the vehicle along the bumpy trail back to the main house. Her stomach started grumbling as she pulled up to the back-back door. Sadly, there was no sign of Robert in the laundry room as she unloaded the dirty linens and started several loads of wash. Nor was he in the kitchen, which probably meant he was still shopping—so she would have to forage for lunch.

Ugh. She'd gotten spoiled by his cooking, and by his using her as a guinea pig for the stuff he wanted to rotate into his menu for the guests. The refrigerator yielded nothing promising in the way of food to test, only a sadly depleted stock of lunch meats. She settled for folding a few slices of ham into a piece of bread, then grabbed a banana and a water bottle as well. The weather was still nice, and there had been a breeze earlier. If the front porch was still in shade, the swing there would make a nice place to sit and eat while the washers ran.

Juggling the fruit, water, and sandwich, she struggled to get the front door and screen door open; she had already closed the screen behind her before she saw the man standing by the porch swing. Startled, she gasped and dropped her sandwich.

"*Shit*. Um. Sorry." Wait. She was a grown-up and she had *earned* her quiet break with that ham sandwich. And he wasn't even supposed to be here. "You know what, Daddy? Never mind. I'm not sorry at all. *Shit*."

Chapter 16

Her father eyed the sandwich like it was the main problem and stuffed his fingers into his pockets. Dad jeans, a striped golf shirt, boat shoes with no socks. Weekend clothes. At least he'd made himself comfortable for the drive down.

"Hi, sweetheart. *I'm* sorry. I didn't mean for you to . . . lose your lunch. So to speak."

Victoria was closer to that than he realized. Her stomach had knotted itself so tightly, the idea of introducing food was completely off the table now anyway, so the loss of the sandwich wasn't that big a deal. "Why are you here? Did Alex . . . Oh my God, she told you, didn't she? She *swore*. I've been working my *ass* off to get stuff lined up by her deadline." No wonder her dad couldn't look her in the eye. He thought she was working at an illegal den of iniquity. "I'm not leaving here with you."

"I don't . . ." Thomas Woodcock shuffled a toe, then looked up, finally meeting her gaze. "I'm not planning to take you anywhere. Alex didn't tell me where you were. You said it in your email, Vicky. Hilltop Ranch. It was easy enough to look up. Damn . . . Well, your mother said this was a bad idea, but I figured if I came right away, you wouldn't have time to realize you'd forgotten to ask us not to."

"Did I forget?" She tried to remember the exact wording of her email, but she was still trying to wrap her mind around the sudden realization that her father thought she'd been blaming Alex for giving her the address. Was it possible he really had come on his own and knew nothing about Giddyup?

"Yep. I'm glad to hear you've lined up some interviews, though. Or . . . I assume you meant interviews. I know, I know." He held up his hands, as if she'd protested aloud. "I need to stop assuming. Hey, you look good. Alex said you were a wreck. I don't know what I was expecting."

"I am good." For the first time in a long time, she truly meant it.

Her father nodded, then shrugged. "Little too thin, maybe."

"Don't let any of Mom's friends hear you say that, please. And I've been working really hard, so probably I've lost some weight. I have no idea." She hadn't done it on purpose, at any rate. Lord knew she'd been eating enough to choke a horse.

"Yeah. You're the cleaning lady and stable girl around here? That's . . . I didn't mean to say that like it's a bad thing. Alexandra said it was—ah. Anyway."

"Oh. No." Victoria strode to the porch rail and put down the banana and water bottle so she could cross her arms while she faced her father. She had never seen him this way—conciliatory, quiet, unsure of himself—and it was throwing her off. "No, I really want to hear what Alexandra said. I wonder if it's right in line with what you said." Not how she'd planned to bring up that topic, but what the hell. If people were going to barge into her life when she was trying her best to distance herself, they deserved whatever they found there.

"Before or after she chewed my head off?"

"Alex chewed your head off?"

"Yes indeed. Do you wanna get off your feet, Peanut?" He gestured toward the swing.

She didn't want to sit beside him, swinging, relaxing, growing to feel at ease. She didn't want to hear *Peanut*. Even from here, she could smell his aftershave, the familiar dad smell of her early childhood. It made her kind of want him to scoop her up in a hug, tell her it would all be okay, the way he had when she was five or six and had faced a setback. Skinned a knee, gotten a noseful of water while learning to swim, failed to do as well at a horse show as she'd hoped. Instead of steeping herself in the fragrance of memory and old patterns of behavior, she stepped back to the rail and hopped up, perching there with her legs wrapped around the posts.

She waited for him to sit down on the swing before speaking again. "Yes. I'm cleaning cabins and occasionally mucking out stalls. Doing some baking. I go on shopping runs, help serve the guests at meals sometimes. Basically, I lend a hand wherever anyone needs it." She censored out most of the Giddyup-specific duties but offered up one relevant tidbit. "I'm even getting to do some textile work here. They have an old-fashioned ropewalk and handmake a lot of the rope they use around the place. Plus, they demonstrate that process for the visitors. So I've been able to help with that, and also show Ethan—one of the owners—different ways to dye the ropes. He sells handmade halters and bridles and stuff. And is a vet. A veterinarian, I mean, not the army kind. He's the large animal kind." *I'm not babbling;* you're *babbling.* She bit the inside of her cheek, shutting herself up. The less her dad knew about her sort-of employer with kinky benefits, the better.

Her dad lifted his eyebrows, displaying none of the disinterest or indulgence he usually did whenever she started talking about what she was studying or doing in her spare time. "That's some good, practical stuff. The rope and whatnot. The other work, too. It reminds me of . . . did I ever tell you this? I think I told Alexandra about it one time. The job I used to do in summertime, when I was in high school?"

Wary of a father who was suddenly into fond reminiscences, she shook her head.

"Well, you know where I grew up, the next town over was Newgulf. It was built for the oil and sulfur workers. And me and a few of those guys I've known since I was a kid—you've met 'em, you know: Bob Blanchard, Ken Scott, Oscar Tanning, those old guys—we would work for Newgulf in the summers, washing and painting the houses. We had this big water truck with a hose, sort of like a junior fire hose. They didn't really have the pressure washers then, like they do now. So we'd spray the house to get off most of the dirt and algae and any loose paint, then come in with brushes and scrub with some kinda . . . Oh, God only knows what that stuff was, probably the reason so many of us are ending up with cancer now. Then once the house was dry, we'd come back and put on the primer, then two coats of the fresh color. White or gray or blue, those were the choices. And the trim was all white. It always felt so good to finish one up because you'd really made a difference you could *see.*" He made a semicircle in the air with his hand, as if he were cleaning the window of his mind's eye. "And then you were *done.* I sometimes miss that. Feeling like I knew exactly how much I'd accomplished because the whole result was right there in front of me."

"And you can check it off the list."

"Mm-hmm." He sketched a check mark with one finger, then lowered his hand to the seat again and pushed the swing into gentle motion with both feet. "Welp. Your sister has been sending me a lot of links."

"Okay . . ."

"To manufacturers' organizations. She also bought me a subscription to *Textile World* magazine."

"Oh my God. Alex."

Her dad chuckled. "When she gets the ball, she runs with it. But I'll hand it to her, it's interesting reading. I just . . ." He looked down at his shirt for a second, plucking at the fabric and shaking his head. "I had no idea what you were actually doing. And I didn't know anything about that school of yours except how much it cost me. It's not just some art camp, it's the big dog, huh?"

She felt like she was in an alternate universe. Her dad paying this much attention to her, having an actual conversation with her? Complimenting her choice of college? "For design overall it's . . . second, I think? Second in the U.S., at least. MIT is the top, and I thought about accepting. But Rhode Island is closer to New York, and there were some teachers there I wanted to study with, so I went with RISD." Would things have turned out differently if she'd chosen MIT? Looking back, she realized that at least her father would've known she was at a *real* university.

At the moment, he was staring at her as if he'd never seen her before. "You . . . were accepted to MIT?"

"Yeah. But RISD was really my top choice all along."

He shook his head again and rubbed a hand over his face. "It was worth the money either way, I guess. But—" He held up his hands again, as if he already knew the argument because he'd heard it before; Victoria hadn't given her mother and Alex nearly enough credit. They'd obviously been schooling Tom Woodcock. "But it shouldn't have been about that. It should have been about respecting your choices, and you, the way I did for Alex. Even if I didn't understand you like I did her. She said not to bring that up, so I won't push, but I . . . I don't know. I still wish you'd finished."

Victoria closed her eyes against the wave of unaccustomed emotions threatening to swamp her. "I will someday."

"Dammit. None of that's why I was supposed to be here, Peanut."

"It's not?" She opened her eyes to find his trained back on the sandwich. He looked supremely uneasy. The *dammit* hadn't been directed at her, she gathered, but at himself.

"No. Alex said you'd talk about all that when you're ready. And I want to respect that. I'm doing my best. But she *did* tell us what happened to you at that place you were working. Before you drove back to Dallas. I came here because I needed to see with my own two eyes that you were all right, and to let you know that whatever you need to handle that—lawyers, therapy, anything—your mother and I want to help you with it. And I hope you'll take our help. I would pay any amount of money right now to put that little shit in jail for laying a hand on you. Or at least sue the bastard into the dirt." His jaw tightened, his lips growing pale from tension. *That* face, she knew. She'd just never seen him look that angry on her behalf before. At anyone else, or at himself. "If I'm the one who made you feel like you had to go and—" He cut himself off again with a shake of his head. "Whatever part I played in landing you there, I'm so sorry. You know I love you more than the world."

One thing was easy enough to address. She led with that. "It's okay, Daddy. I'm fine. Really. I was shaken up and I'm still angry, but I don't think I need therapy or anything to deal with it." The other parts . . . Well, she wasn't ready yet to talk to her dad about what he had or hadn't made her feel. And as for the legal stuff—*ugh*. It made her head ache and her eyes burn to even think about it. Alex had been sending her links, too. To employment laws, to various government sites, to law firms, to articles and what-to-do-if checklists. She had called a state agency, answered some questions, and filled out a form about the incident, but nothing much seemed to have happened since then. If anything *did* happen . . .

"I filed a complaint already," she told him. "After that I don't know what they'll do next. I doubt he'd go to jail in any case, even if I had gone straight to the police after it happened. And I don't want to sue him. He has a wife and kids. I just want . . . I just . . ." *Shit*. Her lip had started to wibble, and the inside of her nose was prickling. A tear slipped down her cheek and then the dam burst. She managed to choke out, "I just w-want it to *not have happened*," before she put her face in her hands and let the tears come.

Fucking hell. Not the way she'd pictured the big, triumphant showdown with Dad.

"Aw, Peanut. If I could buy a time machine and do that for you, I sure would."

A moment later a familiar smell, a familiar touch, an awkward pat—and then a hug. Her father enveloped her with comfort and she soaked it up, crying out the fears and frustrations of the past few months into his neatly pressed golf shirt.

When Ethan walked up the trail from the parking lot to the main house, his mind was firmly on his house. Not on the contract in his hand, not on finding a lawyer to look it over—*hey, Vic's sister might be able to*—but only on finishing the wiring so he could finally put up the interior walls and get the place finished. Although first he wanted to find out who owned the Jaguar in the parking lot. Or maybe before any of that, he'd get in a ride; Sackett had been pastured all weekend and was probably rambunctious. An hour or two on the high trail would settle him right down.

Ethan's focus was for shit. And what little of it he had flew clear out of his mind when he came off the trailhead and spotted a familiar head of honey-kissed locks, leaning on the shoulder of some tall, white-haired old dude. Victoria, sitting on the porch swing with . . .

It couldn't be.

But who else could it be? What other old guy would have his arm around Victoria's shoulders as they sat on the gently moving swing, enjoying the breeze while she shirked her job?

At least this cleared up the mystery of the Jaguar.

Ethan was still a few yards from the porch steps when Victoria turned and spotted him. Gave him a big, watery smile while wiping what looked like the last of a bunch of tears from her eyes. So . . . maybe not enjoying the breeze all *that* much. Guilt nudged at him for judging her too quickly.

"Hey, Ethan." She used the swing's momentum to lift her and stood up, brushing her face one more time. "Daddy, this is Ethan Hill. He's one of the owners—the vet I told you about? Ethan, this is my dad. Thomas Woodcock."

"Tom," her dad immediately offered, putting on a businessman's professional smile as he rose beside Victoria and offered his hand.

Ethan nodded back. "Howdy." He shook Tom's hand automatically, hoping the guy didn't notice his still vaguely pink fingertips and nails and quashing his desire to glare at the man whose unkind words had sent Victoria into a life-altering downward spiral. Victoria seemed to have made up with him; she put a hand on her dad's arm as they shook, smiling at him.

Then, if there was any lingering doubt, Victoria made it clear that they'd buried the hatchet. She patted her father's arm, looking downright wistful. "Are you sure you won't stay for dinner? You could spend the night if you need to. It's such a long time to spend in the car for one day."

Her dad raised his eyebrows at her, clearly amused. And then tapped her nose with his finger. "Says the young lady who drove from Rhode Island to Dallas in three days."

Victoria grinned. "You got me there."

"I appreciate the offer, Peanut, but I have to be back at the office tomorrow."

"Okay, I guess." She grabbed up a grocery bag from the swing, handing it to her father. "I can get the coffee cup back this weekend. Oh, and it's the kind that keeps the coffee *really* hot, so be careful when you first open the drinking part."

Tom turned toward Ethan, shrugging. "Sounds just like her mother." Then, back to Victoria: "We should check your bank app thing—"

"PayPal, Daddy."

"—PayPal, one more time before I go. I want to make sure the money made it there okay. I never quite believe we can do all this from our phones. Back in my day this would've been a job for Western Union or traveler's checks, something like that."

She rolled her eyes—but in a joking way—and pulled out her cell phone. A few taps confirmed that yes, the deposit had made it into her account.

Ethan tried to join in the smiles-all-around mood, but his cheeks were already starting to ache from the effort. She was walking back her stance on refusing her parents' money? *What the actual fuck, Peanut?* He felt like he'd wandered into an alternate universe. He felt like he was intruding. He felt like he didn't know what to feel.

So he made an excuse to escape. "I need to head to the pasture and get Sackett down. It was nice to meet you, sir." *Lies, all lies, and why the hell did I call him sir?*

"You too, Son." Tom gave him a congenial nod.

Victoria smiled at Ethan but seemed distracted, more concerned about seeing her dad off. "I'll see you later, Ethan."

He made a noncommittal noise, tipped his hat, and spun on his heel, forcing himself to walk calmly toward the barn instead of stomping or kicking things the way he wanted to. He was angry and he wasn't even sure *why*. It was a good thing, right, that she was making peace with her parents? Maybe her dad wasn't a piece of shit after all. Maybe he'd apologized. Taking money to finish her degree was the sensible thing to do. Who *wouldn't* be better off without a paid-for college degree? She could angle for even *better* jobs after she had one. And she could probably still find a sweet internship or maybe even a job in the meantime. In Dallas, from the sound of it, if she was planning to go back there by the weekend. Or maybe back on the East Coast, if her parents were going to subsidize her housing again.

His gut ached. When he passed the threshold of the door to the horse barn, he paused on his way through to the pasture gate and slumped down on a bench, dropping his elbows to his knees and his forehead to his hands. He'd folded up Doc's contract and stuck it in his back pocket, and it poked his ass cheek uncomfortably as he leaned forward.

What's more, Victoria had introduced Ethan as "one of the owners." Yep, that was him. Just another one of her employers. Which made sense, because the last thing she probably needed was to explain their relationship to her dad. Especially since they didn't really *have* a relationship, and it was just a short-term thing, and they both knew that going in. *Nothing special to see here, folks, move along.* But still . . .

"*Fuck.*" What the hell was wrong with him?

One thing was for sure, he wasn't going to go on any calming horseback rides at the moment. One whiff of his mood right now and Sackett would be all over the place, taking advantage, and a miserable time would be had by all. Ethan gave his head a final press for good measure, trying to keep all the disorganized thoughts and feelings contained, then slapped his thighs and stood up to head in the direction of his house.

The walk up the hillside did him some good, gave his head time to clear a little. But the moment he opened his door and stepped inside the tiny house, and was greeted by the sight of rumpled blankets and the smell of sex and Victoria, he groaned at his own stupidity. This was probably the *worst* place to work his way through his feelings.

The thick wad of paper was still digging into his muscle, so he pulled it out of his pocket and rolled the contract the other way to smooth the pages out.

Rolling with the flow . . . sure, Victoria had done that. But Ethan had been kidding himself if he thought she'd done it with no safety net. Daddy had *always* been there with the money if she really needed it, hadn't he? For all Ethan knew, she'd had this outcome in mind all along—manipulating her parents, specifically her dad, into a display of affection and support. That didn't seem like her, but neither did her acceptance of money from her dad, or her hugging the guy and warning him not to burn his mouth on the hot coffee.

Ethan was certainly infatuated, but how well did he even know this woman? Or rather, this girl, practically speaking, in terms of where she was in her life. Barely an adult, only out of college because she'd dropped out that semester. So really, what did he know?

He didn't know enough to look at her as a role model, that was for damn sure. But he'd been very close to doing just that—to telling himself he was following her great example by turning down the contract and accepting whatever fate threw at him next.

Ethan didn't believe in fate. And Victoria had abandoned her principled stance, apparently, as soon as Daddy had shown up with an apology and an open checkbook.

He looked down at the contract, the packet of pages that represented what he'd been working almost his whole life to achieve. And he was planning to throw all that work away to make rope and go to kink conventions? To be second banana at a dude ranch that probably wouldn't even be a going business concern if it weren't for the secret BDSM sideline? Jesus Christ, what had he been thinking?

Cold feet. That's what it had been. He'd had cold feet, like a bridegroom the night before the wedding. He was making a huge decision, and it was scary to make that kind of commitment. Perfectly understandable. But that same guy usually still went through with the ceremony and often ended up happily married for life, right?

In Ethan's toolbox, in the top tray under some loose nuts and a hex wrench, he found a pen. Not giving himself time to reconsider, he attacked the document with it, holding the pages against an exposed stud, stabbing his initials into the stamped boxes at the foot of each page, scraping his signature on the lines where indicated. When he was through, the paper looked slightly beaten up, but it was all done and signed. The cover page had fallen off somewhere, but he figured it didn't really matter. It was just about the only page he hadn't needed to write on.

He'd need to get an envelope and stamps from the main house if he wanted to mail the contract. It seemed like less trouble—and more of a declaration—to deliver it back to Doc in person. He could do it right now, in fact. And if he walked to his truck the long way around, he wouldn't have to risk running into Victoria and her dad again on the way. He folded the packet, stuffed it into his pocket again, and headed back down the hill, aiming straight for the parking lot.

Ethan knew who he was and what he wanted. He'd never relied much on anyone for help. He'd set his course and stuck to it and succeeded. So he'd let a beautiful rope bunny distract him near the end, let doubt creep in for a brief time—all that was nothing, a mere hiccup, not some new truth or grand personal insight he had to adapt to if he wanted to be happy.

He had signed the contract. He would deliver it to Doc. He would start living the life he'd always dreamed of. And some Giddyup weekend he'd find the kinkster of his dreams, too. It would all work out, just as he'd always planned.

Everything was going to be *great*.

Chapter 17

Victoria could have sworn she'd seen Ethan heading up the hill toward his house as she started off the porch to walk her dad to his car. She'd been no more than ten minutes in saying good-bye, then following Ethan up the trail, so she was surprised when she didn't meet him on his way back down or find him at the house.

The door was unlocked, as usual, and she went inside without thinking twice about it. Then she wondered why she felt so confident she had the right. Possibly because it wasn't quite a house yet. The pipes and wiring were mostly done, all the interior framing was complete except for the stuff where the cabinetry would go, and if Ethan had wanted to, he could have already started sleeping up in his loft . . . but the space was a skeleton still, and felt more like a workshop than a home.

It also felt strangely empty with neither Ethan nor Roxie there. Roxie was spending the day in the big dog run behind the main house, and Victoria was surprised to find she missed the click of the Border collie's claws, the low sweep of her wagging tail. The dog liked to circle, then settle with an audible sigh, between Victoria and Ethan on the tumble of blankets . . . once they'd stopped moving around and making noises, at least. That contented sigh seemed such a constant already, and Victoria wasn't sure why, any more than she knew why she kept turning toward Ethan like a flower to the sun.

She wished she could ask him to come with her to Dallas the following weekend. Her dad had given her more than enough for a first-class ticket—*You might need a little running money*—so she could easily afford two coach seats. But it might be a tense, awkward few days, the wrong sort of time to bring a new element into an already volatile mix. And he'd seemed upset earlier, when she'd introduced him to her father; his tight posture and closed-off face had reminded her of the way he'd acted the day she'd arrived at Hilltop. What was that all about? She definitely didn't want to find out in the middle of a fraught weekend when she was trying to clear the air with her parents.

Perhaps a better way to use the money would be to buy a coach ticket for herself, then get some sort of thank-you gift for Alexandra, who might have been unduly biased against Giddyup but had apparently also been Victoria's biggest defender. Bringing all her negotiation tactics and litigation skills to bear, she had completely turned around their father's perspective on his younger daughter's capabilities, prospects, and life choices in general. Which was especially remarkable given Alexandra's own doubts about all those things.

Maybe a *small* gift. And save the rest against future legal fees if Victoria decided to go that route. She might, if for no other reason than to make creepy Larry think twice before trying anything with future employees. But she wasn't ready to decide right away.

She had more immediate concerns, asking for time off and securing a ride to the airport Friday being only two of them. Her dad had offered a lot of things besides airfare for a visit home, and they were all tempting as hell. He'd pointed out that letting him and her mother each give her gifts worth up to the estate tax exclusion amount each year would benefit her now and the whole family down the line. So . . . maybe not a BMW, but a less luxurious, reliable used car. Some interview clothes and a work wardrobe to get her started if she ended up getting hired somewhere she couldn't dress like a wild child.

Given that her current outfit consisted of a borrowed plaid shirt, grubby jeans, and some knee-high green rubber boots from Walmart, she had to wonder what exactly her dad thought was *wild* about it. But she'd just smiled and nodded and said she'd think about his offer and let them know that weekend.

Lucky. Lucky, lucky girl. She was rolling in so much privilege, she had enough left over to decline those gifts if she chose to, without even experiencing too much discomfort. If her worst-case scenario was staying at Hilltop, she was still doing pretty damn well. She'd have a roof over her head, three squares a day, enough money to cover her expenses, and all the use she could desire of the crappy borrowed truck. But that scenario was looking less and less likely to be long-term. Pascaline—who apparently had stopped sleeping alto-gether—had already written her a short email to say she had heard of another designer with a possible Paris opening. Details to come as soon as she'd investigated. And another small company based in New York had asked to set up a phone interview. It was a contract position but might lead to something full-time.

Hell, maybe she could even turn Ethan's rope project into an ac-tual job. Expand the product line, start Web sites to advertise to the two very different client bases involved . . . she knew people who'd turned less-promising ideas into paying concerns. It seemed there was a market for just about anything if you could connect with the right buyers. Of course she'd have to talk Alex out of her puritanical objections to Giddyup, but she was more optimistic about that possi-bility now that she felt less panicked about meeting Alex's deadline.

Victoria would have liked to share all her news with Ethan, and maybe even get his thoughts on whether she should take the car and other stuff her parents were offering. She also would have liked to find out what had happened at his meeting with Doc. But she needed to get back to work, so she couldn't wait indefinitely for him.

As she reached for the door handle, wondering whether she should text him to see if he was anywhere close by, a flash of white behind the temporary loft ladder caught her eye—a piece of loose paper. One of Ethan's house-plan sketches or some construction notes? It should probably be in the toolbox, secured with the others. She picked it up, glanced at it automatically while she took the few steps to the tool-box, and then stopped in her tracks when her mind finally put mean-ing to what her eyes were seeing.

Some law firm's letterhead. Then, in bolded caps, right in the mid-dle of the page:

CREEKSIDE LARGE ANIMAL PRACTICE
OWNERSHIP AGREEMENT BETWEEN
LIONEL B. TAYLOR, DVM
AND
ETHAN M. HILL, DVM

The top left corner of the page was slightly torn, obviously ripped off a staple. But impressed on the page—as if it had been folded back under another sheet that had been signed with a heavy hand—was a scrawling design that looked an awful lot like a not-quite-legible signature.

Victoria glanced around the house, looking for whatever the page had been stapled to. There were no other loose papers. Even a quick, guilty peek inside the toolbox yielded nothing but the actual construction documents. She remembered that when Ethan had walked away from the main house, he'd had what she'd thought was a rolled-up magazine stuck in his back pocket. Could it have been the contract this page had been torn from?

Ethan had gone to breakfast with Doc to *maybe* talk about joining the practice. He'd come home acting weird, made a quick exit with a lie about going to the pasture for Sackett, gone to his house instead, and then . . . disappeared. With a contract he might or might not have already signed to buy Creekside from Doc Taylor.

So. Strike one possible career path off the list. Even if it hadn't been a serious offer from him in the first place, apparently making and selling rope with Ethan was no longer among her options.

She folded the paper absentmindedly, stuffing it into her pocket. It had been a taxing day already, but in about an hour she needed to somehow transform herself into the fresh, stylish, confident designer she'd been when she interned at Max & Magda so she could wow her prospective employers. Or, since it was Skype, at least wow them from the waist up.

Ethan wasn't sure what to make of Doc's reaction to the contract. He'd looked startled to begin with, and then sort of concerned. Not quite the warm welcome Ethan had anticipated. After barely glancing at the contract, Doc had put it to one side on his desk and handed Ethan a fresh copy from the shelf next to his desk.

"For your records," he said. "Or if you change your mind about taking it to a lawyer to look over before you tell me it's ready to sign. You really should, you know. Big investment, big commitment. I can hold off as long as you need. I think the agreement's fair, but it's nothing to enter into lightly."

"Just like marriage?" Ethan was being flippant, but he knew practice partners who'd stayed together longer than they'd stayed with their spouses. It could be that long term a commitment—if the partner in question weren't planning to phase into retirement.

Doc drummed his fingers on the ratty-looking stack of signed papers Ethan had handed him, then slid it back toward him. "Keep it. Burn it. Take the clean copy and don't come back with it for a week." He looked almost irked, and possibly even disappointed, and Ethan's heart leaped into his throat at the sudden notion that he might have just fucked everything up. By acting too hastily, by making Doc think he didn't take this seriously, when it was the only thing in his life he did take seriously.

So, so seriously.

He gathered up the papers and nodded solemnly, trying to project calm, businesslike confidence. "All right. My mind's made up, but I'll have someone look it over and get it back to you next Monday."

"I'll take it then. In the meantime, what do you say you come on some jobs with me for an hour or two?" Doc pushed himself out of his desk chair with an old-man noise, then grabbed his hat from the hook by the door. "I need to vet a pony over by Pizzitola's then head to Bewliss's to check up on a mare Janie thinks is lame."

"Thinks?" Jane Bewliss had practically grown up at the family stable she now ran. If anybody would recognize a lame horse, it would be her.

Doc shook his head. "I wanted to see the horse first, but it sounds like it could be stringhalt."

"Aw, damn. Uh . . . sure, I'll ride along." He'd only seen one case of stringhalt—in an elderly gelding in London who'd been donated to the veterinary clinic for research. In that horse's case, no cause had ever been found for the strange neurological disorder, and it had been so severe they'd eventually had to put the animal down. Ethan hoped Jane wasn't looking at the same outcome for her mare.

As for the ride-along, Ethan couldn't think of a good reason to decline. He and Doc would be partners soon, after all, right? Once they were on the road, however, the mood wasn't as easy as it had been in Ethan's high school days, when he'd accompanied Doc on many a trip to act as occasional semiskilled assistant and frequent muscle.

Doc clearly had things on his mind this afternoon. So did Ethan. It didn't make for scintillating conversation—or much conversation at all.

Ethan's mind was filled, for some reason, with images of his house. He wanted to have it completed already. If Doc wanted him to wait on signing the contract, maybe that should be his focus in the interim. Who knew, maybe if he really pushed he could get it all done before the worst heat of the summer. Then he could hitch it to his truck, haul it away in the night, set it up in some field in . . . wherever. Rural Montana or somewhere in the Pacific Northwest.

He reminded himself he was over the idea of becoming a kinky vagabond, making and selling rope all over the country at whatever conventions he could line up. It probably wouldn't have been all that much fun anyway, most likely. Not as a solitary kinky traveling man. Roxie was a great companion, but his vision of the future had changed recently, and now there was a space for an actual . . . *partner.*

Not necessarily Victoria, he insisted to himself, even though she kept floating into the scene. *It could be anyone. She was Miss Right Now, not Miss Right.* That space might be roughly Victoria-shaped. She might have been the one to make him aware of it. But he could find somebody else to fill it.

Somebody would eventually come to Bolero who lit him up the way Victoria did. Or he'd find her in San Antonio or they'd meet on a plane or . . . however those things happened.

And in the meantime, he could get started on his real life, his settled-down grown-up life. Which included things like helping Doc look over Scooter Pizzitola's Shetland-Welsh cross. Scooter's granddaughter had outgrown Patches and he was thinking of selling him, so they'd pulled blood for a Coggins test, checked overall fitness, looked at the pony's gait and manners. Doc knew the sturdy little critter from years of care, but he still paid close attention to the job, as if he were appraising an animal he was considering buying for his own child.

If Ethan was going through the motions, he excused that with the fact that he knew the motions so well; he'd screened so many horses for big stables and large-scale auctions that he could do it in his sleep. But he should have read the room better once Doc stepped back and let him do the talking, after Scooter asked what the verdict was. After a moment's surprise at Doc's deferring to him, Ethan started listing everything he'd observed about the pony, reading from the notes he'd taken.

He mentioned the possible conformation flaws: pasterns bordering on too long; a possible slight tendency to cow hock. He discussed potential corrective strategies, like Hill Therapy and some new stretches he'd been reading about, then ran down their relative merits and costs.

He'd gone on for some time before he realized Doc was staring at him and tugging on one ear.

When they made eye contact, Doc looked pointedly over at his truck, clearly trying to nod his head in that direction without Scooter noticing.

"Um." *Shit.* What had he done wrong? "I think Dr. Taylor can probably sum it up better than I can, though. I just remembered I need to make a quick call and check on something back at the ranch. If y'all will excuse me. Good to see you again, Scooter."

He got out to the truck as quickly as possible and actually pretended to make a call in case anyone walked by. Then he "hung up," feeling chagrined and ridiculous. A few minutes later Doc climbed into the cab with a bemused expression.

Ethan expected a chewing out, not the gentle headshake and eye roll his mentor gave him as they pulled out of the small farm—just a home with acreage really—onto the main road back to Bolero.

"What'd I do wrong?" God, had he missed something huge and obvious? A hock spavin? A walleye? "I've been distracted lately, I know, but I thought—"

"Ethan. You didn't do anything wrong." Doc steered with one hand draped over the wheel, occasionally raising his index finger and nodding to cars that passed.

"Then . . . what?"

"Welp. You told the guy everything he needed to know and then some. It's the *then some* you have to watch out for. Lemme ask you something. You ever been involved in a private horse sale around here, or an auction where they handle ponies or grade horses?"

Ethan had to think about it for a second. "Not since I was a kid. Plenty in California, though. I got a ton of practice there. And I went to a few really big auctions in the UK, mostly jumpers, some dressage horses—"

"Right, right. So here's the thing. What ol' Scooter there wants to know is, is his granddaughter's old ride gonna be safe for the next kid? Is it healthy, is it basically sound? Does it have any big red flags? Because he'd feel awful if he sold it and then something bad happened to his neighbor's son or his wife's friend's grandniece or what have you. And most likely that's all the buyer will be looking for here. Nice, safe, unremarkable pony for their kid to start on, maybe take to some novice events or hack around on."

Ethan nodded. He was getting a headache, the same familiar tension spreading into his brain from his shoulders that had so often plagued him in school when he took on a new subject and worried he wouldn't be able to handle it. "So, tone it down. Gotcha."

"Nah. That ain't it exactly." Doc sighed, drumming his fingers against the steering wheel. "This job, you know, it's not one long oral exam, or clinic rounds where they try to stump you. You don't get extra credit for a more detailed answer. It's about the people, not just the animals. And these folks here, they aren't your high-powered commercial-ranch types or researchers. Most of 'em don't have thousands of head of cattle or a big Thoroughbred breeding operation. They won't be impressed by . . . Not that it's your *job* to impress them—you're there to treat the animals—but you also have to consider your audience and the environment the critters are in. And out here . . . it ain't fancy. And it's usually not complicated. Even if the cases are sometimes, the people aren't."

"I grew up here," Ethan reminded him. "I know what it's like." He knew every tree and rock along the road they were driving like the back of his hand.

Glancing down, he sighed at the sight of his nails and cuticles. He'd worn work gloves at the client's place to hide the stains but taken them off in the truck because they were too warm. At the moment he hardly recognized the back of his hand because his fingers were still *so* pink. But Bolero never changed. There was no painting this town red.

Doc turned onto the main road that would take them through town; the Bewliss's stable was located only a few blocks from "downtown" Bolero. "I know you're from here. But you've been a lot of places since then. Seen a lot of things, done a lot of things most folks here never dream of. Lived in another country. Worked with the top vets in the world. You've impressed the hell outta me, kid, I won't lie to you. Your qualifications are . . ."

"Too much," Ethan suggested. "You think I've outgrown it." After he'd spent twenty years—most of his life—training to do this one job? The person whose approval probably mattered more to him than anyone's, even his family's, wasn't sure he was right for the position after all? He thought of something Trudy had said about Marguerite maybe getting along with one of their grumpier clients. God knows he hadn't been able to charm Rusty. And now, apparently, he was putting off simple hobbyists trying to sell their kid's ponies. "All this time working on animals and I should have been working on my folksy people skills, is that what you're saying? That's what I'd need to cut it here? Hell, why did you offer me the buyout at all, Doc?"

"Ethan Hill." Doc looked cut to the bone and baffled by Ethan's response. And Ethan knew there was something he still wasn't grasping. When Doc clarified, he wasn't sure whether he felt better or worse. "It's not that I don't think you can cut it. Chrissakes, Son, do you think I'm a fool? Look at all you've done. You think I'm worried you can't handle a lazy backwater operation like this, where the tough cases usually get referred off to places like your old practice in San Antonio, or over to A&M? You can learn to talk to people. You're not too big for your britches, you're not trying to prove anything to them, it just takes practice and getting a feel for it. Hell, I've seen you do just fine at it before. The problem is I worry you're *bigger* than this place now and you won't be happy with your choice. You're still single, your career should be on the rise, you can go anywhere in the world. Instead, you're looking to tie yourself down here, and I have to ask myself why you wanna sell yourself short like that? Why're you aiming so low?"

Low? "Low?" But as much as Ethan wanted to yell *How dare you?* for the slur on his hometown . . . he knew what Doc meant. Tiny town. Tiny practice. A few medium-sized cattle operations, some small vanity and specialty herds, quite a few hobby-level horse breeders, and a handful of dude ranches running a few dozen head of cattle to lend the place some authenticity. Other than that, mostly individual owners and FFA kids. Doc worked hard because he wore a lot of hats, and his practice was vital to the area . . . but it wasn't a starting place. It was a place to end up. A damn good one, but unless Ethan was ready to spend the rest of his working days in Bolero, maybe it wasn't the spot he needed to be in right now. Assuming, of course, that he planned to spend the rest of his working days as a vet.

It was what he'd always wanted. Still did want. The question remained: Was he ready to get what he'd always wanted? Or did he need to be thinking bigger? Was that really the cause of all his doubt in the first place, not some wild hair about traipsing around the country as a bondage rope peddler?

Doc hadn't responded. He was back to tapping the steering wheel with his fingers, waggling thumb and forefinger back and forth in a steady beat. His hands had always been weathered, but now Ethan saw the age spots, the look of arthritis about the knuckles. Doc wasn't close to done yet. He'd said so—that he wasn't ready to retire, that he wanted the slow buyout partly because he didn't want to give up the work he loved. But in another five years? Ten maybe? Ethan realized he didn't actually know how old the man was. He was kind of like Lamar—he'd *always* looked like an old guy, partly because his hide was so tanned it seemed to have done all its aging already. These old cowboys, it sometimes seemed like you'd open up their coffin fifty years down the line and find their corpses looking exactly the same, preserved by the sun like pieces of jerky.

Ethan picked at a magenta hangnail. "You haven't signed the paperwork yet."

Doc waved at somebody on the sidewalk in front of the general store as they cruised past. "Yup. We could tear it up. Revisit the whole thing another time. Or not." After a few minutes of silence, he changed the subject. "Say, what've you been doing with all that leisure time since you left Malik's practice? I could use some pointers, maybe, for when I retire."

Suspension bondage and making more rope to do more suspension bondage didn't seem like the best answer, so Ethan gave him a qualified version of the truth. "Working on my house. Doing some projects. Finishing the rope for a custom halter Marguerite wanted. Helping out at Hilltop."

"Mm-hmm." Doc flicked the turn signal and one-handed the turn onto the long driveway of the Bewliss stables. "Y'all had one o' them private parties up there this weekend, right?"

"Yup."

"Fancy."

"It's an interesting group of folks."

Doc shot him a skeptical look, then shrugged and pulled into the long driveway at the practice, parking in his usual spot: in front of the big sign that said "Reserved for Mayor Bewliss."

He'd arm-wrestled the mayor for that privilege some thirty years or more earlier. Nobody needed to be told; everybody knew Doc got to park there. Ethan wondered if he should offer to arm-wrestle his cousin Chet for his reserved spot at the new county justice center. But he wouldn't have much occasion to visit the station; the only police dog was Chet's Bloodhound, Bevo, and Bevo was pushing twelve, so it probably wouldn't be worth it in the long run. There were more useful people for the vet to challenge to feats of strength for preferred parking.

"You ever seen springhalt before?" Doc asked as they climbed from the truck.

Ethan opened his mouth to launch into a description of the gelding at the Royal Veterinary College. Then he stopped by the flower beds that flanked the front door to the office building, adjusted his hat brim, and nodded slowly. "Yep."

Doc flicked the brim of his own hat lightly. "You're learning, Grasshopper. Now c'mon. Let's see what's up with this mare."

Chapter 18

When Victoria headed to the main house for dinner, she saw Ethan sitting on the porch steps, holding a stack of paper that looked at least twice as big as the one he'd had in his pocket earlier.

His copies, she supposed, of the contract.

He watched her approach without waving, a somewhat wary, stony expression on his usually active face. She got to the step and sat down beside him, then flapped her interview shirt out from her skin to create a breeze. It wasn't all that hot yet, but it was already getting humid.

Ethan remained silent and Victoria broke first. "So, I had the interview."

He bit his lip, looking guilty for a second. "I forgot. Sorry. How'd it go?"

"They offered me a job." It still didn't seem real to her. The interview had apparently been a formality. The creative team at Max & Magda had not only remembered her, they'd seen her work for Balenciaga and had already been planning to feel her out about working with them when her résumé hit the in-box. They had been *thrilled* to move their timetable up instead of waiting for her to finish her degree.

"Oh. Wow. Congratulations, that's amazing."

"Thanks." Remembering she was still in her same jeans, she stretched out one leg enough to dig in her front pocket for the folded, and now slightly wrinkled, contract cover page. She handed it to him and he unfolded it, puzzled. "I gather I should also be congratulating you."

Ethan finally got the page open enough to see what it was. He folded it back up, shaking his head. "I haven't signed anything yet."

She couldn't help turning to look at him, aghast at the blatant lie. "Well, it had an imprint of *somebody's* signature on it. E squiggle H squiggle. That doesn't seem like Doc's John Hancock. Or his E Hancock. Or . . . Oh, you know what I mean."

"Yeah, no." Ethan shook his head again and waved a hand as if he was physically clearing the air. "I signed it, but he wouldn't take it. He gave it back, gave me a fresh one, and then basically told me to go away for a week and . . . think about what I'd done. Then we went to see some folks about some horses, and first I was an asshole, but then I was a hero. Best day ever."

She didn't know where to start with a response, so she shrugged, hands up. Ethan looked slightly abashed, but he elaborated on at least part of his story. "There's this gait disorder in horses called springhalt. It's actually a neurological condition. Every time they try to take a step, instead of just going forward, their back leg spasms up toward their belly." He demonstrated the motion with his arms; even though the joints were different, Victoria could get the gist. "If it gets severe enough, the horse can't really walk and may have to be put down. Sometimes the cause is never discovered, but there are a few plants that are known to cause it, especially if the horse is eating them over a long period of time. One of them is sweet peas. But since we don't exactly have pastures full of sweet peas around here, it's not something people tend to look out for."

"Did they have a planter box of them or something?" Victoria might not have been very happy with Ethan, but it was still a good mystery, and she wanted to know how it turned out.

"*No.* That was my first thought, too. I'd seen some pink flowers out front and I thought for sure that was it. But those weren't sweet peas. They were just impatiens and begonias."

She made a sad-horn noise: *"Wah-waaah."*

Ethan held up one finger. "But. I had a hunch. So while Doc was talking to Jane, I did a quick perimeter of the small pasture where this mare was. She's Jane's riding horse, and right now she's usually the only one in that enclosure because the boarded horses go into the big pasture when they're out. And she gets cranky and nips them sometimes. Anyway. This thing is about a hundred yards around, and at the far end of it there's an old gate from when the Bewlisses used to own the next few acres over, too, and an old feed trough that's kind of overgrown and rotting. And right next to *that*, and also climbing all over the old trough, in what I can only assume was the perfect microclimate, what do you think I found?"

"Sweet peas?"

"Sweet peas," he confirmed. "Once I came back and told them, Jane was horrified. But it was good, because all they have to do is get rid of the sweet peas and the mare should be okay. She'd already eaten all the ones she could reach, and it's getting too warm for them to have grown much more anyway. So the prognosis is good."

"Wow." She was genuinely impressed. "Veterinarian supersleuth."

"It felt like that." He leaned back against the top step, resting on his elbows and stretching out both legs, crossing them at the ankles. "So when do you leave for New York City?"

Victoria studied his posture for a moment, then imitated it deliberately. It wasn't all that comfortable for her, but fuck it, sometimes you had to suffer to be a smart-ass. "I haven't accepted the job offer yet. I told them I'd let them know tomorrow."

It was Ethan's turn to sit up and pay attention despite himself. The look on his face was almost comical. Then he tempered it, as she watched, bringing things back to a near frown. "You going home instead or back to school?"

What? "Uh . . . neither. What makes you think . . . ?"

"The money. From your dad? He PayPaled you, remember? It seems like something you'd remember."

The cynical twist of his lips made her want to slap him. Just straight-up slap that look off his annoying, goofy, inexplicably handsome face. "He gave me money for a plane ride home this weekend. My parents have been very worried about me. And I have to talk to them at some point. Daddy called home and talked to Mom, and apparently she knows a family therapist up by them who's willing to meet with us on Saturday so we'll have a safe space or neutral ground or something to clear the air. I thought that was a really good idea. My dad offered to pay for a plane ticket so I wouldn't have to borrow a car, and I accepted because I couldn't afford the ticket myself and I really didn't think the farm truck would make it. I didn't feel that compromised my values."

"No, but—" Ethan blinked. "Oh. Shit. I thought—"

"Wait. You thought I just . . . gave up? He comes here one time, we have one decent talk, and suddenly I'm fine with the things he said before and everything goes back to the way it was?" She sat up, unable to glare sufficiently at Ethan from a semiprone position. "Have you ever *met* me? Were you paying attention at all?"

Ethan flinched, looking baffled. "But I saw you swinging on the porch swing with him. He was *cuddling* you like you were Daddy's little girl. Then he's putting money in your account. What was I supposed to think?"

Slap him or kick him right in the nuts. Either would feel great right about then. "Yeah, he was hugging me because I'd burst into tears when he asked about what happened in the coffee shop with Larry. And he offered me all the money and lawyers and mental health care I needed, if I was willing to take it. So yeah, I cried, and he hugged me because he can be kind of an asshole but he's still my dad. We sat on the swing and he told me it would be okay, and that if I'd rather, he could just fly to Rhode Island himself and punch Larry's lights out."

"I hope you didn't accept."

"I did not."

"About the punching, I mean. You should probably accept the lawyers and—"

"I know what you meant," she assured him. She started to rub her hands across her face, then remembered she'd put on mascara and eyeliner for the interview. "Okay. If I agree it was reasonable for you to assume what you did about the money, would you agree it was reasonable for me to assume what I did about your signed contract with Doc Taylor?"

Ethan pursed his lips for a few seconds, then nodded and stuck out his right hand. Victoria shook it, trying to ignore the instant urge to stroke, to pull him closer, to turn it into an embrace.

"Well," Ethan said after a second as they reluctantly ended the handshake, "we've been in kind of a fantasy bubble here, you know? It's been *amazing*. But if we were both so willing to believe the worst of the other over stuff that a few questions or a five-minute conversation could easily clear up . . . then maybe we don't really know each other as well as it felt like we did."

Victoria's heart sank. He wasn't wrong. But she would've rather stayed in the fantasy bubble. "I just wish we'd had more time."

"Me too." He plucked at her sleeve, rubbing the silk back and forth between his fingers. "I would have liked to find out if we had anything. Because I won't lie, Victoria, I think we could have had something. Outside of kink."

She leaned forward, resting her forehead against his and letting her fingertips play along the fabric beside his pink-tinted ones. "We already know we have show tunes."

"True. And a mutual interest in fibers." He gripped a handful of silk, then released it and slid his fingers between hers. "We both have a lot we coulda taught the other person about rope, I tell you what."

God. So Texas-y. But so accurate.

"If you don't join Doc's practice, what'll you do instead?" She suddenly realized he didn't have a job lined up like she did. He was back to being a free agent. Maybe he could become the traveling rope peddler after all. He could look her up if he was ever on the East Coast; she'd be the one envying his square footage as she tried to live out of the coat closet she *might* be able to afford on the modest salary she'd be making. Part of the reason she hadn't jumped at the offer, honestly. She loved Manhattan but *damn* was it ever expensive to live there.

Ethan sat up straight, pulling away a little, looking like he'd suddenly thought of something. *"Time."* She must have looked confused because he laughed and repeated himself. "Time, Victoria. You needed more time. We both did. But that's the one thing we *can* get."

Two days later Victoria was reaching down for a spirit level when she heard Ethan's phone buzz in his back pocket. She ignored it and took the level from him so she could confirm she'd hung the cabinet straight. It was right on the money.

"Aw yeah." First time, too. She was a natural at this construction stuff. And after only a few rocky moments yesterday Ethan had stopped looking panicked every time she climbed the ladder or picked up a tool.

"You got it? Good job!" He reached up for an awkward high five

She slapped his palm, then scooted down the ladder. "Did you just get a text?"

Ethan put his hand to his pocket automatically but didn't pull his phone out. "Uh, yeah."

He looked uncertain, a little worried ... *young*, all of a sudden, like he must've looked as a teenager.

Victoria put the level down on the newly installed kitchen counter, then put her hands against his chest, palms flat, feeling the heat of the skin beneath cotton and the steady beat of his heart. "Hey, you know what?"

"What?" He slid his free hand over one of hers—the other one stayed near his phone.

"This construction thing is really fun. I was worried we might fight or something."

Ethan chuckled and brought his other hand up, weaving his fingers with hers. "It *has* been good, hasn't it? You're much better with a hammer than a toilet brush."

"That just means if we ever live together, you should probably do all the cleaning and I'll take care of all the home maintenance." *Whoops*; probably too serious, too soon. Smirking, she tugged one of his hands toward her lips, kissing his knuckles gallantly. "You could get one of those ruffled aprons. How would you feel about stiletto heels, like a 1950s housewife vibe?"

He shrugged, then shook his head. "Nah. I got bunions. I could do those fluffy slipper things, with the . . . ?"

"Maribou feathers?"

"Is that what those are called?"

"Mm-hmm. Are you going to see who was texting you? Or calling, whatever?"

With a sigh, Ethan freed his hands and pulled his phone out to check it. "Well. It's not Doc." He swiped his screen, apparently reading something that seemed longer than a text.

Resisting the urge to peek at the screen, Victoria stepped back toward the ladder and perched uncomfortably on one of the rungs, looking around at the rapidly changing interior of the tiny house. With the walls mostly in place, the larger loft finished, and the kitchen cabinets installed, the space should have seemed smaller; instead it felt cozy but also roomier. All the windows kept it open and airy, giving it a treehouse quality.

She could imagine living in a space like this. All too easily. Ethan's idea of working on it together this week, as a way to spend quality time and get to know each other better outside the fantasy bubble, had been a good one . . . except that Victoria was only becoming more and more sure she would miss him too much to bear when she left for Manhattan in a few weeks.

That was the current plan, at least. Summer in Manhattan getting to know the team at the new company and then—if all went well, if she was accepted back at RISD and could get the classes she needed—back to Providence for the fall semester.

She had taken the job with Max & Magda, and they'd been so happy to have her that they'd quickly agreed to let her telecommute once she was familiar with the job. As long as she came in for an occasional meeting—once or maybe twice a month—she could do the rest of her work from anywhere with an internet connection, as long as she could procure the workspace and equipment she'd need.

She'd spent almost an hour on Monday working out possibilities, talking them through with Ethan's help, researching every angle. There was an Amtrak from Providence to Penn Station and it was only about sixty bucks each way. If she telecommuted, she could set her own daily work schedule. That meant she could pick up a course at RISD in the fall and possibly even do an independent study to get credit for things she was working on with Max & Magda. She'd already gotten approval for her senior project the previous year, so she should be able to pick up where she'd left off on that. If she used Wintersession to start on it, she could finish it up in the spring term without having to scramble too hard.

That evening, after her dad got home, he and her mom had called her. Firming up weekend plans, ostensibly, but really just to talk, she thought. Among other things, they'd offered her an interest-free loan for the rest of her tuition if she wouldn't take the money outright. She was still thinking about it; it would definitely be smarter than financial aid. But she didn't want to commit to anything until after they'd talked in person . . . and her father actually understood what he'd been apologizing for. Whatever she chose, she wanted there to be full transparency on both sides going forward.

Her eye fell on one of the spots in the loft frame that Ethan had marked for a ringbolt. *Well, maybe not* full *transparency*. But at least financial and philosophical honesty.

Ethan had looked askance at the loan idea but then admitted that he wasn't sure how he felt because *Victoria* clearly wasn't sure how *she* felt. "If you're saving on rent by not staying in Manhattan and you manage to keep your other expenses low, maybe you could afford the tuition by yourself."

She'd happened to be looking at the relevant page on RISD's

Web site, so she'd turned her laptop to let him read the tuition figures on the screen. He'd widened his eyes and blinked, and Victoria had snorted. "That's without books and supplies."

"Ah. So no, then, you'd definitely need help."

"Probably. But I'll take things one step at a time."

Time. He'd been right about that. Victoria didn't have to decide anything immediately. And neither did Ethan; he'd taken his own advice and finally admitted he also needed some time to work things out before he committed to taking over Doc's practice.

"Doc didn't really want to retire yet anyway," he'd explained on Monday night as they watched the sunset from the front porch of the main house. "And if he ends up changing his mind and selling to somebody else, it's not like I'm out of options. We're talking about a year off. I never had a . . . what do they call it? When you do a year before you start the next school thing?"

"A gap year?" Victoria had nestled closer to Ethan for warmth. They'd spent most of the day on the porch; soon it would be too warm for that, and she couldn't quite believe that by then she would be in New York again. It was easier to pretend she could stay at Hilltop forever, watching sunsets from the comforting confinement of Ethan's arms.

"Yeah, a gap year. Not to work, and not to go backpacking around Europe, whatever. Driving around to kink cons, selling rope, setting up the house in different places . . . that can be my gap year." True, it might set him back when and if he tried to get back into practice; but hell, he could figure that out when he got there. "My world is opening up *right now*. For once I'm going to embrace that and stop worrying so much about what might happen down the line."

Embracing his new world had included embracing Victoria at that moment, so she'd supported him wholeheartedly. She still did, even though they'd be apart sooner than she wanted to think about. Who knew where they'd be in a year or so? Maybe his nationwide rope tour would bring him to the East Coast. Maybe after she finished her degree she'd move back to Texas for some career opportunity. Stranger things had happened. And she hadn't known him long enough to feel like she was sacrificing one need for another . . . right?

Ethan had been texting rapidly, apparently in an active back and forth with his correspondent. When he finally put the phone back in his pocket, he wasn't frowning anymore, but he wasn't smiling either. Not sure what to make of his expression and not wanting to pry into the details of whatever he'd been texting about, Victoria dove into the conversational breach with a new topic.

"So you know my dad called again this afternoon?"

"Oh, yeah? His new hobby. I'm glad you're talking to him, though. You seem happier."

"I am happier." Not least because of a certain irresistible rope nerd. "I'm not sure what to do, though. My parents have this thing with estate taxes. They want to give me a car. Not the BMW. A cheap car, under fourteen thousand dollars. So, should I take it? Once I get to Rhode Island, not when I'm in Manhattan."

He lifted his eyebrows. "A free car? Hell yeah, you should take it. But . . . *but* I haven't been in your shoes." Suddenly restless, he shifted his weight and ran his fingers through his hair, spiking it up and not bothering to smooth it back down. "Look. Okay, here's the deal. You want to live as cheaply as possible, right?"

"Well . . . within reason." Her notion of what *reasonable* meant had changed drastically over the past few months, but she still had standards. Indoor plumbing, for instance, was nonnegotiable; peeing outside in the dark at Ethan's had shown her it wasn't *necessary*, but also reminded her how much she valued it.

"Sure." He finally stilled enough to make eye contact again. "Uh, you like the tiny house, right?"

"Oh. Yes. But it's . . . here. I mean . . . I like it, it's just that—"

"Right. But what if it was there? In Rhode Island. Or close. Canterbury, Connecticut, to be exact. It's about an hour away from Providence, maybe a little less." He looked at her very earnestly and took one of her hands again, pressing it between both of his palms.

Victoria could hear her heart pounding, blood rushing in her ears. "You're . . . are you offering me your house or . . . ?"

"I'm offering me *and* the house. Package deal."

Ethan exhaled slowly, trying to keep his composure, while Victoria processed what he'd just said. After a moment he lost it and started talking again to break the silence. "My friend Trey owns this horse farm in Canterbury. We've known each other since Davis. See, earlier I remembered how small everything is over on the East Coast, so I checked the map and found out his place was really close to Providence. So I texted him just in case, and asked if he'd be hip to me parking the house there for a year or so, and he said—that was him, just now—he said sure, come on over. And it would only be a few hundred a month, plus we can cook at home a lot, so it would be a huge savings. You could still take the loan if you wanted, but maybe you wouldn't have to."

Victoria inhaled, then paused. "That's . . . that's a lot to think about. I wasn't expecting that." She picked up the level again, contemplating the movement of the air bubble as she rocked the device back and forth. Her next words made Ethan's heart race. "Could you have a ropewalk there, though?"

"Yeah, yeah. He's kinky. It's how we know each other. I mean, we met in class, but then . . . you know." He knew she was going to say yes. He had to play it cool because she was dragging it out, but he had felt things click into place so firmly that all his anxiety had turned to pure anticipation in an instant. "And the East Coast is good for kink, he says."

She grinned, finally letting him see the growing spark of delight and hope in her eyes. "Oh my God, yes. There are *so* many kink events within a few hours' drive from there."

He nodded, feeling almost light-headed with possibility. "Maybe you can do your senior project on ropes."

"Nope. I already have a topic. God. If we're doing this, I guess I should tell my parents this weekend. Uh . . ." She stopped and contemplated him, her face unreadable again. "'Mom and Dad, I got that job in Manhattan and I'll probably go back to school in the fall, but I'm also moving to Connecticut with . . . some guy.' Would we be . . . what would we be? Roommates? Fuck buddies? What's the Facebook status, here? I can't tell them I'm moving in with 'It's complicated and he ties me up a lot.' Accurate though that might be."

"Is it?" He was starting to think that assuming things were complicated might be part of his problem. "Complicated, I mean? I think it's pretty simple. 'In a relationship.' We can decide what that means as we go along, right? Tell them the truth: We started seeing each other after you got here, we want to spend more time together, and now we want to try living together. And if the worst happens, and after a few months we start to annoy the hell out of each other, at least you'll have a few paychecks under your belt. You can go to Providence and continue with your original plan."

She looked like a series of emoticons come to life, and it was adorable. "I wouldn't even need that car. It's a farm, right? I could just keep borrowing the farm truck."

"No, you should absolutely accept the car." There, he'd said it.

She glanced up at him and stage whispered, "Of course I'm taking the car; I'm not an idiot. Free car."

"Oh thank God."

"On the other hand, I do already have a line on a supercheap apartment in Providence . . ." Her forehead wrinkled and she looked off at the horizon. "It would be better for the environment not to commute by car at all."

He shook his head. "I can't recommend that." Folding his fingers over hers, he pried her hand free and brought it up to his lips, pressing a kiss to each of her knuckles as she'd done to him minutes earlier. "For, oh, let's say three reasons at least. One, Roxie would miss you terribly."

A smile flashed over her lips, so swift he almost missed it. Her gaze flickered toward his as if she couldn't help herself. "Well that *would* be bad."

"Two, *I* would miss you terribly."

She tilted her head from one side to the other, then finally let her smile stick. "Okay, I would miss you, too."

"Because you're falling in love with me."

"Yeah. I am." She squeezed his fingers and her smile deepened until her dimples showed.

"Oh good, because if you hadn't been, that would have been *really* awkward. And I'm falling in love with you. And we need time to see how that plays out, right?" He dropped a kiss on her smiling lips, intoxicated by her proximity.

"What's three?"

"Huh?"

"You said three reasons at least," she reminded him, standing on tiptoe to kiss him as if that might help him remember.

Fortunately, he didn't require help. "Three," he said, pulling her into his arms, "is obvious. Your tiny, crappy apartment in Providence almost certainly wouldn't have a big-ass bondage frame in the middle of the living room."

She was giggling when he kissed her again, and it was like kissing a glass of champagne. A toast to their future, which was suddenly full of possibilities.

Chapter 19

Victoria had put the wall hanging up while Ethan was checking the trailer hitch. She jumped down from the door and closed it firmly behind her, dusting her hands off on her thighs as she approached him. It didn't help; her hands stayed grubby. It was almost ninety, the humidity was insane, and between the sweat and the dust, she felt grimy pretty much all the time. But that would change once they got far enough east.

"Everything's secure, hatches all battened down for traveling. Or rather, all the cabinets are latched and the books are strapped in. But I left the throw pillows and bed linens on, and the wall art all stays up in transit, so it's still ready to show off before we leave."

"Attagirl. So glad you know something about decorating, because this thing would have turned into a complete crapfest otherwise. I did *not* research that part sufficiently."

"I knew there was a reason you loved me."

He grinned, stepping away from the hitch and grabbing her before she could escape. "Are we talking about your ass?" He shifted his grip so he could squeeze the body part under discussion.

Victoria reached around his neck to pull him down for a kiss. Hot, sticky, whatever. He'd earned a solid kiss. They both had, after all the work they'd put in on the house. They hadn't quite beat the heat; it was late May, and they would have preferred to leave about two weeks earlier. But now Victoria was glad they'd waited for all the last-minute pieces they'd ordered, and finished everything completely. It felt better to start off that way. Solid. Prepared for whatever came along. Feeling completely at home in their handmade home.

They'd worked their asses off the past few months—both of them putting in time on the house, Victoria getting increasingly into her new job, and Ethan doing everything he could to make sure the ranch wasn't impacted by their absence. And they'd spent hours each week building up stock for the rope business. They'd earned every square inch of their portable retreat from the world.

Ethan released her with a final pat on the butt. "Okay. Let's get this baby rolling. Keep your fingers crossed."

They got in the cab, and Ethan spent what felt like an eternity to Victoria carefully maneuvering the trailer off the space it had been parked on, over to the gravel service road that trailed around the property, and down to the turnoff where the service road merged into the main driveway.

When they finally made it there—without incident, although there had been a few hair-raisingly tight turns—most of the ranch staff, plus Victoria's mother and sister, were there to see them off. And to finally see the completed tiny house, which Ethan had been denying access to for the past month. He'd wanted a reveal. Robert was even taking a video with his phone to record the moment for posterity.

Ethan stopped the truck, engaged the brake, then turned his head and shot her a smile. "Ready for this?"

She nodded. "Let's do it."

They got out at the same time, Victoria rounding the truck to join the group as they oohed and aahed over the reclaimed wood and rust-finished metal of the tiny house's outside.

"I thought these things all looked like cottages," her mother said, putting an arm around her waist. "This is beautiful, honey. So modern. I've gotten a ton of pictures already for Daddy."

Alexandra made a skeptical noise. "I still think it'll look like a boxcar on the inside too." She still wasn't entirely easy with the situation—Victoria'd had to do a lot of education and an equal amount of wheedling to get her to give up her outing plans—but she hadn't tipped their parents off so far. That didn't keep her from expressing her displeasure through less direct means.

Mindy gave them all a smug look. "Nah. It's gorgeous. I peeked through the windows a few days ago."

"Cheater!" Ethan finally located the right key and put the short step stool under the door, climbing it to open the house up, then stepping inside to make way for the visitors. "Okay, right this way, folks. Watch your step. Okay, c'mon up, Audrey." He took Victoria's mother's hand, helping her clamber up and in. "Of course this'll all be easier with the permanent steps, but I'll build those in on site. No, Mindy, you were a cheater so you can come in last."

One by one, they filed in to join Ethan in the small space—Logan, Diego, Robert, a couple of the part-timers, Audrey Woodcock, Alexandra, and finally Mindy. Victoria brought up the rear, curious to see what the house looked like with ten people in it.

Crowded as hell, frankly, but not nearly as bad as she'd feared. Some of the guests had moved into the couch area already; they all knew Victoria's mom was vanilla, so they may have noted the cleats and rings, but none of them commented on that feature.

Ethan was already happily explaining everything in front of them, demonstrating the versatility of the kitchen with its extendible counter that could double as a dining table or temporary desk. He moved on to tell the crowd more than they probably ever wanted to hear about the bathroom, including his decision matrix for choosing that particular incinerating toilet. Then he showed them *almost* all the hidden storage; it was everywhere, from smuggler's panels in the floors to removable couch cushions that revealed compartments.

He still hadn't seen the wall hanging—there were too many people between him and the right-hand loft, so the one free section of wall she'd utilized was obscured from his view.

She got her chance when he ran out of words trying to describe what they'd done with the décor. He didn't have many words for that, other than to say he liked it. Victoria took over, explaining the limited palette of colors, the use of neutrals throughout most of the space to make it look bigger and less busy.

"And then when you do have a piece of art, it needs to be something really significant. Because the space is so limited. But I just put this up and I think it fits the bill really well. Plus, it adds a lot of color." She stepped closer to the piece, caught in admiring the infinite hues of red all over again. Most of it was hemp, with some bits of sisal and jute woven in here and there. Down each side of the piece of cedar the woven panel hung from, strips of red leather sharpened and neatened the outline. But it still had a rough, handmade look, with as many variations in texture and thickness of the rope as there were in the colors. Up at the top, natural undyed jute blended to a soft watercolor pink. The pink weft continued into a row of hemp dyed the same color. The next pick was deeper in tone but with less consistent coloration. For a few rows the rope was almost magenta, and then it finally warmed to a rose before it darkened to red. The weft strands grew longer toward the bottom of the two-foot-wide panel. The next-to-last one was a thirty-foot, six-millimeter hemp, its top a jewel-bright claret, its end a deep, almost plummy black cherry; it took up fifteen rows, nearly a vertical foot of the panel. It was the test piece where they'd finally perfected the ombre process.

Below that, a shorter weft—twelve feet, if Victoria recalled correctly—took the color in a new direction that she and Logan had just started on the previous week. A warm, deep purple, almost as dark as the near-black row above it, blended into cobalt blue, and from there into teal. Below that, the undyed hemp warp strands hung empty for the final foot or so.

"That's cool." Even Alexandra was willing to admit it. The kinksters were busy explaining the different types of rope to Victoria's mom, who thought it was amazing how much the ranch folks all knew about the subject.

Victoria glanced over to Ethan, whose eyes were fixed on the colorful piece. She couldn't tell whether he liked it or not. Whether he *got* it or not. A chronicle of their relationship, from their rough early days straight through to the current patch of unaccountably smooth sailing even though the waters weren't charted.

She made her way through the group to his side, looping an arm around his waist and trying to see the hanging through his eyes. No good. She knew too much about it already. Knew what each component meant and where each slip had come from.

"Thank you," Ethan murmured, low enough that only she could hear it.

"Happy moving day," she replied, kissing him on the cheek.

He bounced on his toes, as if he were about to leap out the door. "It's about time to go, isn't it?"

"Just about. The GPS is all set. The stops are all mapped out. We've triple-checked that everything is packed. Trey isn't expecting us for two weeks. The open road is ours to conquer."

Ethan chuckled and pulled her closer, pressing a kiss into her hair. "Love you."

"Love you, too."

"I even made you a playlist."

"Seriously?" She made them for him all the time; he'd never made one for her before.

He nodded. "Mm-hmm. So what do you say we clear the house and hightail it outta here?"

"I say it's the best idea I've heard in weeks."

Five minutes later, with all the last-minute hugs applied, the final farewells and cautions and reassurances exchanged, they settled into their seats. Ethan started up the truck and handed his plugged-in, open phone to Victoria. As he pulled out of the service drive and on to the last section of the main driveway, she looked at the title of the playlist he'd pulled up.

"*Super Kinky XXX Don't Show Audrey.* Nice. She'll never suspect."

"I knew you'd like it. You can press Play whenever you want to start; it's already cued up. So, I noticed the wall hanging isn't quite . . . finished. Or is it supposed to be that way at the bottom? I don't know these things sometimes."

"Oh. Well." Victoria flushed, looking down at the phone and running a fingertip around the Home button a few times before sliding her fingers quickly up and down the page to keep it from locking again. "It isn't finished, that's true. But it's *current*."

"And the space at the bottom?"

She shifted one hand over to his thigh, squeezing through the denim for a moment. "It's up to us how we fill it. But thanks to you, you know what we have?"

He flicked his signal on, looking left to right before pulling out onto the main road cautiously. "What?"

She chuckled. How quickly they forgot. "*Time.*"

"Oh, that. Yeah, we do. I'm looking forward to it."

Victoria was, too.

They were finally on the actual road, heading to the highway that would take them east. Into their future together. She pressed the Start button on the playlist and laughed with delight when she heard the first song spill out into the truck cab, all mellow, husky voice and subtle background.

"Ella!"

Ethan grinned. "Of course."

He picked up speed and they both started to sing along to "You Do Something to Me . . ."

Love visiting the Giddyup ranch?
Be sure to read
RIDE 'EM
Available now
and keep an eye out for
the next book in the series,
coming soon from
Delphine Dryden
and
Lyrical Books

ABOUT THE AUTHOR

Delphine Dryden has written contemporary and erotic romance for Carina Press and Harlequin, and mainstream steampunk romance for Berkley Publishing. She has also self-published. Her writing has earned an Award of Excellence and Reviewers' Choice Award from *Romantic Times Book Reviews*, an EPIC Award, an IPPY Gold Medal, and a Colorado Romance Writers' Award of Excellence. She was also the inaugural winner of the Science in My Fiction contest. When not writing, she can be found editing for various freelance clients and for Riptide Publishing. Visit her at delphinedryden.com.

DELPHINE DRYDEN

A
GIDDYUP
NOVEL

RIDE
Em

RIDE 'EM

SADDLE UP
Mindy has come to Logan's dude ranch to convince him to sign
away his land's mineral rights to her stepfather. She doesn't want to
beg, but she will if she has to, like she does Friday nights when she
submits to her master's desire . . .

BUCKLE DOWN
Logan doesn't like to be jerked around, in business or pleasure. And
when he learns what Mindy is up to, he's ready to teach her a
lesson. In fact, he'd like to tie her up, strip her down, and give her a
spanking she'll never forget . . .

RIDE HARD
With passion riding high, Logan and Mindy indulge in carnal play
that leaves them both wanting more. And with their jobs on the line,
they realize that their erotic fantasies might be their ticket to

www.ingramcontent.com/pod-product-compliance
Lightning Source LLC
Chambersburg PA
CBHW050736250626
47155CB00005B/1804